THE ROGUE

Hideaway Springs Book 3

ROXANNE TULLY

Copyright © 2024 by Roxanne Tully

All rights reserved.

No part of this publication may be reproduced, distributed, or transmitted in any form or by any means, including photocopying, recording, or other electronic or mechanical methods, without the prior written permission of the publisher, except as permitted by U.S. copyright law.

The story, characters, and incidents portrayed in this production are fictitious. No identification with actual persons (living or deceased), places, buildings, and products is intended or should be inferred.

Illustrators: Francesca Weber, Caiden Woodard

Book Cover by: Bernadett Lankovits

Edited by: Looking Glass Editors

Proofread by: Emma Cook | Booktastic Blonde LLC

Contents

About	1
Author's Note	3
Dedication	5
Playlist	7
Prologue	9
1. Tessa	21
2. Levi	29
3. Levi	35
4. Tessa	43
5. Levi	57
6. Tessa	63
7. Levi	71
8. Tessa	81
9. Levi	91
10. Tessa	97
11. Levi	107

12.	Tessa	116
13.	Tessa	122
14.	Levi	129
15.	Tessa	139
16.	Tessa	153
17.	Tessa	165
18.	Levi	178
19.	Tessa	185
20.	Levi	193
21.	Levi	198
22.	Tessa	209
23.	Levi	217
24.	Levi	223
25.	Tessa	229
26.	Levi	241
27.	Tessa	251
28.	Levi	261
29.	Tessa	271
30.	Levi	283
31.	Tessa	291
Epilogue		295
Thank You		301

The Runaway - Excerpt	303
Also By Roxanne	314
Connect with Roxanne	315
Acknowledgements	317

HELP WANTED

Single dad rancher seeking live in nanny for 9-year-old boy.

Must have experience, playful and <u>not</u> looking for a real-life love story.

(Temp job - 6 weeks only.)

ROXANNE TULLY

TRIGGER WARNING

The Rogue is a small-town single-dad cowboy romance. It also contains some suspense (both flashbacks and present). For a list of possible violence-related triggers and mental health triggers, please visit the book page on my website and scroll to the bottom of the blurb,
https://geni.us/therogue_tw
thank you.

Dedication

For the women who've been hiding too long, waiting for that spark to pull you out of the shadows...

Here's to finding a love hotter than a summer day, friendships that bloom like wildflowers in the rain and a cowboy who knows exactly how to handle you.

Playlist

Cowgirls – Morgan Wallen

Every Rose Has Its Thorn – Poison

Austin – Dasha

Broken and Beautiful – Kelly Clarkson

Unstoppable – Sia

Show Yourself – Idina Menzel, Evan Rachel Wood

PROLOGUE
Three years ago

THE SUN HANGS LOW, casting long shadows over the sprawling fields of Hideaway Ranch.

My ranch.

My home.

I tighten my grip on the steering wheel, my calloused hands proof of the countless hours of work put into the land. A land I carved out of the wild seven years ago.

It was nothing but a stretch of earth when I first laid eyes on it.

A hidden treasure.

A future for my growing family.

Before I saw this place, I wanted to be a boxer like my father, Aiden Reeves. Travel, fight, and become a world champion.

But everything changed when Lilly told me she was pregnant. I didn't want to leave either one of them for one moment.

As good a man as my father was to his wife and four boys, he was still absent for a good chunk of our upbringing because of his job.

I didn't hate him for it. We were proud. He'd always look at me before he walked out of the house. A tiny wink reminding me to take care of my little brothers.

I always winked my promise back.

Until the day I didn't.

The day he walked out after mom died. There was no fight. No championship to win. Nothing but his need to escape and grieve the only way he knew how. On the road. Where his boys couldn't see him break down every time he thought of her, missed her, craved her.

I vowed to be better. Present. I was going to be a father to one hell of a little man, and I'd die before I missed one second of his life.

I proposed to Lilly—it was the right thing to do. Took every penny my mother left me in her will, bought this house and the land behind it.

Not a single regret.

That was years ago. A lot's changed.

Lilly changed.

Dad came home for good, too. Got his act together. Not just with his family but with our community. After a hefty donation toward enhancements in our small town, he used what was left of his boxing fortune to buy Hideaway Springs Inn—the only hotel in town—and renovated it to be more than just a place to stay. But a place to bring people together. Starting with the lobby, which he turned into a bar open to the public, not just hotel guests.

It's where I'm headed now.

Sliding on my sunglasses, I raise the window and turn up the AC in my truck. Jackson—my six-year-old pride and joy—wiggles in the passenger's seat.

I can't help but smile at the kid's boundless energy. Always looking for our next adventure.

That's what I tell him in the summers. He's on an adventure with Dad. Summer camp is boring. Swimming pools are contaminated. Arts and crafts are for winter.

All of which is a hell of a better reason than, "*Well, son, you can't go to summer camp because I don't trust your mother not to come and pull you out of there outside her visitation days.*"

My ex-wife barely gave motherhood a chance before she decided to play *Where's Waldo*, disappearing and reappearing like it was some game.

The private school he attends during the year is different. They know the drama with Lilly. They run a tight ship when it comes to releasing children.

Our one camp in town operates a little more...informally.

And I'm not taking chances with the one person on this green earth I care more about than my next breath.

"Dad, do you think Sheriff Woody will let me see the jail cells?" Jackson asks, his eyes wide with curiosity.

I chuckle the way only this kid knows how to make me. "You know his name isn't Woody, right, bud?"

"But he looks like Woody from Toy Story. And he's a sheriff."

"I wear a cowboy hat sometimes. Does that make me look like Woody?"

"No. You're daddy. You look like my dad."

For some reason, that makes me smile. I want to be that safe space for him. But it quickly fades when I need to break the news to him.

"Actually, bud, I gotta take you to Grandpa's. Sheriff and I are just having a quick bite at the station to talk about security in town."

"Why?"

My chest tightens.

Good question.

Hideaway Springs was never perfect and quiet. We've had our fair share of newsworthy crimes. But over the last few months, surrounding towns have had an uptick in graffiti, vandalism, and auto theft—not just petty theft, like stolen bikes. We're talking residences and businesses that have been victims of late-night break-ins and shootings.

And I'm not sitting back and waiting for it to start happening *here*.

We drive out of the fields and onto the streets of our small town. I turn onto Main Street, lined with familiar shops. Their once colorful awnings now worn and distressed, showing their age.

Most of these small-town shop owners refuse to raise prices to keep up with inflation. Appearances are usually the first to go where a budget is concerned. Never the quality service.

It's noble but not very sustainable.

It's become one of the main topics of conversation at Sunday dinners at Dad's. My brothers and I trade updates on shops we check in on from time to time to make sure people are staying afloat.

I'm the oldest of four. Second to me is Noah, the town lawyer. He's not the *only* town lawyer, but sure as hell acts like he is, taking nearly every case brought to him. If you're a broke town resident in a jam, you're almost guaranteed a pro bono attorney to take you on.

Chase is the hockey player. A sport he'd spend hours on Hideaway Springs Lake perfecting in the winters. Never would have imagined he'd go pro, but here he is, playing center for the Denver Kings hockey team.

Then there's Elliot, the youngest. He's still in college, but at least he's close enough for us to keep an eye on him. He's the only one out of all of us who doesn't remember Mom during her good days before she got sick. He's quiet, guarded, and to be honest, I never really know what's going on in his head. Chase seems to be the only one who connects with him on a deeper level.

"Tell ya what," I start with the good news as usual. "Let me see if I can sweet talk Sheriff *Bradshaw* into letting me bring you along next week. He can show you around then. But for now—"

"Grandpa's?" he grumbles.

"Aww, come on. You two always have fun together," I remind him, glancing between the road and my son. Seeing he's not convinced, I sweeten the deal. "And when I pick you up, I *won't* ask if you had an ice cream sundae two days in a row."

He considers for a hot second, then nods curtly in agreement—not giving away that he's getting the better end. Just like I've taught him. "Deal."

I pull onto the gravel lot of Hideaway Springs Inn. Elliot's outside, releasing smoke from his mouth before flicking his cigarette down and crushing it with his heel. His grin is wide as I pull to a stop and roll down my window.

"He-ey," he calls cheerily, crossing to my truck and searching for Jackson. "Where's my favorite little man?"

Jackson struggles with his seatbelt before jumping out. "I'm here. And I'm not little."

Elliot rolls his eyes. "Yeah, good luck with that, kid. I was the little one for thirteen years, so you've got a long way to go."

Dad steps out and gives me a quick nod before wrapping my kid in a giant bear hug. "'Bout time you got here." Then whispers something I'm not intended to hear before taking him inside, making my kid giggle with excitement.

I'm still in the driver's seat, a hard scowl as my eyes flick to the cigarette on the floor. "What's that shit about?"

He sucks his teeth. "I'm in college. Everyone smokes in college."

I pull out my phone.

"What?" he sighs melodramatically.

"I'm fact-checking you."

"Well, don't. I don't need all of you to keep parenting me just because you all got nothin' better to do."

"I'm messin' with you. Just keep it to a minimum, okay? I'd like to keep you—and your lungs—around for a long time."

"I'm fine."

"Thanks for watchin' him for me again."

He shrugs. "It's all good. Dad and I were expecting him. See you later."

Worry gnaws at me as I drive away, and I need to remind myself this isn't the same thing. I'm not abandoning my son the way my ex-wife did. The way *Dad* did.

But these drop-offs are becoming too frequent and it's only a matter of time before Jackson notices. Before he starts thinking I don't have time for him.

That *anything* is more important than him.

It's not.

Nothing will ever be more important than him and keeping him safe.

Part of my meeting with the sheriff today is to see how the Reeves family can help keep crime down. The other is finding out exactly what preventative measures they have in place. Because if anyone with an ounce of no-good shows up in my town, I will personally run them out.

"Little late for lunch." Hideaway Springs town sheriff, Wyatt Bradshaw, grumbles as I hop out of my truck and walk toward the police station.

"Did you at least save me any donuts?" I ask as I follow him into the air-conditioned building. It's modest, like everything else in Hideaway Springs, but serves its purpose.

The smell of bad coffee and a burnt-out copy machine fills the lobby as we make our way to his office.

"You get quotes for the new security system?" I jump to the point of my visit.

Wyatt shakes his head with a grunt. "We uh…we'll need to put that off for a while."

"Put it off? Thought you said you'd fit it into next month's budget?"

"We were counting on funds from parking violation payments, speeding tickets and such to cover the cost."

"And?"

"There aren't any," he answers tightly.

That doesn't add up. "Isn't that a good thing? I mean on the bright side—"

"No bright side. We had over a hundred and fifty tickets last month. All gone."

"I'm not following."

He glances at the glass-enclosed room. Several tan-uniformed officers crowd a young woman. I can't see her face since she's sitting in a chair facing away from us.

But the situation is as clear as the glass wall—she's being interrogated.

I remove my hat. Legs pulled in her direction. Wild and curly auburn hair hangs down to the middle of her back. And when she pushes off her chair, my eyes dip down the rest of her.

She's slender with a heart-shaped ass in fitted blue jeans. Skin that looks smooth enough to touch is exposed from the hem of a crunched-up plaid shirt tied at the waist.

An officer twice her size pushes her back down, and I'm on the move—weaving across the cubicle-crowded floor.

"Hell is going on in there?" I call out like I'm in charge.

"That's Tessa Banks—a recent new hire and the reason we're low on funds for the security initiative."

"Theft?"

He sighs. "No. Messed with the computer. Somehow deleting all pending and delinquent violations in our system."

"On *purpose*?"

"Probably. Holding her until we figure it out." Wyatt sighs with frustration.

"I'll help," I tell him—no question in my tone.

He gives me a hard glare. "Levi, we've been over this. I appreciate your help, but you don't have a badge. I've already broken all kinds of policies keeping you in the loop here, but—"

I put my hands up in defense. "I hear ya." I glance to my right. "But doesn't look like your boys are gettin' anywhere over there. Perhaps someone without authority will minimize tension."

He grunts, running a hand down his face. "Suppose it couldn't hurt. Think the others are too charmed by Little Miss Country."

Sure didn't look like the man who pressed an unwelcome hand on her shoulder was *too charmed*. Fucker practically shoved her down like she's a criminal.

I follow Wyatt into the room, hanging my hat on the hook by the door. The woman he referred to as Tessa earlier glances at the newcomers and does a double-take when she sees me.

"Who's the stray?"

Sheriff crosses to the front of the room. "This is Levi Reeves. Local rancher and a good friend of the police department."

I'd have answered for myself, but I'm too busy catching the breath this woman stole from me when I circled the room to stand before her.

Chestnut hair frames a beautifully freckled face—full pink lips, bright golden-brown eyes—whiskey eyes.

And a smirk that tells me she's guilty as fuck.

I clear my throat, breaking the spell. But not my eyes, which are held tight by her fiercely determined ones.

The Sheriff nods his officers out of the room as I take a seat on the other side of the table.

Her cocky smirk widens as she leans forward. "Clever. Sitting across from me instead of hovering over my shoulder."

"Thought your neck could use a break."

She assesses me, then leans back in the chair. "So, no uniform, no badge. And I'm supposed to answer to you?" She releases a breathy laugh, brightening her face.

My reply is tight. "Tampering with police files isn't something to smile about."

Even if I could watch it all day.

"No. But being innocent is." She flashes me her pearly whites.

I keep my eyes on her. "Wyatt, I'll be out in a minute with a confession. This won't take long."

He hesitates, then nods and steps out.

She folds her arms. "Exactly when does 'this won't take long' business start? After you're done eye-fucking me or during?"

I smirk back, not bothering to deny it. "Look, I don't work here. I'm not a cop, but I know a guilty face when I see one. My family and I make hefty annual donations to the station to ensure they can do their job with the necessary resources."

Whiskey Eyes stares back at me. I nearly lose my train of thought as I study every feature, wondering how I've never seen her here before.

"Sheriff is a good friend of mine. I tell him you're innocent, he'll let you walk out of here. Just answer me this. Was it a mistake?"

She looks me dead in the eye. "No."

"There a reason you robbin' the police station of income they depend on?"

No response other than a slight twitch of her brows as she considers it.

"Fine. I'll take a guess." I cross my arms and settle back in the metal chair. "You knew about the security plans for the town, so you and your buddies decided to sabotage it."

She jerks, looking genuinely confused. "My *buddies*?"

"The crimes in the other towns."

She scoffs. "Paranoid much?"

"Protective," I bite.

Straightening her spine, she glares back at me. "Did you know that traffic violations *doubled* in the last three months in this town? Did the population double? I don't think so." She extends a tattooed arm dramatically. And it catches my eye. A snake wrapped from her elbow down to her wrist. "Did driving laws just not exist before? Also no. I think it's a little unjust for the department to take out low funding issues on innocent citizens."

My eyes flick back to hers. And damn, she's one captivating woman. My chest burns when I realize who she reminds me of. I sit up. "What do you think happens when the department doesn't have money? We lose good workers. Less overtime, less night shifts. Less motivated cops. Our town needs—"

"Then do something else. Raise money for the cause. *Tell them* what it's for. Don't just slap tickets on cars."

I'm one heartbeat away from smashing my mouth against hers. "Where'd you come from, anyway? Never seen you around."

She rolls her eyes. "Don't worry, Indiana Jones. I won't be sticking around."

"Oh, you think you're walkin' out of here? After they slap those fines on you—you're going to prison. That kind of shit ain't—"

Sheriff steps back into the room, exasperated. "Tessa, you're free to go."

"What?" I bark. "I just got a confession."

Wyatt ignores me as Tessa stands with a bored sigh.

"Unfortunately, you can't keep your employment here so—"

"Got it," she cuts him off and mutters a quick 'thanks' on her way out of the room.

"And Tessa?" He clears his throat uncomfortably. "Hideaway Springs is—well, you're welcome here anytime."

She considers it, grins to herself, and nods once. "Cool. Thanks again, Woody."

My head snaps at the nickname.

Turning on her heel, she moves to a desk I can only assume was hers, and tosses a few items into a large tote bag.

I grab Wyatt's arm. "You wanna tell me what that was about? She did it—she's guilty."

He doesn't look me in the eye. "Appreciate you stopping by today, Levi. I need to go uh..." He clears his throat again, muttering *damage control* on the way to his office.

The fuck?

I turn, finding Tessa halfway out the door and race after her until we're both outside. "You think you're some kind of hero?"

Her eyes drop, but she keeps walking. "No."

"Then stop acting like one." I slide my hat back on. "Do yourself a favor and stay away from Hideaway Springs. We don't need rogues like you tryin' to save the day."

"No."

"Excuse me?"

"I'm just getting started here, Indie." She sweeps her gaze over me. "See you around."

She disappeared after that. Only to pop into my head like a bad song I couldn't shake.

And just like Lilly—smokey eyes, fiery red hair—Tessa Banks kept reappearing. She would stick around for a bit, cause more trouble, then take off like a squirrel caught ransacking your apartment.

She's the kind of addictive trouble I don't need.

The kind I won't be tempted by ever again.

1

Present

Frank: *You need to leave again.*

Fuck.

I duck out into the back alley at the sight of the message on my phone. I wish I could say it's cryptic. But it's not.

I know exactly what this is.

It's also a sign that he's about to call. I breathe in the hot summer air, waiting for that shrill of a ring tone that always cuts through the stillness of my heart.

A reminder of what I'm running from.

His calls are never casual or routine; they only come when something's gone wrong.

I'm in danger again.

With a deep breath, I lean against the rough brick wall and answer the call. "I *just* got back, Frank."

"Unless you prefer the safehouse? I can arrange for it."

"No. Place felt like a prison. I need to *live*, Frank."

He sighs. Knowing I won't have my life back until the Brunetti Cartel—the crime organization responsible for my boyfriend's death and the bullet hole in my lower back—are all behind bars.

And that will never happen.

Frank's been working on my case for over three years. Anyone else would have retired early, having been stuck with me.

I swallow my fear and man the fuck up. "They back in town?"

"Eddie Graves was traced to a warehouse on Emerson. He was one of them that day, Tess. We need to get you out of here—like tonight. Or..."

"Or what?"

"If you've no place to hide, we've got to bring you back to the safehouse."

"You can't just—"

"With a court order—and for your own protection—we can, Tess."

"Fine," I grit. "I'll get out of town."

"And Tess. No more funny business."

I roll my eyes and push off the wall. "Come on, Frank. You only had to bail me out once."

Hardly. All the man did was make one phone call and give his FBI badge number, and it was 'no questions asked' by my old boss, Sheriff Bradshaw.

The only fucker I liked in that whole building.

"Tess, this isn't a joke. Can you try to blend in for a few weeks this time without drawing attention to yourself?"

"A few weeks, huh?" Usually, when Frank sends me out of town, it's for two to three months at a time. Except for late last fall, when members of the cartel were here for over six months on a job.

"I think so. This will all be over soon, Tess. We're closing in. We'll have you back here in no time."

"Sure takin' a long time to 'close in'," I mutter.

He sighs again. "It's complicated. Can't arrest one of them just based on one witness. The rest of 'em will disappear without a trace before we have enough on the others."

"I know. My testimony is useless."

"It's not useless, it's just that we need more. When we have more on the others, we'll have you testify."

I shake my head. All I'm hearing is *you're not getting your life back any time soon*.

"Where you goin this time?" Frank asks.

"La La Land."

"Good answer."

The agreement was that every time I needed to disappear, I would go to a different town to avoid suspicion or recognition.

If Frank knew my escape route had been Hideaway Springs for the last three years, he'd toss me right back in that safehouse and throw away the key.

"You got a fear of flying or somethin'?" Bessie asks. She's the head chef at Dolmentos, a diner I work at when I'm in Summer Hill.

It's a shithole of a town. One I ended up in because Eric—my dead ex-boyfriend—had some quick business to take care of.

I didn't know what he was involved in.

And he didn't know he was being set up after screwing up a delivery.

God, I hope he didn't suspect a setup. Because if he did, the fucker deserved what he got for bringing me along.

Bessie is the only one who knows my story. She knew something was up with me the moment I walked in begging for a job—somewhere in the kitchen. Where no one could see me.

I'm in witness protection. And regardless of what I've been told, the FBI can't keep me locked up in a safehouse against my will. So, Agent Frank Mercer and I came up with a mutual agreement. I cooperate by staying close to town and answering when they call, and they don't take every legal measure to take away my freedom for my *'own safety'*.

"You know I can't go far, Bessie."

I wish I could. I'm so tired of this life, I could cry.

I *crave* normal.

I crave sanity.

Hell, at this point, I'll take a full night's sleep. I still wake up in cold sweats because of what I lived through.

Even with the freedom of roaming about outside a safehouse, I'm not free. I'm *chained* to this town until the entire organization is locked away.

"What if I go with you? Make sure you're not being followed and, when the coast is clear, I'll catch a flight back."

I wrap the green apron around my waist. "I wouldn't put you at risk like that."

She purses her lips. "When do you leave?"

"As soon as I find a job in Hideaway Springs," I whisper as if anyone could hear us.

She perks a brow. "Haven't you exhausted all their resources by now?"

I wince.

She may have a point. I've worked nearly every job in that small town and they all ended terribly.

Not to mention, the dust barely settled after I fled the place over a month ago.

The last time Frank sent me out of Summer Hill—last fall—happened to be right around the time Aiden Reeves, owner of Hideaway Springs Inn, needed a new bartender in the lobby bar.

I jumped at the chance at that job. Unfortunately, I wasn't able to secure a place to live. Not an affordable one at least. So…I snuck into one of the guest rooms…every night…for several months.

One evening in late Spring, I finished a shift, closed up, and went up to my room. I found Aiden leaning against the small window, hands in his pockets and an expression that told me I needed to explain.

Aiden was…*reasonable*, to say the least. He even offered to work something out if I could be honest about my situation. But I was too mortified to stick around.

Exhausted or not, I can't help *wanting* to go back. Perhaps it's the irony of the town's name and my need to hide away.

Or maybe I'm drawn to its charming existence. There's life on those streets. People *care* about their community. Friendships grow like wildflowers and families are as tight as a handmade quilt, each piece bound together by love.

I'm not looking for a permanent home there.

Nothing and nowhere is permanent—or safe—for me.

But because I'm a little bit of a masochist, I continue to choose a place where I'm known as the *Town Rogue*. My welcome party will likely consist of 'you owe us money' and 'go back to where you came from'.

I wave her off. "Oh, I'm sure there's something I haven't done yet. Good labor is hard to find. And I'm ready, willing and able."

Bessie sighs. "Could you at least try to find something that's not as *public* as bartending this time."

I wince. "Yeah, that wasn't the smartest choice."

She rolls her eyes and turns back to the hot stove. "Read me off the classifieds, and I'll tell ya if it's a no or a go."

With a deep breath, I settle onto a stool with my phone and type into the blank fields.

Here goes nothing.

Job Search – Hideaway Springs

1 result.

Single dad rancher seeking live in nanny for 9-year-old boy. Must have experience, playful and **not** looking for a real-life love story.

Temp job - 6 weeks only.

I chuckle but at the same time, want to cry. This can't be it. There can't just be *one* job in the entire town.

Hell, I have a better chance at Aiden hiring me back than his oldest, grumpiest son, Levi.

I toss my phone across the counter with a growl and wince at the sound of a crack.

Bessie jerks and lifts it off the floor. "I've got to see this." She sets her glasses over her eyes. "Oh hey, look at that. That's somethin' new. *And you get a room.*" She hands it back to me. "Doesn't get any better than that. Put me down as a reference. I'll tell 'em you used to babysit my niece or somethin'."

I snatch it back and feel a scrape of cracked glass against my fingers. *Ouch.* I flip my screen over to her. "*This* is Levi Reeves. *If*—and that's a very big if—the grumpy cowboy hires me to watch Wiggles, I'd be sleepin' with the horses. Not his house." I shake my head and hit refresh. No change.

Bessie frowns. "Wiggles? Thought it said nine-year-old boy, not a pet."

"Yeah. Kid wiggles a lot. It's kinda cute."

"Cute? You don't like kids." Bessie perks a curious brow.

I shrug defensively, smirking as I remember the ruffle haired small-town boy who just wants to have fun. "This one's cute. He used to get dropped off at the Inn when Levi was working. I'd make his fries extra crispy. And Aiden taught me how he likes his ice cream sundae; vanilla only, a touch of hot fudge, two cherries."

Bessie watches me. "You 'bout done?"

I shake it off. "Anyway, that's all. Doesn't mean I qualify to be anyone's *nanny.*" I say the word with enough disgust to disqualify me immediately.

She oils a pan. "You sure it's the same guy?"

"There's only one ranch in that town, and it's his. I'm positive."

"Well, who cares? Tess, the man's offering a *bed*. I'd at least give it a try. Especially since it sounds like you could somewhat stand the kid."

I hold up the phone to her again. "Look at that last line. What does it tell ya about the guy?"

She scoffs. "That he's got a sense of humor?"

"That he's a conceited jackass who will laugh in my face."

"Tess. Look again. That last line is your ticket! *That* guy—as grumpy as he may be—is looking for *exactly* your type. Get in, do your job, and get out."

I flip the phone around with a scowl. *Huh.*

I shake my head. "What if he doesn't, Bess?"

Her tone softens. "Then you get over your infatuation with that town and go to the next one over."

At this point, I'm not sure what's more daunting. My life in danger... Or facing the gorgeous grump who hates me the most.

2

"Tell me again why you're holding interviews for a new nanny at the Inn instead of, say...at the job site—a.k.a your house?" my father asks as I sneak behind his bar refilling my coffee after the first horrendous interview of the day.

I grunt. "Tried that last week. Cuts out the '*hey, if I'm going to be living here, I'd love a tour*' part of the interview process."

Dad chuckles. "Look, I'm all for you getting someone to watch over Jackson until school starts, but you need to be a little more open-minded."

"Dad, she asked if 'the kid' had a regular sitter she could leave him with if she had a date or somethin' better to do."

Another laugh. "Yeah, heard that."

The bell above the door jingles and a young woman steps inside, scanning the lobby bar before spotting me. She's petite and perky with a wide smile as she makes her way over.

Keeping an *open mind*, I suppose "perky" is good for keeping up with Jackson's energy.

"Levi," she announces brightly, like we're old friends. We only spoke on the phone once when setting up her appointment. Other than that, I don't know her. "I'm Sophie."

I shake her hand with a firm grip. "Nice to meet you, Sophie." Then stretch it out to a nearby booth. "Please have a seat."

Sophie settles in. "Thank you for meeting with me. At first, I was surprised it's not at the actual home, but I can understand that."

Intrigue captures my attention. "Can you?"

"Absolutely. And I totally agree. Bringing around random people talking about your son in front of him must be super uncomfortable for the little guy."

I grin, impressed at her consideration—even if she is way off. She also clearly forgot his name since referring to 'him' and 'little guy'. Giving her the benefit of the doubt—I drop his name. "Jackson's with one of my brothers at his place right now."

She bats her lashes at me.

"So, tell me about your experience with children."

Sophie takes a breath and launches into a well-rehearsed speech about her time babysitting for various families in town. She seems enthusiastic. But I'm not loving the way she stretches her hand out to mine every few words expressing how hard it must be for me and how she's looking forward to getting to know "him" and me.

It's forward and intrusive.

I sigh, glancing at Dad. His brow is perked almost as a reminder to keep that open mind.

"And what do you like to do in your free time?" If bar hopping or skinny-dipping is on this girl's list, I'm saying 'thank you for your time' immediately.

"I'm really into yoga," Sophie replies, her eyes twinkling with delight. "You'll have to try it with me sometime."

I smile, and just for shits, I ask. "Do you have any questions about...Max?"

Sophie blinks, seeming momentarily lost. "Oh, right. Um, what's he like?"

My jaw tightens. *You don't deserve to know what he's like.* I'm about to tell her exactly why she's not getting the job when my father interjects.

"Hey, Levi, I think your next interview is here so you should probably wrap up. Now."

With a tight jaw, I nod at his warning glare for me to take it easy. When he walks away, I thank Sophie without so much as a grin and tell her I'll be in touch.

I rub my temples with a groan.

Fucking useless.

Am I the problem?

Barely a moment passes before the door opens again, and a stern-looking woman in her fifties walks in. Her posture is rigid as she approaches me with a brisk stride.

"Mr. Reeves? I'm Margaret," she introduces, shaking my hand firmly—and briefly—before sitting down.

My eyes flash to Dad, and he presses his palms down, mouthing the words, "*Cool it.*"

"Nice to meet you, Margaret. Thanks for coming," I offer robotically. "Can you tell me about your experience?" I don't bother masking my lack of enthusiasm.

Margaret opens with a detailed narrative of her years as a nanny and her strict approach to childcare. Including structure of the home, schoolwork and maintaining a schedule.

"I believe children thrive on routine," Margaret says with a tight-lipped smile. "It's important to set boundaries and consistency."

Somehow, I don't think her definition of boundaries is the same as mine.

I nod slowly. "Jackson is very free-spirited. He loves to explore, ask questions, get a little dirty, and stay up late. How would you handle his energy and curiosity?"

"Curiosity is good, but it must be channeled appropriately."

I frown at that. "In other words, you'd steer him away from being himself?"

Where are these people coming from? Really? Is someone playing a practical joke on me?

Margaret's smile doesn't reach her eyes as she regards my question. "Children need to understand their place. If his questions and *curiosity* fit into our activity, then I'll address it."

She reminds me of the strict nanny Jackson had last fall. She was an acceptable temporary solution. But I knew Jackson didn't like her. Only kept her around because I was desperate.

The last straw was at Jackson's birthday party where a certain bartender went rogue and nearly killed the woman with alcohol poisoning.

Okay, so maybe Tessa knew *exactly* how much to give her to knock her out for a few hours, but she had no right to mess with an innocent woman like that.

Even if the innocent woman *did* yell at my son at his own birthday party in front of all his friends because he was having too much sugar.

Damn spitfire always causing trouble in this town.

I still remember the fierceness in Tessa's eyes when I confronted her. There was no remorse, just anger—but not raging anger—it was...protective.

For a kid she barely knew.

Hard to believe someone as destructive as Tessa Banks has a heart—but I won't be fooled by a beautiful woman again.

Jackson's mom was plenty for that. And I'm one wrong move away from a restraining order against Lilly.

"Thank you, Margaret, I'm afraid you and Jackson won't see eye to eye on—well anything—but I appreciate your time."

She blinks. "Mr. Reeves, I didn't respond to your first ad three weeks ago—the one that just asks for experience, references, and immediate availability. Then I saw an updated version a few days ago—the one where you added 'not looking for a real-life love story'. I can only imagine the type of candidates you've been getting up 'til now and I can assure you, that won't be the case with me. You're *desperate* to find a caretaker for your son—I'm more than qualified. You are clearly not looking for a woman looking to play wife—neither am I. But I will make sure your son has what you haven't been offering him—a good *dependable* home."

I perk my brow. Color me impressed. I'm about to extend an offer on the spot when my father cuts me off—a hard edge in his tone.

"Lady, you heard my son. You're not fit for Jackson. Thanks for stopping by." He points sharply to the exit.

She humphs and pushes to her feet. "Good luck, Mr. Reeves."

Dad takes her seat as I stare in astonishment. He rubs his temples. "Please tell me there's another one."

"I was about to offer her the job."

He looks at me like I'm crazy. "Because she was bullying you into it. The same way she'll bully your son into seeing it her way. Is that what you want for Jackson?"

I drag a hand through my hair. "Fuck, you're right. I'm losing my mind."

"I said keep an open mind—not punish the kid."

I stare blurry-eyed at my list. "There's one more tonight, but I'm not sure I have the energy. She's from out of town." I check my watch. "Told her to meet me here at six."

A woman by the name of Bessie. She sounded nice enough on the phone. Sweet, actually. Early fifties if I had to guess. She'll be my last for the day before I leave to pick up Jackson from Noah's and head home.

Dad stands. "Leave no stone unturned. I'll get dinner started for you and Jackson."

"Thanks, Dad."

"A fresh pot of coffee too. Looks like you might need it. And one for your candidate since she's coming in from out of town. Where from again?"

I shrug. "I didn't ask." I look at my phone to check the area code, then flip it back to him. "Familiar?"

Dad frowns. "Think that's Summer Hill. It's about two hours from here." His eyes flick to mine with doubt. "Let's hope it's not a wasted trip to Hideaway Springs."

3

Levi

I STAND AT THE kitchen sink, scrubbing the last of the dinner plates while Jackson clears the table, gently stacking the remaining dishes.

The kitchen is large in its square shape. It's an open concept with a 'rustic charm' as my sister-in-law, Pepper, calls it. With wooden beams overhead and a window offering a view of the expansive ranch.

The last interview didn't show. And I take it the woman realized it's too far and not worth the drive. It was too bad. She sounded super laid back and…well, motherly. She also had somewhat of a sharp tongue which tells me she doesn't beat around the bush. Her whole vibe told me she'd fit in just fine here.

I almost want to call her back and ask her if she'd like to interview by phone if she's concerned about the long drive for nothing.

I glance over my shoulder at my little boy. "Thanks for helping out, buddy."

He opens the freezer like it's routine or something.

"Hold it right there."

He turns to me, all innocent.

"Didn't you have an ice pop at Uncle Noah's today?"

"Just one."

"One is plenty. Go brush and get ready for bed."

He closes the freezer with a look I accept as *worth a shot*. "Can we read a story before bed?"

I bite down a grunt. "Sure we can. Pick one out, I'll be up in a minute."

Jackson's footsteps echo through the wooden floors as I dry my hands on a towel, wondering if it's really all that hard to just...do this all myself.

We don't need anybody, do we?

Except maybe our family. I'm grateful to my brothers for always stepping in to help when I need it.

Both of them.

We lost Elliot two years ago to a skiing accident. His death ripped us up inside. But the four of us stuck together, refusing to let another death in our family destroy us.

Dad checked in on us daily. He was the opposite of the man he was when Mom died.

Chase thought he was hovering.

Noah called it overcompensating.

I saw it as Dad needing us as much as we needed him. Regardless of the motive, we survive better together.

And hell, with both my brothers settling down with the loves of their lives, I may never need a mother figure for him. Pepper and Charlie will be plenty for that.

I suppose.

But still, I can count on them. They're not Lilly. They're not going anywhere.

I toss the leftovers into the fridge and shut off the lights. Thank heavens Dad took pity on me and prepared take-out dinner. Otherwise, the kid would have had mac and cheese while I picked at a can of tuna.

I'm usually an enthusiastic cook—hell my gourmet kitchen is built for it—but summers are long and hot on the ranch. Good help is slowing down, and I've got Jackson at my hip or on my mind all day to worry about meal prep.

The bully candidate was right about one thing. The kid needs stability. Routine.

I find Jackson already in pajamas, eagerly flipping through a comic book. The room is a blend of childhood treasures—both mine and his.

I pluck a book from the shelf. Noah and his live-in girlfriend, Charlie, are opening a bookstore in the fall. Charlie brings a new book for Jackson every Sunday dinner at Dad's, impressively keeping up with his interest.

That woman is as talented at reading young minds as she is at stealing the heart of my grumpy little brother.

They met when Noah was in law school, and Charlie was a lost undergrad—dated briefly until a horrible misunderstanding tore them apart. A few months ago, she was wrongfully evicted, and instead of suing the bastard landlord on her behalf, my little brother moved her into his place. It's no surprise those two gave up their stubborn feud and ended up in the sack.

My voice is steady and warm as I start to read. Jackson snuggles close—something I know he'll be getting too old to do soon enough—so I soak it up, pulling him against me. His eyelids grow heavy before I even get to the second page.

About halfway in, I close the book, watching Jackson's small chest rise and fall in a peaceful rhythm.

I bend to kiss his forehead. "Night, cowboy."

Back downstairs, I survey the rest of the floor. Place wouldn't mind a housekeeper either. I read something about a messy home causing unidentifiable stress.

I wonder if we're both affected by it.

Jackson seems fine, but hell, what if the mess symbolizes how chaotic his life is? How I need to be careful that his mother doesn't come back into his life. How protective I am of his heart. His expectations.

His need for a mother Lilly never wanted to be.

I check the time. Only nine o'clock. Why the hell does it feel like midnight?

I sigh, shutting the lights to blind myself of the mess in the living room.

Worry about it tomorrow.

I don't get far up the stairs when the doorbell rings.

Who the hell?

I peek out to the driveway, the porch lighting doesn't give me much, but there is a car—a small, old car—now parked next to mine.

I yank the door open and blink—my breath catching in my throat.

Tessa's chest hikes as she lifts her chin. Those wild auburn curls hang longer over her shoulder. Her freckled skin now slightly sun-kissed. Her lips, still full and smooth, with that little part in the middle still drawing my gaze like it's begging for me to part them further.

"You've *got* to be kidding me," I finally say.

She grins and holds up a hand. "Sorry, I'm late. I'm your six o'clock."

I frown at her delusion. "You're not my six o'clock. My six o'clock was a no show by the name of—Tessa, what the hell are you doing here? At my door, after dark."

"Bessie is my closest friend—and occasional colleague. The job you posted required a quick call before setting an appointment, so...she did me a solid."

"Did. You. A. Solid."

She rolls forward and back on her heels. "Yep. Clever, huh?"

My glare is hard. Icy, hopefully. But as usual, she's not fazed.

"Bessie is super cool. You'd really like her."

I raise my brows. "Great. Is she looking for a job?"

"Come on, Levi, what was I supposed to do? This is the only job opening in town. Trust me, I hit refresh seventeen times on my drive over. I mean yes, I expected you to laugh in my face, but hear me out, I've already written your pros and cons list."

Her face is no laughing matter. Even in the moonlight, she's a vision and a half.

Tearing my eyes off her pouty features that are about to do a number in my pants, I scan the rest of her. She's in jeans and a white crop top, highlighting her toned, tanned arms and neck.

And hold the fuck up.

I drag my gaze back to hers. "Did you say *only* job?"

She rolls her eyes and whips out her phone, swiping the screen open and shows it to me. "See?"

I wince. "The fuck happened to that thing?"

She tucks it in her back pocket and keeps her eyes on me. "Chucked it across the room when I saw the post."

I cock my head. "Disappointed I don't need a love interest?"

"You kidding? That's the best fu—" She glances over my shoulder. "*Freaking* part. Which is a pro on this list. Aren't you even curious to see it?"

Yes.

"No." Then I step out onto the driveway and close the door behind me. "Now I get why you didn't show up at my dad's inn. You've really got some nerve coming back here. I should have you arrested for trespassing and theft."

"Theft?" She scrunches her nose nervously, and fuck, it's cute. "Is staying at a hotel room without ever booking it really considered theft?"

"It's a goddamn crime, Tessa," I bark, taking a step toward her, getting a whiff of baked goods and flowers off her skin.

She pulls her face away from my advancement but not her feet. "Can I interview for the position of Jackson's nanny?"

"You just did." I back up. "And you didn't get the job."

She sucks in a deep breath, her eyes drifting like she's buying time. With new determination, they meet mine again. She pulls out a worn piece of paper from her other back pocket.

"Pro: Wiggles already knows and *adores* me, I mean come on, even you have to admit that."

I fold my arms, my chest puffing with irritation.

"Pro: I may not have experience, but I'm playful and totally not looking for a love story."

I feign sleepiness.

Her eyes flutter from me to her list. "Pro: Job comes with a free room—" She scrunches her face. "Shoot, that one was for me only."

Now *that* makes me laugh in her face. "When do we get to the cons?"

She flips over the list, scanning it.

"Not mine. I already know them. Tell me *yours*."

She deadpans me. "I don't want to work for you any more than you want me."

My eyes sweep over her. Intrigued as fuck how she ended up here. But the last time a woman intrigued me enough to trust her, I got burned. I step back into the house. "Then it's settled. Goodbye, Tess."

I shut the door, releasing a ragged breath.

With a heaviness in my chest, I pace my living room. This has to be some sick joke. Tessa knows I'd never in a million years hire her.

Hell, I even made it clear last year when she offered to watch Jackson for one night for Chase's bachelor party.

I hated how much I wanted to take her up on the offer. And being the dick that I am—overcompensated for it in my response when I told her she wasn't exactly the ideal candidate to care for a child.

The hurt in her eyes that day haunted me all night.

I release a breath and stride back to the door, swinging it open. Tessa is seated on the hood of the beaten-up Camry she arrived in. Her chin resting on her knees like she's waiting for a pickup truck.

Folding my arms, I lean on the doorframe. "Need a place to crash before you head back to where you came from?"

Tessa hops off and dusts her hands on her hips. "Thought you'd never ask." Then she strides over to the door, stopping at the threshold like she's afraid to pass me.

"Don't you...have a bag or something?" I ask.

She smirks. "I'll leave it in the car. Wouldn't want you thinking I'm making myself comfortable or anything." She's a breath away and I try to convince myself I haven't missed that raspy, sassy voice.

I give the front door a little kick. "Fine with me."

She enters and I lock it behind her. "I'll bring you down some linens." I point to the small den just past the foyer. "You can crash on that couch."

I have two empty bedrooms upstairs but there's no way I'm letting Jackson see Tessa here.

He grew a little too fond of her last year, and I don't know what Kool-Aid she'd been feeding him, but I'm not having any of it.

"Help yourself to the kitchen if you want anything, but if you don't mind, I'd like you gone before Jackson wakes up tomorrow. The kid asks too many questions as it is."

"I'll be up before he is," she assures me sharply, scoping out the den.

If I'd ever heard a guarantee from anyone, *that* was it. "Great," I mutter before rushing up the stairs, shaking my head at myself as I round up a pillow and light blanket.

She's got one part right—I wouldn't have to worry about her looking for a real-life love story because one thing I'd learned about Tessa is that she's a flake. A flight risk. Temporary.

She has every intention of leaving.

Who's to say I'm not going to come home one day and find Jackson scared and alone because she decided it was time to go again?

Something's up with that girl—there were times I was curious as fuck to know what it is—but that's just asking for trouble.

And I don't want trouble anywhere near Jackson.

Or me.

I toss the linens on the couch.

She smiles. "I won't let the bed bugs bite."

I point a finger at her. "Seven. The sun will be up, and you will be gone."

"Seven," she repeats.

4

Tessa

*P*ANG.

I jolt at the violent sound, the sharp pain in my lower back and suck in a jagged breath.

It's fine. I'm fine. It's just my internal alarm clock.

If I told you it gets easier waking up to the subconscious sound of a gunshot, I'd be lying. It always hits the same.

My eyes sting, but I shake it off.

Thankfully, I always wake up alone. Not for the obvious reason that no one will ever have to witness my permanent trauma. But when I wake up—no one is pointing a gun at my chest, threatening to finish the job.

But…it does take me a minute to remember where I am.

That's right. I'm at Indie's castle of a home. The one he graciously let me crash last night.

I pull the covers off and slide my jeans back on. The sun won't be up for another three hours, but I don't bother staring at the ceiling until it does.

With a yawn, I stretch and glance around. Certainly doesn't give off those *Indiana Jones* vibes. It's clean. Sure, a bit untidy, but no dead skeletons or muddy boots in sight.

But he does still wear that hat, so the nickname stays.

The man's got sweet digs. It's not a mansion by any means. But Levi does own the biggest residential property in Hideaway Springs.

I never understood why. It's just him and his son here. It's not like members of his staff live in the house. He's got cabins and small villas built for a handful of cowboys along the ranch.

Not that I've ever gotten a tour, but Pepper—who befriended me last fall with zero judgment—pointed them out from her backyard since her cottage is on the opposite side of it.

Barefoot, I wander out of the den and into the main room.

Rugged yet charming are the words a realtor would use to hook buyers for this place. Other than its owner, this home is one hundred percent *inviting*. With wide-plank wooden floors, exposed beam ceilings, a large stone fireplace, and an oversized rustic chandelier overhead.

I scan the messy space with a peaceful smirk. Imagining the erratically arranged plush couch cushions used for pillow fights or fort building.

It may just be the two of them but it *breathes* love, comfort and security.

I move to the stained coffee table with scattered Lego pieces next to an unfinished pirate ship. I gather the magazines, piling them evenly on the edge and place the three remote controls over them like a paperweight.

Cracking my knuckles, I flip to a page in the Lego manual and get to work.

Two hours later, I'm mixing pancake batter with swift, practiced movements the way Bessie taught me. It's almost therapeutic as my eyes peer through the large kitchen window to the open fields.

It's still somewhat dark out, but I see movement near one of the barns and some by the cabins. Levi's men already at work.

Hell of a better view than Bessie's trailer, where I've lived the last six weeks since leaving Hideaway Springs.

I wash and slice fresh strawberries, mixing some into the batter, then set some on the edge of the plate.

The man did say I could help myself to the kitchen, he didn't say I couldn't make enough breakfast to feed a farm.

Occupational hazard, I suppose.

The man *also* said he wanted me out before Jackson wakes…and as grateful as I am for a place to crash last night…I'm a little ticked off that this desperate man won't even give me a shot.

So I'm doing the predictable thing and…*going rogue.*

Muffled voices and footsteps are above me and I pour a second helping of coffee into the *Cowboys Do It Better* mug I found. Grinning once again as I sip.

Heavy steps pound the stairs, and I stiffen, surprised to find myself a *wee* bit afraid.

What is with you? Get a grip, Tess.

"Buddy, hurry up, got a late start agai—" Levi stops short before he even rounds the corner to where I'm standing in the kitchen.

"What the…" Levi pulls his gaze from the living room and turns to the kitchen.

I hold up my mug with a grin. "Morning, grumpy."

His eyes drop to the stacks of pancakes and fruit on the counter, then to the *Cowboys Do It Better* mug in my hand.

He points to it stiffly. "That's not mine."

I cock my head innocently. "Was in your cabinet." I lean in like it's a secret. "Right up front."

"I thought I made myself clear last night. And what happened to not making yourself too comfortable?"

I shrug.

He glances back at the living room. "Did you *clean*?"

"Calm your horses. Yes, I touched your stuff. Can you wait until *after* I leave to set it on fire?"

"Why?" he practically grits.

"I was up early."

"*How* early?"

Little footsteps race down the stairs. "Tessaaaa," Jackson cries as he rounds the corner, zooms into the kitchen and wraps his arms around my waist.

I nearly fall back at the embrace.

What is going on? The stupid question flies out of my mind as fast as it flew in.

He's hugging you. It's what people do when they don't judge you.

"Uh—hey, kid. Morning. Want some coffee?"

"No," Levi barks.

"I was *kidding*." I really wasn't, but the moment was awkward, and I just wanted to shimmy the little slugger off me.

Plus, I'm used to offering people coffee instead of a glass of milk or juice.

I grip his shoulders and twist him to the counter, where I have a special plate prepared for him.

"Sit. I'll get you some milk."

Levi scans his son's plate with a scowl. "Where'd you find powdered sugar?"

"Far left cabinet behind the flour."

"I don't use flour."

"That's why you didn't know you had powdered sugar."

"Did you check the expiration date?"

I give him a one-shouldered shrug with a wink. "It won't kill him."

He focuses on his son and exhales. Then flicks his gaze to me. "Can I talk to you in the other room for a sec?" he grits.

I set the mug down and follow him to the den.

He sweeps his eyes around the tidied-up room. The linens have been folded and set to the side. Tugging my arm, he twists me, his breath inches from mine. "I know what you're doing and you might as well quit now. I'd be a fool to hire you."

Ocean-blue eyes roam my face like he's studying me rather than threatening.

"Yeah, 'cause I'm a danger to society," I mock.

But he doesn't laugh. Instead, his jaw tightens, and he pulls me close, his breath hits the tip of my nose. "I know you think your actions in this town are heroic, but they're deceitful and illegal."

I swallow.

"My father was kind to you, offered you a job when no one else would. And you stole from him, too."

"I didn't—"

"It cost him revenue. So it's stealing."

I release a shaky breath, and he lets me go, stepping back. Then runs a frustrated hand through his hair. But his frustration isn't with me. It's like he's angry with himself.

"I appreciate the breakfast you made for Jackson, but I'd appreciate it more if you said goodbye and left."

I nod, my voice raspier than usual when I mutter, "Thanks again." Brushing past him, I make my way to the kitchen with a bright smile. "Hey, Wiggles."

The kid turns to me with a milk mustache and powdered sugar on his chin.

I ruffle his hair. "Thanks for havin' me. I'm going to head out." I avoid saying *I'll see you soon.*

"These were so yummy, Tessa. Did you have powdered sugar on yours too?"

I set my used coffee mug in the sink. "Nah, I don't eat breakfast."

Levi scowls, and I already know what he's grumbling about internally. So I add, "*But* it's the most important meal of the day, so I'll grab a donut or something at the gas station."

Jackson frowns. "Dad says you can't concentrate if you don't have breakfast. But you finished my pirate ship Lego."

Levi's head turns back to the living room.

"Only because you did the hard part."

"How'd you find the missing pieces?"

"Under the couch cushions." I wink as I circle the counter. "Well, this was fun. See ya around."

"Will we?" Jackson asks, hopping off his stool. And Levi was right, this kid and his questions.

I'm about to answer when the kid adds, "Because when you left before, Dad said we'll never have to see you again."

Yep, that tracks.

With tightness in my chest, I flash him another wink. "You never know."

Levi walks me to the door. His voice low and annoyed as he speaks, "You've been up for hours and haven't found time to eat anything?"

I don't bother answering the question that doesn't concern him. "Thanks again for the bed."

"It was a couch," he grumbles.

I run my hand down his cotton-covered chest. "Doesn't make you any less of a gentleman for letting me stay."

He swallows hard, averting his gaze. "Goodbye, Tess."

A moment later, I'm in my car—mentally preparing myself for plan B, which isn't very thought-out. It involves calling Frank to tell him plan A didn't work out and that I'll be at a hotel for a few days until my cash runs out. Then...he'd better have some good news on the men after me so I can go home.

And it sure as hell isn't going to be Summer Hill.

I twist the key in the ignition, praying for the usual reassuring rumble. I sigh in relief when the engine cranks, filling the air with familiar whirring—but then it pauses.

A sinking feeling grips me as it falls silent.

No worries. We almost had it. Just...try it again.

I twist the key again with the same result.

Levi's front door pulls open and Jackson runs out. Levi is behind him, holding a duffle bag.

The man squints at me through my windshield then focuses on something behind me.

Through my rearview mirror, I see a car pulling up, stopping inches from my bumper. Levi follows Jackson toward it, making small talk with the driver and thanking him as the kid hops in. I tune out the muffled voices behind me and try the engine a third time.

Come on, girl, work. Just this once. Just get me out of here.

I squeeze my eyes shut as it dies and hit my forehead against the steering wheel. I keep my head down even as I feel his presence at my open window.

"Trouble?"

My head feels heavy as I lift it. "I *swear* to you, I'm *not* doing this on purpose."

"No, no. The author of your life just seems to hate us both. Pop the hood."

"Hood," I repeat and blink down, pulling on a small latch. Before I do, I instantly know that's not the right one.

"That's the trunk, Tess."

I don't bother telling him I know cars probably as well as he does—because actions speak louder than words.

And I'm just all out of sorts this morning.

"Thanks," Levi mutters into his cell phone before hanging up.

We're standing outside his house in the driveway after he's concluded that my car—which, I'll be honest, I'm just as shocked as the next guy that it got me here—needs a new alternator.

And it's going to cost…oh, roughly my plan B money, so there's that.

"My buddy Beau has an auto shop not too far from here. He'll tow 'er over there today. Should have it ready for you in two days."

"*Two days?*"

"Yep. You're in luck, I'm going to save you an Uber ride this morning and drive you to the Inn myself."

"I can't go back there," I snap.

He grins, but there's no humor. "Oh, you're going back. Because you're not staying here." He lifts my trunk and pulls out my suitcase, tossing it into the bed of his truck. "While you're there, maybe you can apologize to my father for screwing him during a busy season. Get in."

I open my mouth again to protest, but he cuts me off.

"The man prides himself on helping people, and you made him feel like a fool. So I'd make it good if I were you." He pulls open the passenger door for me.

I inhale a sharp breath. "You're right. I'll apologize and... ask for a room for a night or two."

"At full price," he states.

"And not a penny less, got it." Maybe Bessie will lend me some cash since my car just blew all of mine.

"Good."

We drive out of the ranch in silence, and I roll down my window. A habit I don't allow myself when I'm in Summer Hill. Or hell, anytime I'm in my car alone.

No one will be looking for me here. But just in case, I slide on my sunglasses.

Levi glances at me. "You didn't have to do that, you know?"

"What?" I call over the wind against my face. "Tamper with my own vehicle just so I could stay close to you a little longer? Sorry, Indie, couldn't help myself, you're just *so* irresistible."

"Very funny. Even *you* couldn't pull something like that." He squints at the road. "I meant cleaning and...breakfast and all."

I shrug. "I was bored."

Another quiet minute rolls by, but it's not awkward. It's not comfortable either. It's just...us. Old rivals in the same space, waiting it out until we're not.

"So why don't you eat breakfast?" he asks dryly.

I roll up the window before answering. "I usually wake up nauseous." It's probably the most honest thing I've said all day.

"Sorry to hear that."

I scoff.

"I'm serious," he says casually. "It can't be pleasant."

"It's not."

His eyes sweep over me. "You uh, alright now?"

"Jesus, I'm not going to hurl in your Jeep, Levi."

"I was being a gentleman by asking, but you know what—now, I hope you do."

"The way *you* drive? I'd be careful what you wish for."

A hint of a smirk touches his lips before it disappears. "What are you doing back here, anyway?"

Like I'd tell you.

I shake my head with a laugh. "You don't think I'm on to you?"

"What?"

"I know your angle. I get all distracted telling you where I'm from and why I'm here while you take a detour to the Hideaway P.D."

He grins like he's enjoying the fact that I'm at his mercy. "I'm not taking you to the station."

"Why not? Cause I'll cost them more money than I'm worth?"

He perks a brow, sparing me a glance. "Depends. What do you think you're worth?" He sets the car in park, and I'm glad his question didn't assume an answer. Shutting off the ignition, he stares at the storefront of my longest-running job in Hideaway Springs. "We're here. Ready?"

I inhale and tighten my jaw. *Not like I have a choice.* "Yeah," I mutter and hop out.

That familiar bell jingles as we step into the Inn. It's quiet and empty—typical for a Monday morning.

Aiden is behind the bar, stopping short when he finds me at the door, then glances at his son behind me.

"Tessa!"

I swallow. "Hey, boss."

His warm eyes harden, and he checks his watch. "You're about two months late for work."

"Six weeks, actually, and—I know." I wince.

His eyes shift to Levi. "Did you two happen to walk in here at the same time?"

The jerk behind me leans against the doorframe. "Tess ran into some bad luck. First, she got shot down hard for the only job opening in Hideaway Springs, then her car broke down."

Aiden glares at him, and I assume it's for more information.

Levi pushes his spine off the wooden beam and strolls in. "I brought her here because she owes you an explanation. An apology, and while we're at it, maybe a repayment plan."

My heart thumps hard against my chest. It's been a while since I've been this worked up. Not because of the debt I undoubtedly owe this man, but the betrayal. He was good to me, fair even. Treated me more like a partner than a temporary bartender.

And I cheated him and his business.

I swallow the hard lump in my throat. Leaving Levi behind me, I move toward the older man I'd grown too fond of over my time here. "I am so sorry for what I did. It was—"

"My fault for trusting you?"

My shoulders sag as a rocky exhale rips from my chest. "No...I just didn't have many options." My voice is abnormally small. I swallow to get it back.

Aiden's hands are on his waist. "Well, I probably had it coming. I mean, that's who I hired, wasn't it? The town rogue? Always causing trouble, then running off?"

I open my mouth but he cuts me off. And it's just as well, I have nothing good to say.

"Why are you even here? Let me guess—car broke down and you need a place to stay?"

I flinch at his tone.

"Dad." The deep rumble comes from behind me, sounding like a question mixed with warning.

Aiden turns to his oldest son with a scowl like I'd never seen. "Stay out of it."

Levi moves forward, stopping a foot in front of me. "Maybe take it down a notch?" he says quietly, and I can't tell if it's suggesting... or *threatening*.

Aiden scans the room briefly. "I'm sorry, am I being disruptive? There's no one else here." He takes a breath and slaps a smile on his face. "Thanks for bringing her by...I'll take it from here."

"I'm not going anywhere," Levi howls.

"Stop," I shout, then step between the two men.

Aiden's expression softens when he turns back to me, but only slightly.

"When I came back to Hideaway Springs last fall, my living arrangements...didn't work out. I thought I could stay here a few nights until I found a place, but..." I shrug and wince. "Got too comfortable."

Aiden shakes his head. "That's on me for hiring you on the spot without references or proof of residence."

What is going on? Why is the kindest man I know acting like...well, like his oldest, grumpiest son? He seemed so sympathetic to my situation when he found out.

"You know what, I've heard enough. I'm calling the police." Aiden turns and lifts the receiver off the wall.

My eyes stretch, but I don't protest. I'm frozen in place. Hell, I won't even try to run.

Maybe Frank will find this funny when he bails me out?

"Put it down," Levi roars behind me, moving toward the bar.

Aiden hangs up reluctantly with a sigh. I catch a quick wink in my direction before he faces his son with disappointment.

"This was a mistake," Levi mumbles.

Aiden shakes his head at me. "You're not staying here."

"Damn right she's not," Levi confirms through gritted teeth.

There's a hint of a smirk on my old boss's face as he watches Levi storm out from behind the bar and toward me. Grabbing my hand like I'm his property, Levi hauls me toward the exit.

And this…might just be why I *love* this town.

5

Levi

"Where you takin' her now?" my father calls after me before the door shuts behind us. "To apologize to someone else she screwed over?"

I pull open the passenger door and Tess doesn't need to be asked to jump in. "Wait here," I order, half certain that when I come back, she'll be gone, and half ...not.

Pulling the door to the inn open, I stalk over to the check-in desk, where my father is casually looking over the day's ledger like he didn't just act like the biggest asshole on the planet.

"The hell is going on? Something bite you in the ass this morning?"

"Don't worry, I called a buddy of mine—not a cop. He'll take her off your hands and see that she leaves town quietly."

"Wha—who did you call?"

"Who cares? She's not our problem anymore."

"Do you know she woke up before dawn this morning, cleaned up my wreck of a living room, dusted the goddamn curtains, and made *pancakes?*"

Dad doesn't look impressed.

Or surprised.

"With *sliced strawberries*. All before Jackson even came downstairs."

He points a finger at me. "She's up to something."

I'm outraged. "She's out of work. Cut her some slack."

A smirk spreads across my father's face, followed by a laugh.

"What?" I snap.

He shrugs like it's nothing.

"You're not going to tell me why you just turned Hulk on her?"

"I wanted to see something." Scratching his chin, he scans me like *I'm* that something.

"I'm out of here." I curse and stalk to the door.

Dad calls after me. "The next time you think about bringing someone over here to humiliate them, I'd like a heads up."

"That's probably never going to happen again."

"Glad I could still teach you something." He checks his watch. "Oh, and make sure Tessa grabs something to eat soon."

I turn back. "What do you mean?"

"She's been up for almost five hours. She'll need fuel soon."

I'm static for a brief moment. Snapping out of it, I head back and hop into the driver's seat of my truck with a grunt. "You knew he was faking all along?"

A grin that brightens her eyes spreads across her face. "Not until just before we left. He had me goin'."

I confirm she's buckled before turning back to the road. "You ever cause any trouble at Township Bakery?"

"Not that I can think of. Why?"

I put the car in drive and steer onto Main Street. "Because we're having breakfast there."

She watches me like we're having a moment where I don't despise her. Like she's waiting for me to turn to her and confirm our newfound friendship. Well, it's not going to happen.

"So...are we like, cool now?"

And there it is.

"Far from it. I'm feeding you as a thank you for this morning, and then I'll throw Beau an extra few bills to speed up your repairs."

"Okay—"

"After that, I'm going to *personally* follow you to the highway until you've cleared some border—town, state, doesn't matter."

She stares at me with wide eyes, which I pretend I don't notice as I keep mine on the road.

"What's your damage?"

"I don't like to be fucked with, that's all. And I really don't like that my father fucked with me for *your* benefit."

She laughs. "Oh, is that all? Well, then, let me cancel my master plan to fuck with you until you're blue in the face."

"Am I dead? Is this purgatory?"

She laughs again—but with her whole body. My pulse stumbles at the sound of it. The sight. It's not at my expense. It's *real*. As if all the sarcasm typically inside her melts away and in its place is warm, genuine amusement.

Okay, it's a little at my expense.

But I don't mind it so long as I get to witness it.

She swipes at a tear at the corner of her eye. "Oh, that was good, Indie. Breakfast with you might just be tolerable."

I turn onto a side street. "So, how does my father know you need fuel soon?"

She sighs, coming down from the high of her laughter. "I'd...forget to eat something in the morning once my shift started and...may have fainted once. Twice."

"So you're a troublemaker and a damsel in distress."

"I'm no damsel. I laugh at women who complain about morning sickness for a few months. Because I literally live with it."

"Ever try and find out why?"

"Sucking candy, ginger tea, I've heard it all. They give you solutions instead of finding out what's wrong with you."

"Maybe it's all in your head at this point."

"Maybe," she mutters, her thoughts drifting her away.

She's quiet as we enter the bakery. Tessa sits by the back wall while I order at the counter. I join her with two cups of coffee and pass her one.

"Thanks." She pops the lid and blows softly while I struggle to pull my gaze off those pouty lips. "So, who got you the mug you claim isn't yours?"

"Lonnie," I answer flatly, blinking away.

"Pepper's friend?"

"Technically, she's Pepper's boss." My ex Lonnie, is the Denver Ice Queens choreographer and trainer. When Pepper returned to town last year as a runaway bride, Chase got her a gig at the arena in an effort to disguise her. They had it all worked out, even faked an engagement so no one would figure out the woman with the million-dollar reward on her head by the name of Penelope Walker—was our very own Pepper Woods.

Even after the debacle with her ex was over, Pepper stayed an Ice Queen, working with her—now real—husband, the team captain of the Denver Kings hockey team, and my brother.

She sips her coffee, watching me like I'm keeping a secret. "Hmm...but you kept it. Could that be because you're still hot for her?"

I scoff. "No, because cowboys really *do* do it better."

She humphs. "Doubtful," she says as the eggs, bacon and toast platter is placed between us.

I'm going to regret asking. "And why's that?"

"Well…if you were really that good"—she points her fork at me—"she wouldn't have bought you a parting gift."

I laugh. "I can assure you, Lonnie's breakup with me was *not* because of that."

But apparently, my ex-wife's was. Since I found out she was sleeping with anything that moved in between her sporadic appearances.

She holds up a hand. "Actions speak louder than coffee mugs."

"False," I say. "That coffee mug is still speaking. Through you…"

"Hmm… you've got a point." She takes a bite of bacon, scrunching her nose at the eggs.

"You better eat these eggs, woman. I'm not having anyone pass out on my watch."

"Maybe just a bite." She pouts at the platter of four over easy eggs.

I lift my fork. "I'll help." My phone pings, and I lift it off the table.

Beau: *Got a new estimate for you.*

I clear my throat. "Excuse me," I tell Tessa while I type out a response.

Levi: *What do you mean new?*

Unless there was more damage to the car after he left with it, there shouldn't be a *new* estimate.

Beau: *Part going to cost more. Not worth it in my opinion.*

He sends me a figure that basically doubles what he told us initially. And if I remember correctly, Tessa's jaw practically fell to the floor when she heard it.

Levi: *I'll send you the difference now if you get it done by tomorrow.*

Beau: *Tomorrow before supper.*

Levi: *Perfect.*

"Everything alright?" Tess asks.

I set my phone down. "Why wouldn't it be?"

"Your jaw is tight. Your body is tense, and well, you basically look the way you do when I walk into a room."

I smirk. "You've noticed."

"And yet you hide it so well."

I lift my fork. "Good news is your car will be ready tomorrow."

"And the bad news?" She winces.

I picture the figure Beau sent and he's right; it's not worth the extra cash to save that thing.

But neither is telling her.

"Bad news is you're spending another night in my den."

She leans back in her chair, her brown eyes searching mine like she knows there's something else.

But she drops it. "Can I bring my toothbrush in this time?"

6

Tessa

I AVOID CALLING FRANK until I figure out plan B. If the man has even the slightest clue that I'm on the streets, he'll insist I go back into witness protection.

I will not live like a prisoner just because there *may* be a killer—or several—still looking for me.

They never give up, Tessa. They move on, but they always come back for the person who could ruin them. And you have that power.

"You get the job?" Bessie asks when I call her on my walk along the ranch.

"No."

"Cripe. He fill the position before you got there?"

"Nope. The job is still open. Just not to me."

"You're kidding. This guy really is an ass, isn't he?"

I consider it. If she asked me this yesterday, it would have been a hard yes. "I'm not sure."

"You still broke and homeless out there?"

"Don't forget without a car. Yes."

"Then he's an ass. What's his problem? You'd be terrific at—what's the job again?"

"A nanny."

The line is quiet and then Bessie sighs. "Maybe refresh the search again?"

"Goodbye, Bess."

"Bye, hun. Call me tomorrow."

I hang up and glance down the street. Levi went to work at the ranch after breakfast and I took myself on a tour.

It's the first week of August and the weather is scorching. Not to mention impossible finding any shade as I walk along.

I spot a familiar home on the other side of the ranch and realize where I've seen it.

It's Chase and Pepper's cottage.

The hockey king and his queen are off for the summer so they must be staying in town.

I suppose it would be rude not to say hello. And it would be just like Pepper to be annoyed if she found out I was next door for two days and didn't stop by.

Within a few feet, I'm standing in front of the cottage, beads of sweat trickling down my face and chest as I knock.

A blast of air conditioning hits me sweetly as Pepper swings the door open.

"Tessa!" Without hesitation or judgment, she throws her arms around me and pulls me inside. "Come in, come in. I am so happy to see you. Also, I win a bet I had going with my husband about you coming back." She shakes my shoulders cheerfully like we're old high school besties.

I chuckle awkwardly. "I'm glad. Think I could get a cut of that?"

"Oh don't be silly, we don't bet cash."

I frown. "What'd you bet?"

Her eyes flash devilishly. "Can I get you a lemonade?"

"Please." I follow her to the kitchen. "Is Chase home?"

"Nope. He's over at the Web."

"The what?"

"Charlie's Web?" she says like I know what that is. "The new bookstore opening at the end of the summer. The one Noah had designed and built for Charlie."

I blink. "Oh. I didn't know about that."

She exhales a dramatic breath. "That's right. That all happened after you left. *On* my wedding day."

I wince. "I'm so sorry. I'm sure you heard about my sleeping arrangements at the Inn."

"That no one but you had arranged that arrangement? Yeah, I know. Look, I get ditching the town because you think everyone judges you—" She raises her hand. "Um, been there. But we were really worried about you. A simple text to me or Charlie would have been cool."

"I guess I didn't think anyone would notice."

But not only did she notice, she bet on my coming back.

"Where'd you go?"

The question is so simple, but the answer...too loaded.

"Umm...I was staying with a friend not far from here." Two hours actually. "She needed my help so I had to go."

Bessie's given me a perpetual license to use her as an excuse anytime.

Pepper nods slowly. And I know she doesn't believe me. "You don't have to tell me where you go. But can you tell me how long you're staying?"

I'm about to answer but curiosity gets the best of me. "Why?"

"Because I like you and I want to be friends. You remind me a lot of my New York friends; cool, mysterious and a little badass."

I laugh. "Thanks. I think. So, as a friend...can I ask for a favor?"

"Anything," She beams, then backtracks suspiciously. "Probably."

"Can I use your shower?"

A little later, I'm climbing the steps of Levi's back porch. It's a wide and welcoming structure that stretches the length of the house, shaded by an overhanging roof. To the left are a pair of rocking chairs that sway in the light breeze. On the other side of the steps is a suitable yet weathered bench swing that could use a decorative pillow or two.

Reaching the door, I try my luck—which is laughable at this point—and turn the knob.

Finding it unlocked, I push it open and step inside.

Well, he *did* invite me to stay the night, so this should be okay.

"Tessa," Jackson calls excitedly from the living room. Almost like he's been waiting for me. The T.V. is on and he's sitting cross-legged on the rug.

"Hey, Wiggles."

He chuckles at the nickname. "Dad said you were coming over again. Wanna watch Star Wars?"

I flick my gaze to the screen. It's some sort of Jedi cartoon series. "I guess. But okay if we sit on the couch? I might hurt my neck watching that close."

Jackson moves his neck around like he's feeling for aches. "Good idea." He stands and settles into the cushions. I scooch in next to him.

"Where is your dad, anyway?"

He shrugs. "I don't know. He was here a minute ago. We just got home."

I hear the front door swing open with a grunt. "All good, buddy, I've got the groceries."

Jackson hops off the couch. "Oh, right. Sorry, Dad, coming."

I follow him as Levi sets four paper bags of groceries on the kitchen counter.

"All this for two people?" I ask.

"There's more in the truck," he says on an exhale. He's wearing the same T-shirt from earlier. The one that hugs his puffed chest and muscled biceps so deliciously, it's a shame. Because guys who are clearly sworn off women like this scorned single dad shouldn't look this good.

"Need a hand with the rest? Or four?" I lift one of Jackson's hands.

He winks, and I'm not entirely positive it's for me. Could just be a habit. "Nah, I've got it, thanks. Besides, we don't let women do our heavy lifting, do we, bud?"

"Nope," Jackson calls as he races back into the living room in front of the television.

"So I'm suitable to wreck an entire town but not strong enough to lift a grocery bag?"

"Not on my watch," he mutters without waiting for a response. Then steps out to unload the rest.

I peek out the window at the sunset, imagining this being their daily routine. Just the two of them. Levi running the ranch from dawn to dusk, worrying about Jackson throughout the day. Then spending every moment of the evening giving him as close to normal as he can. When does the man rest?

"I brought your suitcase in earlier, too," he calls on his way back with two more bags.

I stroll over to the den to take a peek, not seeing my things anywhere. "Thanks...where'd you put it?"

"Upstairs."

I frown. "Why? There was nothing wrong with the den. I'm only here for one night."

"Figured you might want some privacy, a good night's sleep, or…" He scans me. "A shower. But it looks like you took care of that."

"I took a quick one at Pepper's."

He glances toward the cottage from his back porch but doesn't say anything.

"Can I make dinner?"

"No." His response is sharp.

"Okay, maybe I can help get Jackson cleaned up or something?"

For fuck's sake, let someone do something.

He whips out scallions from a paper bag and points them at me. "I don't need your help, Tessa."

I hold up my hands. "Okay."

"This isn't an extended silent interview. I'm not hiring you. You're in a jam and I'm helping you out with a place to crash one more night. Nothing more."

My chest burns but it fades quickly. I've never been the type to cry. Never. Not even when I woke up with excruciating pain in my lower back three years ago. But just in case the stinging in my eyes doesn't fade soon, I should go.

"Gotcha." Swallowing hard, I back up. "Did you say my things were upstairs?"

His hard features neutralize. "Third door on the left."

"Thank you."

I plug my phone in and wait for it to charge so I can turn it on. It finally ran out of juice after I ended my call with Bessie earlier.

The guest room Levi put me in is rustic and clean. Smells nice, too. A queen bed with a solid white down comforter and linens. A wooden desk.

A standing dresser.

My stomach twists.

It's sad that a piece of bedroom furniture strikes more fear into my heart than a killer spider.

I need serious therapy.

I'd ask if I could sleep in the den again, but it doesn't seem like Levi is in the mood for me right now.

I get it. The man is protective of his town, his family—and I'm the threat to all that is good in his world.

If I had any pride left, I'd march out of his house and this town on foot before I let a man speak to me that way.

But I'm too tired to be proud.

And this bed is warm. I haven't slept on a mattress since those nights I'd sneak into the Inn. Back in Summer Hill, I sleep on Bessie's couch.

I lie over the bed covers and watch what remains of the sunset from my window, my eyelids falling heavy until I give up the fight to stay awake.

The voice next to me is hoarse and familiar. "Hey."

I blink my eyes open.

Groaning, I turn. Levi is at my side. "Oh good, you're awake," he says softly with a grin.

"I'm not."

"Don't make me splash cold water on your face, Tess."

I sigh with another groan. "What did I do now?"

"Nothing," he answers gravelly, running a hand across his brow. "I was just wondering if you'd like to have dinner with me."

He can't be serious. I'd like to splash water on *his* face for even considering that I'd have a meal with him. "No."

He's not fazed by my glower. I'm losing my touch. "Jackson's asleep." I sit up. "Indie, I'm going to make this very easy for you. I'm going to personally disqualify myself for the job right now. I don't like kids. I don't want them. I have no experience. And I don't. Like. You."

He inhales a small breath, ready to speak.

I hold up a finger, remembering his ad. "I take that back. I totally see myself falling in love with you. Ergo, I don't meet your requirements. I will leave here the minute my car is returned, and you'll never have to see me again."

His face is tight, but there's compassion and remorse in his eyes. "Okay." Then, he holds his hand out. "Now, will you have dinner with me?"

I stare at it uncommittedly.

"You offered to help me before. I could use some help finishing dinner. It's chicken. There's veggies. You like wine? I prefer beer, but should have a bottle of red somewhere—"

"Please stop." I take his hand. Shocked by an electrical current that zips through my veins. "I'll have dinner with you."

His eyes dip to where we're connected. "I may not have wine…"

"I prefer beer."

7

Levi

Tessa's up early again.

I can smell the bacon from my bedroom upstairs.

Yesterday was an off day. I overslept, waking at seven instead of six. The failed interviews from the previous night took a toll on me and Tessa showing up at my door threw me off kilter.

She's the woman I'd fought to leave my town every time she turned up, and knowing she was right downstairs kept me up longer than ideal.

But now I'm up an hour before yesterday, and it's like she's keeping up with our internal clocks the way she manages to be up before me.

The steps creak as I make my way down.

Tessa is in a new outfit. Denim shorts and a plaid blouse. Her smooth long legs are toned and tanned. Her hair is tied in a ponytail over one shoulder, strands of curls falling loose at every end.

The dark circles under her eyes suggest that, once again, she didn't get more than five hours of sleep.

She glances up at me mid-task. "Mornin'."

"Mornin'." I look down at the spread she's preparing. It looks suitable for a bed and breakfast. "You gonna eat any of it this time?"

She scrunches her nose like I'd just asked if she'd consume a raw egg. "No thanks. And I'm gettin' out of your hair soon. Pepper said I can wait in her cottage till my car's ready."

"Why?"

"Assume you're all leaving the house this morning, and I can't stay here alone." She shrugs like it's the obvious reason. "Might wreck the place."

"That's not your style," I say with confidence, pouring myself a cup of coffee from the freshly filled pot.

"What's my style?"

I fold my arms across my chest and lean against the counter, assessing her. "You cause trouble, not vandalism."

"Maybe I'll surprise you and switch it up." She holds my gaze and perks a brow, and damn, it's too sexy.

I ignore the flirtatious comment and push off the counter. "Besides, I'm home all morning, so you don't need to rush out. Car should be here by noon."

She plates pancakes and glances over at the ranch. "Thought you cowboys work round the clock."

"Daylight mostly, unless there's an emergency. My men are out there, but I've got a few more interviews this morning."

She sets an empty batter bowl in the sink and runs the water. "Indie, come on. Who are you kidding? You are not going to find the perfect nanny."

"I don't need perfect. I just need someone responsible and experienced to watch my kid."

She holds out her arms. "I'm responsible."

I scoff. "You're responsible for a heck of a lot that no one bothered holding you accountable for."

"Look, you know I'm good for feedin' the kid and he's safe with me—what more do you want?"

"Trust, Tessa. I don't trust you."

"I don't trust anyone either, doesn't mean I can't work with them."

An annoyed grunt rattles my throat, and I pinch the bridge of my nose.

"Okay, fine, don't have an aneurysm. Forget I said anything."

I drop my hand with a sigh. Tessa's back is to me. Lifting on her toes, she puts away breakfast ingredients in the cupboards. Roaming through my kitchen like she belongs here. And looking damn good doing it, too.

Add *that* to the con list for hiring her. I can't keep looking at her the way I want to.

Not to mention those full lips and the level of sass coming out of them.

But she's right. If today turns out to be anything like Sunday's interviews, I'm screwed.

I look down at the plate she so delicately arranged for my kid. And can't stop myself from offering her a fighting chance.

After all, it's not forever.

"Look, if the people I've got coming today turn out to be disasters—and I mean total unworkable disasters—"

She slaps a hand down on the counter. "You'll hire me!" Her eyes brighten with a smile that stops my heart.

"*Give* you a proper interview," I finish.

She rolls her eyes.

"See, that right there? If you're not going to respect your boss, that's a giant red flag."

She sucks her teeth and does it again.

"Seriously?"

"Fine. But I'm sticking around for them."

"What do you mean you're sticking around for them?"

She points to herself. "I can call bullshit when I see it. You need me as backup out there."

"You're not sitting in on my interviews. That's creepy, and how am I supposed to explain that?"

"I'll be in the background. Tell them I'm your cleaning lady."

Jackson races down the stairs. "Bacon!"

Tessa's soft laugh fills the kitchen as she pushes the plate in front of his chair. "Extra crispy."

I walk over to my kid, brushing his unruly hair back. "Why you up so early?"

"I smelled bacon and thought Grandpa was here to pick me up."

"Grandpa's not the only one who can make bacon."

The kid shrugs and takes a bite. I guess it has been a minute since I bothered. I just stock up on the stuff, expecting to make time to cook, but lately, it's been takeout from the Inn or a quick bagel on the go.

Tessa tears the bacon out of his mouth like it's licorice and replaces it with a silver dollar pancake.

I point a finger at her with a warning, like I'm the one doing her a favor. "You can stay for the interviews, but not a word."

She zips her mouth shut and winks at Jackson.

I'm going to regret this.

The second contestant of the day is Becca Fischer. She's thirty, relatively new in town, and keeps staring at my biceps like she's mentally fitting me for a new suit.

So far, she's a huge step up from the first interview, who looked like she stepped out of a fairytale, ready to fall into song and dance. She wouldn't last five minutes with Jackson.

"So, Becca, where'd you live before Hideaway Springs?"

"Texas. Born and raised. My parents moved here, and I followed them to ensure they were okay. You know people don't want to admit they need their children to care for them when they're older, but I don't think they can function without me."

It's a harsh statement to make but I ignore it. "So they live here too, then?"

She grins and bobs her head. "Yep."

There's something off about her, but I need to give her the benefit of the doubt.

"Why do you want to be a nanny?"

"I love taking care of people." She scans me and licks her lips. "Some say I'm a giver."

Tessa whistles provocatively behind me.

I drop my head and press my lips together to keep from laughing.

A spray bottle and rag in hand, Tessa circles my chair, her tone a little snappy. "It's a live-in position. Would that work for you, given you live with your parents to uh...take care of them?" she asks.

Becca blows it off without a thought. "Oh yeah. They'll be fine without me."

Sixty seconds later, I'm walking Becca out—who Tessa bullied into admitting that her parents allowed her to live with them temporarily as long as she found work.

I shut the door and glare at the temporary intruder in my home, and she lifts her shoulders innocently. "What? They were total jokes. One basically offered you a blow job, and the other wanted to turn your son into a ballerina."

I stride past her, muttering. "I'll take a blow job over a police record."

She extends her hands like we finally agree on something as she follows me into the main room. "Well, why didn't you say so? Drop 'em, Cowboy."

I flip back to her. "I was *joking*."

"Uh...so was I." She winces, scratching her head.

I bite down a chuckle and check my phone to see who's next. Christ. There's only one more.

"And how is living with your parents worse than sneaking into a hotel room every night after your shift?"

"When you give me a proper interview, I'll tell you." She pops a blueberry in her mouth and I check the time, noting she hadn't eaten yet.

I tear my gaze off her lips and sigh.

One more. I've got one more and I'm confident about this next one. I know her from town. I know her parents. She *has* to be it.

A few minutes later, the doorbell rings and Tessa grabs a duster as if someone just called "*Places*". With a headshake, I pull the door open and plaster a smile.

"Carol, hi."

A kind, warm smile greets me. "Mr. Reeves, hi." Carol is in a pale pink blouse and flowy skirt that falls to her knees. It's summery and appropriate.

"Please, come in."

"Thanks so much for meeting with me, and I'm sorry I couldn't make it yesterday. I had to take my little brother to practice. He's on the little league team."

"Oh, how fun. No worries, I'm glad you could make it today." I point her to the couch and take a seat on the armchair.

Tessa hangs back, fake dusting the banister.

Carol blinks, scanning my *cleaning lady's* outfit. But doesn't say anything.

"So, I know I emailed it, but I wanted to bring my resume anyway." She passes me a crisp folder. "As you'll see, I have three years experience at the daycare and eight months at the elementary school."

I wait for Tessa to comment on the short-term at the school, but she doesn't.

"It's where I did my student teaching."

Ah.

"I also don't have a boyfriend, by the way."

I nearly sigh. *And there it is!*

But I'll let Tess take this one. Then kindly thank Carol before walking her out.

"So you'll never have to worry about me sneaking boys in when you're out. This is your home, your rules, and I totally respect it."

I blow out a breath, scanning the resume. That sounds rehearsed. And definitely Googled.

Also, I appreciate the note but who does that? Is she dropping 'I'm single' hints?

Am I paranoid?

Or just conceded?

"Besides," she says. "I have no interest in relationships until after I finish my master's in education. I only have one year to go."

Both, I'm definitely both.

Blowing out a harsh breath, I nod, considering if there's anything left to ask her. "That's... impressive."

She sighs at her accomplishment. "I'm excited. Teaching and children have always gone well for me. It's my passion. Oh and I love to cook. I get it's not part of the job but every kid needs a homemade meal. And every kid should learn to cook, so I do plan to slap an apron on Jackson."

Child labor. Red flag.

Again, I wait for a comment from the peanut gallery and glance behind me. But Tessa's not there.

"Also, I think Jackson and my little brother Thomas know each other from school. If it's alright with you, I could arrange playdates or trips to the library or the lake..."

I nod at Carol as she goes on and subtly scan the floor for my fiery redhead.

"I think I saw her go in the den," Carol offers.

I frown, turning my focus back.

"Sorry, I pay attention when someone needs something. Occupational hazard."

Give it a rest, Sunshine.

Glancing outside, I see another car in my lot.

Tessa's car.

Beau Hamilton is out there with her, counting cash as she loads her suitcase into the trunk.

Moth to a flame, I fly to my front door, yanking it open. Like a hypocrite, I glare at the guy I paid extra to help me get rid of the town rogue faster.

"That was quick. You sure it works without a problem?"

Tessa shuts her trunk, squinting from the sun in her eyes. "Car starts like new." Then, with that same bright smile she had given me earlier, she points to Beau with her thumb. "This guy works miracles."

I'm nothing but scowls as I approach the two of them, and there's not a damn thing I can do to help it.

Picking up my vibe, Beau backs up and gives me a solute. "Appreciate the business."

Tessa glances behind me at the house, her bottom lip between her teeth. "Hey, thanks for everything. Give Wiggles a high five for me."

God, that raspy voice is going to be the death of me. "Where you goin'?"

She shrugs. "Wherever the road takes me."

I step closer. "I don't recall giving you a day off."

She frowns then glances behind me again.

A voice slices through the air between us. "Sorry, should I wait inside, or is the interview over?"

"It's over," I say, feeling like someone else is talking for me. Keeping my eyes on my redheaded rebel, I seal the deal. "Appreciate you coming in, but the position's been filled."

"Oh. Guess...it must have slipped your mind."

Breaking my gaze, I turn to Carol. "Sorry about that."

"No...worries." Confused, she gets back in her car and backs out of my driveway.

Tessa smacks my arm. "Hell was that about? She was perfect."

I shrug. "She was too late. My new nanny started yesterday."

"Levi...even I'm not that selfish. Jackson needs someone like that girl." Her genuine concern for my kid wraps around me. It reinforces my decision.

"Maybe I don't want a girl taking care of my kid. Maybe I want a woman."

8

Tessa

I'M SEATED ON THE kitchen counter stool, biting the shit out of my bottom lip. A nervous tick I've been fighting my entire adult life.

Levi and I hardly spoke since Beau quietly reversed out of the driveway during the awkward moment where…I think Indie *hired* me to take care of his kid.

I've been in his house all afternoon processing after he left for the ranch, returning with Jackson at his side and take out from the Inn.

We ate dinner quietly—well, *we* were quiet. Jackson talked up a storm about a rock he and a kid named Rowan found. And how they cracked it into pieces finding a crystal center.

About an hour ago, Levi announced bedtime in a way that almost made it sound fun and disappeared up the stairs with Wiggles.

Meanwhile, I've been sitting here practically banging my head against the marble counter because *what in the actual fuck did I get myself into?*

I needed to get the fuck out of town.

I needed a job and a place to live.

I *wanted* it to be in Hideaway Springs.

I didn't want to be responsible for another human.

I'm not a kid person. Hell, I don't even remember being one. I'm an only child.

My only frame of reference for parenting is dad leaving mom a year after I was born, reappearing every so often only to take off again. Once I was old enough to care for myself—around seventeen—they *both* left.

Not that I see myself ditching the kid or anything, but who's to say I won't screw something up the way my parents did?

How much time is too much to spend with a kid until you've somehow managed to fuck with their innocent little mind?

I like Jackson too much to mess up his beautiful soul.

First time I met the kid was at his birthday party last fall when I was part of Aiden's catering crew. The moment I laid eyes on him, I knew who he belonged to.

The mean rugged cowboy that makes you want to cock your head to the side and ask, "Who hurt you?"

Still boggles me how the two boys upstairs are related.

Jackson is warm, trusting, and bursting with exciting energy that makes you want to ruffle his hair and pull him in for a squeeze.

Levi is a grumbly, rugged ice-cold skeptic who makes you want to scream. And not in a good way.

Which is unfortunate.

I stiffen when I hear him making his way back down. What the hell now? Do I act like I know what I'm doing? Tell him he won't be disappointed? Will he see right through me?

A cedary scent lingers when he moves past me to stand across the counter. "Thanks for not saying anything to Jackson yet."

"I'm not exactly sure what to say."

"Me neither," he grumbles, and it makes me swallow.

One of us should know how to do this.

I push off my seat. "This was a bad idea."

"Sit down."

I drop back onto my seat. His intimidating energy doing a number on me already.

"Tell me about yourself, Tessa." The question doesn't come out casual or conversational. Reading between the lines, he's asking me to give him a reason to change his mind.

"I'm an only child. Natural redhead."

"Where are you from?"

"All over."

"Tessa."

"What does it matter? What East Coast takes care of kids better than the West Coast? Who cares?"

"So, West Coast?"

"Chicago."

He considers that for a moment. "How old are you?"

"Twenty-seven."

"Why'd you come to Hideaway Springs?"

"Which time?" I ask, already putting up my defenses.

"All of them."

"These are not the questions you asked the other candidates today."

"Doesn't mean I don't expect a candid answer."

Our gazes lock, it's raw and intense and it makes me look away. I hate being the first to look away. "I'm not answering it."

"Well, I can't exactly ask what your experience is since it's non-existent."

"I can cook."

"So can I."

"I can tell by all the takeout containers." I blink with a grin.

His biceps tighten, flexing with the pressure against the counter. "Summer's really busy at the ranch."

"You're welcome," I remind him with a snap.

He crosses to me. "You'll protect him."

The word jolts me into hyper-awareness. "From what?"

His gaze drifts. "Anything that could hurt him."

"With my life," I say it with every bone in my body. I'd protect the hell out of that kid.

His gaze drops to my mouth. "The job is temporary. Just till the end of summer. That's six weeks. Can you make it without skipping town that long?"

"Pretty sure."

"Tessa."

"Yes," I say tightly instead of storming out that door like he deserves.

He nods like he doesn't know what to do with himself. But it's clear as day. Someone did a number on this guy. Or his kid. Maybe both?

"Do I get a question?"

"Sure," he answers just as tight.

"Is every conversation going to be this intense?"

"Can't handle it?"

I narrow my eyes. "I'd like to be prepared."

"Probably." He glances at my small suitcase at the bottom of the steps. I'd brought it down this morning, prepared to leave. "Where's the rest of your stuff?"

"This is it."

"It's one bag. People pack more on a four-day cruise."

"I live with someone back...where I'm from. She doesn't have a lot of space."

"You don't have a place of your own?"

"If I did, I wouldn't have been living at the Inn for six months."

He watches me—clearly another question on his mind. But lets it go. Shifting his gaze, he crosses to a calendar on the refrigerator. "Jackson has a handful of activities planned for the rest of the summer. Some with friends from town, some with family. It's all here. I'm up at six every morning and then head down to my gym for thirty minutes before heading to the ranch. You're free to use it after that."

"Or before," I mutter.

"And about your early hours." He turns to me. "I don't like it."

"I'm sorry?"

"That may have worked for you before, but you're responsible for a child now. I need you focused and alert."

This makes me want to scream. Because my internal alarm clock is not by choice. It's a goddamn curse. One that no kiss from a frog is going to break. But I don't come with much else to offer, so with this, I appease him. "I'll see what I can do."

"Great. Any questions?"

"Can I stay in the den?"

"What?"

"I like it in the den. Can I stay there?"

"There's no door."

"I'll change in the bathroom."

"What's wrong with the bedroom?"

The wardrobe. The door. Window too high from the ground.

"Nothing, it's fine. It'll be fine." I convince myself.

"Are you overwhelmed?"

"No," I lie.

The tension is so high, and the truth of the matter is, I've been living with enough self-doubt and depreciation to have to put up with it from this guy.

"One more thing." I slide off the seat and cross the space between us. His eyes sweep over me but are unreadable as I stop directly in front of him. "Either you fix your tone when you speak to me, or you'll be right back where you started."

He holds my gaze for a beat, and I can't tell if it's my imagination or if he's tilting toward me. Maybe even smelling the top of my head?

Pulling back, he drags a hand down his face and gives me a quick nod. "Okay."

"Can we get ice cream at Millie's today?" Jackson asks as he hands me dry dishes from the washer that I ran overnight.

It's my second full day with Jackson and so far, so good. Who knew I'd be good at this nanny thing? Who knew it's basically living your day-to-day, cooking, tidying up, and talking nonsense to your customers as you refill their coffee?

Except it's one customer, and it's apple juice.

"Um…" I turn to the schedule. Tomorrow is a big day. In addition to a few errands to run in town, I'm supposed to have him at the Inn for something called a 'Web Party'. "Yeah, we've got room for ice cream today." I scan his snug outfit. "But first, I want to go through your closets and pick out some things that might be a little small for you that we can donate."

"Okay." He closes the empty dishwasher.

I would have emptied the thing earlier myself—when I was up at four-fifteen this morning. But with Levi's warning that I can't be waking up at ungodly hours of the night, I opted for little to no noise around the house.

Bright side is, I got in a good workout in his fully equipped gym, washed my hair, let it air dry, and read a magazine about agriculture. I waited until after the boys were up to start moving about in the kitchen. Least I could do is make it *look* like I woke up at a normal hour.

Levi mostly grunted all morning before leaving for the ranch, and that's fine. Grunting is better than setting more rules and expectations I'm bound to never meet.

With the kitchen sparkling, we head upstairs to rummage through his dresser.

"Dad said he'll take me shopping closer to the school year for new stuff. Says at the rate I'm going, I might grow another six inches before then."

I laugh. "You did get a little taller since I last saw you."

This seems to jog a memory for the little guy. "Grandpa missed you at the Inn."

I glance back. "How do you know?"

"I asked him."

"You did?"

"Yeah. I said, 'I miss Tessa. She used to give me more fries'. And Grandpa said, 'Me too kid, but I could do without the fries'."

I shake my head with a smile I can't help. "Okay, take a look at these." I toss a few things at him. "If you can live without it, I think we should add it to the donation pile."

We pack a generous load to drop off and clean up his room.

"There, now there's room for new stuff."

"Cool." He looks up at me with joyful eyes. "Ice cream now?"

I check my watch. "But we haven't had lunch yet?"

He shrugs.

I narrow my eyes at him. "Yeah, okay." I reach for his hand. "Let's go rogue."

ROXANNE TULLY

"Come out, come out *wherever you are.*"

Sweat drips down my face, my neck, and hell, I'm hot everywhere. It's fucking boiling in here. Who the hell keeps a standing wardrobe anymore?

My eyes drop to the side where my dead body is going to be a minute from now, and my last thoughts are, "Who the hell keeps a standing wardrobe?"

Footsteps grow closer, and I inch further behind the pile of clothes.

Sirens sound in the distance, but it does nothing to settle the pounding of my heart. To the undeniable truth that I am not making it out of here alive.

Those cops could be right outside and I'd still have no shot in hell.

"Eddie, we gotta get out of here." The other voice is urgent, almost as desperate as I am for them to leave.

"She's in here," the voice of the guy who shot Eric grits.

"There's no one here—let's go."

A nearby chair is kicked angrily. "I fucking saw her, Vince."

I bite down a whimper.

The sirens are closer. I chew on my bottom lip as I peek through the cracks. Eddie slams the closet across the room shut. After a beat, his eyes flick across the open space to the wardrobe.

No, no, no, no.

He marches forward and I barely have time to blink before the door is pulled open and I'm thrown to the cold tile floor next to my dead boyfriend. He points the gun at me. The same one that put two bullets in Eric minutes ago.

I stare at his body, a cold, dreadful thought sweeps my mind and I'm a horrible person for it.

You might have deserved this ending, but I don't.

"Eddie, we got to go." Vince presses, his voice ragged. He must be new to the organization.

Eddie flips me over, a sharp strike across my face. "What did you see?"

"Nothing," I breathe.

"What did you see?" he shouts.

Somewhere behind where I lie on the floor, Vince curses under his breath and opens the window, making Eddie snap his head up. "The fuck are you doing?"

"Getting out of here." Vince jumps as Eddie curses and moves to the window.

Shit. The window. Why didn't I think of that when we heard them coming? I could have made it.

But I stupidly let Eric shove me in the damn wardrobe.

"Vince!" he whisper-screams, then points the gun out the window and fires. "Damn it. Wait."

Jesus Christ.

Scrambling to my feet, I'm at the door in two seconds and pull. Locked. It's locked.

I struggle with the knob, twisting the little latch in every direction, desperate to break free, but the damn thing won't give. All I hear is my last jagged breath before a deafening sound goes off.

A wave of agony radiates through me as sharp, searing pain explodes right through my lower back. I'm stiff as my knees give out, my fingers slide off the doorknob, and I fall to the ground.

I jerk forward, gasping for air, my hands clutching at the covers over me as I rock myself back to sanity. Trying not to imagine that if he'd aimed a little higher, I'd either be dead or paralyzed.

Pulling out of bed, I stride to the door and pull it open. If only just a crack.

The laundry list of baggage I have carried since that day is outrageous. The therapy I refused even more.

I change and head down the stairs to the gym, confident that the thunder and lightning outside these walls will overthrow the sounds of my footsteps at four in the morning.

9

Levi

I'M UP BEFORE MY alarm and blame it on the thunder and lightning outside my window and the pattering against my roof.

It's five o'clock. Still dark. I punch the corner of my pillow but know it's no use. That last hour snooze is gone and there's no getting it back.

I rise and slip on my gym shorts. A longer workout never hurt anybody.

Tessa's first two days with Jackson seemed to go off without a hitch. But I'm not buying for one minute that she's been sleeping in. Yesterday, she started making breakfast after we'd come down, but miraculously, the refrigerator was cleaned out and cabinets rearranged in a way that made sense.

Whatever. I could have done that if I had time—and the energy.

Can't wait for the day she oversleeps because my kid wore her out. She has no idea.

The thought should scare me. That she's never done this before. That she doesn't have a single parental bone in her body. But my dumbass is frustratingly intrigued.

One good thing will come out of it, I suppose. No one can ever say I don't give people the benefit of the doubt. Because I've had my doubts about Tessa Banks for years.

And every time she's in town, she proves me right.

I brush my teeth, throw on a clean T-shirt, and toss a towel over my shoulder before stepping out into the dark hall.

I nearly crash with a half-naked body as it passes in front of me.

Tessa gasps, throwing a hand to her chest. My gaze draws up from her bare legs, the tight spandex shorts around her hips and the sports bra covering her chest.

Gripping her forearms, I haul her to the bedroom across mine, shut her door and crowd her against it.

"What the hell are you doing?" I grit.

Breath hitching, she stares up at me. Her hair and face are damp. The top of her breasts glisten with sweat, and I struggle to keep my eyes on hers. Swallowing, she answers. "I think that's my question."

"Jackson could have stepped out of his room. You can't be walking around in your underwear."

Her expression hardens and she pins me with those whiskey-colored eyes. "I can see how this might bother you." She juts out her hips, hitting my erection, causing me to grunt in response. "But how is this a problem for someone who won't be up for hours?"

Lifting her arms above her head, I growl. "Don't do that again."

Tearing her heated gaze from my lips, she meets my eyes. "I think *inappropriate* went out the window when you shut me in here and pinned me against the wall, Indie."

She has a point.

I release her and storm to the wardrobe, pulling the doors apart.

Empty.

"Where are your clothes?"

Sighing, she crosses to the nightstand and pulls at the drawers. "There. Will you be inspecting my room on a daily basis?"

What is wrong with this woman? Who shoves their stuff into tiny nightstand drawers? "This room doesn't have closets. Hang your clothes in the wardrobe."

"No." The answer comes fast and flat.

"Fine, I don't fucking care where you put your clothes, as long as you're fully dressed when you walk out this door. Jackson is nine years old. *Nine*. Not three. You need to be more conscious." Scanning her once more, I take note of just how sweaty and winded she is. "How long was your workout?"

She looks to the side as if she's guilty of something. "I was up at four."

I drag a hand through my hair. "I'll leave you to it. Meet me downstairs in an hour."

Sweat drips down my face as I grip the cold metal again, muscles straining with the weight.

It's a rhythm I'm used to.

It should be mindless. Purposeless.

Instead, Tessa's face, the rise and fall of her chest, and her damp skin linger on the edge of my focus like *she's* my motivation.

I check the time and it's like I'm competing with her, because until I get that full hour, I'm not leaving this room.

I dab my face and pecs with a clean towel and climb the steps back to the front hall. Then start a pot of coffee.

I grip the edge of the counter, biting down a growl.

I've got to stop being a dick to her.

And I've got to keep my hands off Tessa Banks— stealing glances at her skin every chance I get. I damn near lost myself in her bedroom.

It would have been so easy.

Just the feel of her skin under my fingertips sent me soaring past levels of appropriate boss-employee behavior. All that was missing was a taste of that pretty little mouth. The mouth that curved up a tad when she called me out on my hardon.

And yet, somehow, I have zero regrets about not hiring Carol. Because watching Tessa walk out of my life for good was something I didn't realize I wasn't ready for.

I hear her soft footsteps coming down the stairs and sniff some control into my system.

Reaching up, I pull the cowboy mug she seems to favor from the cabinet and pour her some coffee.

"Sugar?" I ask.

No response.

Fuck, did I screw up so badly that I'm getting the cold shoulder now?

"Okay, no sugar," I turn, finding Tessa ripping her gaze off my mid-section before quickly snapping to my eyes.

"Yes, please," she responds in a single breath.

I glance down and fuck—forgot my shirt.

I step closer, keeping the island counter between us, ignoring the fact that I am a fucking hypocrite. "How many?"

"Two."

I drop two spoonfuls into her mug.

She smirks at the one I chose for her and takes a sip. "Perfect."

"Sorry, I forgot to slip it back on after my workout," I say, turning away from her lingering gaze that doesn't help my inappropriate thoughts.

"I suppose there are things we *both* should get used to."

I glance back at her. She's in skinny jeans and an oversized shirt.

"It's supposed to be close to ninety today. You're not gonna make it far in that."

"I'll be alright. Wouldn't want to be dressing provocatively in front of the almost-teenager you're raising."

I grunt. "I overreacted, Tess."

She twists the coffee mug between her palms.

"It's highly unlikely that Jackson would be up that early, but I would still appreciate it if—"

"Won't happen again," she offers quickly.

I release a breath, my shoulders slumping. "Thank you."

She winces and covers her eyes. "And sorry I did that thing where I—"

"It's forgotten." I almost laugh and cross to her, pulling her hand down. "You wouldn't have if I hadn't crowded your personal space."

Her eyes are on my chest, lips parting delicately. "All good."

My gaze drops to where her teeth grab hold of her full bottom lip, and I can consider my self-control fucked.

My hand reaches to pull it from between her teeth. "You're gonna give yourself a bruise like that."

"You almost sound like you care," she rasps. And God, I could get used to that voice.

I may already have.

I drop my hand from the side of her face and step back. "Now, maybe when you're done eye-fucking me, you can get back to work."

The corner of her lips quirk. "Touche, Indie." She moves around me and pulls at contents from the cabinets.

Well, I'll be damned. *She remembered.*

10

Tessa

"Jackson, you almost ready?" I've been overcompensating all morning and I don't need to be a rocket scientist to notice it.

First, with the outfit fit for fall, then with an overly healthy breakfast. Now I'm calling him by his actual name instead of 'Wiggles' or 'kid'.

All this overthinking is throwing me off. It's nearly ten and we're already running late to the first thing on the schedule today.

"Jackson, turn off the T.V. and pack your stuff, we're heading out soon."

"I can't find the remote."

I step into the living room. "I put it on the coffee table this morning. Did you check between the cushions?"

"Yes."

I sigh. "Well, then, shut it off the old-fashioned way."

"The what way?"

I growl and storm over to the flat-screen television, finding the little button on the side and pressing it. Moving back to the kitchen, I load the dishwasher and wash my hands.

My phone pings with a message.

Levi: What'd you have for breakfast?

Tessa: I made him eggs with a side of blueberries and toast.

Levi: That wasn't what I asked.

Tessa: I don't understand the question.

Levi. Then read it again.

Wise ass. I scroll back up.

Tessa: You mean me?

Levi: Yes.

Tessa: Blueberries and toast.

Levi: Protein?

Tessa: No time.

My phone rings with Levi's name on the screen.

I shake my head and answer it. "We're about to walk out the door. You left us a full schedule today."

"Open the top cabinet left of the fridge."

I frown, thinking I missed something. "What am I looking for? There's nothing but protein shakes here."

"That's right, you moved everything. Um...the one underneath it."

I shut the top one and open the one below. "Cane sugar, powdered sugar, maple syrup, peanut butter."

"That one."

I place it on the counter. "Now what?"

"Grab a spoonful and eat it."

"What? No."

"You allergic?"

"No."

"Then what's the problem?"

I stare at the jar like it's growing mold. "I don't like the consistency."

"Tessa, you were up at four o'clock this morning, worked out for an hour, and had berries for breakfast. It's either that or an omelet. You're not going anywhere until you refuel."

My eyes dart to my coffee mug.

"Coffee doesn't count."

I yank open the drawer and pull out a spoon. There's a beat on the other line as I dip the tip into the creamy substance.

"More."

"Wh—are you watching me from somewhere?"

"You're stubborn. Call it a hunch."

I suck on the spoon. "This was not in my contract," I say, my tongue sounding like it's been burned.

There's a smirk in his voice when he responds. "Have a fine day."

I grunt and hang up.

"Was that Dad?"

"Did you find the remote?"

"No. We could just look for it later."

I rub my eyes. "It's going to bother me all day."

Twenty minutes later, I find the damn thing stuffed into the pocket of an oversized sweatshirt.

"Oh, right." Jackson flashes me an innocent smile. "Alright, shoes on, let's move."

"There she is." Aiden's grin is wide as he comes around the bar with his arms extended.

My smile in return is hesitant.

"Come here, let me give you a proper hello."

I shrug coyly before he wraps me in a bear hug. "I didn't mind the first one."

He sighs, glancing at Jackson, who's distracted picking at a basket of mini muffins. "I apologize for my son. If you broke his arm for dragging you in here to humiliate you, I wouldn't have held it against you."

I wink at him. "It was worth it."

He scans me like an overprotective parent. "How are you? Everything okay? Do you need anything?"

"Aiden," I start.

He holds up his hands. "Please, don't. I feel bad enough."

"*You* feel bad?"

He sighs. "I practically forced you out of town. You obviously needed help and..."

"And you offered it," I remind him.

He nods. "You always have a room here if you need it."

"Thank you."

"Have you eaten?"

"Yes, jeez. You Reeves men really need to simmer down."

"Reeves men?"

"Levi called me at ten this morning and wouldn't back off until he heard me eat a spoonful of peanut butter."

The corner of his mouth turns up. "That so?"

"I still can't get the taste out of my mouth." I move behind the bar like I still work here and grab a bottle of water. "So, why are we here? I was told to bring the kid over. Are we late?"

"Technically, you're early since Noah and Charlie are running late."

As if on cue, the charming new couple stride into the Inn mid-argument over whose fault it is they're late. But it doesn't last long since they quickly find something hilarious about it.

They truly are a strange, nerdy—yet adorable duo.

Out of the three brothers, Noah might just be the most charming. Tall, with deep blue eyes, sharp jaw, a head full of dark hair, and a muscular upper body that's always covered in a crisp button-down. The smile on his face looks foreign to me, but given he's looking at the tiny blonde at his side, it suits him.

Charlie is bubbly, outgoing, and friendly—all things opposite Noah.

"Tessa." Charlie beams.

I stiffen on contact when she wraps her arms around me. It's not her who has me holding my breath.

It's her boyfriend.

"I'm so happy to see you." She squeezes me once more before pulling back. "You look phenomenal as usual."

Noah's glare is intense as he approaches, his tone empty. "Tessa. What brings you by? Can't imagine there's much left in this town for you to corrupt."

Charlie elbows him, keeping her smile bright as he grunts behind her.

Jackson skips over. "Tessa's my new nanny. She's living with us."

Charlie gasps happily while Noah chokes out a laugh. "Does my brother know this?"

"As a matter of fact, your brother insisted," I say.

"Really?" He steps forward, lowering his voice. "Did you happen to give him the same stuff you poisoned Jackson's *old* nanny with?"

"Noah," Charlie grits, pulling on his bicep. "That mean ol' lady had it comin'. Lay off her. Plus, I like Tessa, and I don't have a lot of friends."

"I'll buy you new friends," he grumbles.

"Excuse me," I mutter, then walk over to Aiden, who's glaring at Noah. "Would you mind texting me when Jackson can be picked up? I should probably go."

"You're staying," Aiden says softly, then points his son to the kitchen. "Come help me with something."

Noah rolls his eyes and follows the older man behind the wooden door.

Charlie takes my hands and lures me into a booth. "We'd love for you to come and help. With the upstairs of my new bookstore finished, we can start stacking books. Jackson's been looking forward to working on the children's section."

I smirk. "That doesn't sound like my cup of tea. But...I suppose I should stick around and make sure he doesn't hurt himself or something."

Charlie gasps and lifts her phone. "Does Pepper know you're here? I'll invite her. We could make frozen margaritas. We just put in a kitchen and there's an ice machine—"

I hold up my hands. "I'm on the clock, but an iced coffee wouldn't hurt."

She squeals and texts Pepper.

A flutter bursts in my stomach as I lean back in the booth. It's unexplainable—this sudden foreign feeling of joy—but the word *acceptance* comes to mind. Even *welcoming*. Despite my flaws.

A minute later, Noah approaches our table, looking stoic and dry. "Tessa, glad to have you back. Won't you please join us today?"

I smirk up at the robotic stud beside us. "Since you asked so nicely."

Rolling his eyes and eerily reminding me of his older brother, he walks off.

I perk a brow at Charlie. "I guess opposites truly do attract."

She smirks his way. "We're not all that different."

It's four in the afternoon and I'm waiting for the other shoe to drop.

Charlie, Pepper, and I have spent the majority of the afternoon together—painting, stacking, and drinking our guilty pleasures. And neither one has asked where I've been or why I skipped town.

I'm not sure how long this 'no questions asked' will last but I'm grateful for it.

Something in my chest swelled each time they had a chance and opted to make me laugh instead. To welcome me into this small circle of friendship.

My bladder has caught up with my second iced coffee so I head up to the restroom on the second level. I find Jackson and check in on him.

"Hey, Wiggles. How's it hangin'?" I eye the display of plush 'reading buddies' on the round table he's arranging ever so thoughtfully.

I lift one. "These are cool."

Jackson reaches over and flicks a switch. "And look, there's a light if you're reading in the dark."

"*Super* cool."

"Yeah, I wouldn't use it to read, though. I'd use it as a night light."

"You sleep with a night light?"

He nods like he's ashamed. "I get scared in the dark."

My heart goes out to him. "Oh, me too," I tell him honestly. "You know what else? I have to have my door open when I sleep."

Or no door at all. But apparently, it's not appropriate for nannies to sleep in the den.

His eyes stretch at the new information. "You can leave the door open in our house. It's safe. Nothing will happen to you there. Dad's really big on security in our town."

Yes, I'm aware.

I fight the urge to stroke his cheek for trying to make me feel safe in his home. But I settle for a smirk. "Thanks, kid."

I hold up the plush dolphin with the light. "I'm going to get this for you."

He gives me a small smile, and there seems to be thought behind it, but he doesn't say anything.

We're close to wrapping up for the day, and I bring the dolphin to Charlie at the checkout desk.

She lifts the blue and white toy and frowns. "Do you want to pick another one?"

"Jackson seemed to like this one. Why?"

She smirks and rings me up. "He's already got one."

We have a final stop to make before heading home. Yawning hard, I pull up in front of the clothing and shoe drop and hop out, dumping the bagful in the large container.

With another yawn, I square my shoulders and buckle up. "Okay, kid, have enough fun for one day?"

"I guess." He shrugs in the back seat. "*You* look pretty tired."

"Nah. I'm like the Energizer Bunny."

Though maybe today, I'm like the bunny with an old battery. One you thought was full of life but is quickly fading.

"If you say so."

It's five thirty, and traffic on Main Street is heavy. I text Levi that we're on our way back but might be a while with rush hour.

At the rate we're moving, I may as well put the car in park.

Within ten minutes, we've moved one block. "Progress, buddy. We're making progress. You like music? I could put some on."

"No, that's okay. I'm going to play my video game."

I might need music. Loud music.

I blink hard, shaking off the heavy fog clouding my mind. The engine and pulsing surrounding sounds seem to lull me deeper. My eyes flutter for a second, and I snap my head up.

You've gone much longer without sleep in the past. Get a grip.

When we're at another standstill, I do just that, grip the steering wheel with a deep breath. The pull to shut my eyes is too powerful, and I give in.

Maybe just for a minute...it's not like we're going anywhere.

"Tessa!"

I jolt at Jackson's panicked voice. The car veers to the right, dangerously close to a grey Toyota. Heart racing, I steer in the other direction as another vehicle blows its horn violently. Steadying the wheel, I snap us back to our lane with a harsh breath.

Christ.

I'm static and wide-eyed behind the wheel. A hot wave of terror washes over me when I realize how close I was to losing control. To crashing—with Jackson in the car.

I pull over the first chance I get and flip around. "You alright?"

His eyes are wide with confusion. "Are you?"

"Oh my God. Yes. No. Yes." My hand is on my chest. "You're buckled, right?"

"Yeah. I'm okay."

I turn back to the steering wheel, whispering to myself. "What happened?"

"You...fell asleep," Jackson answers, making my blood run cold.

Twenty minutes later, we're climbing the steps to the house and I turn to Jackson, bending to his level.

"Hey, Wiggles. We're friends, right?"

"Yeah." He holds up the plush dolphin. "We're night light buddies now."

I smile thoughtfully, not fully grasping his meaning. "Listen, maybe let's not tell your dad I dozed off in the car, okay?"

He hesitates, then shrugs. "Okay."

I ruffle his hair, my heart still in my throat. "Thanks."

Somehow, our little agreement doesn't make me feel better.

Not one bit.

11

Levi

"It didn't occur to me to ask if you like fish." I say as we clean up. I'm rinsing and loading the dishwasher while Tessa and Jackson clear the table. She fiddled with her food more than Jackson does when I give him a plate of greens and barely looked my way.

"I like fish," Tessa says dryly. Or maybe it's not dry. Maybe her voice is a little shaky.

The three times she's spoken since getting home has been distant. It's setting off all kinds of alarms.

Did I push it this morning when I touched her?

I get my answer when my reflexes catch the salad bowl that slips from her hands.

She's tired.

"Listen, why don't you head upstairs? I can take it from here."

Tessa shakes her head. "I promised Jackson a movie night."

"Yeah, movie night. I'll pick the movie." My kid cheers, racing for the remote like either of us had a shot.

Setting the bowl down, I catch her hand, ready to insist she go to bed.

Averting her gaze, she breaks free. "I'm fine. It's early. I'm good," she claims. "But I am a bit warm. I'm just going to change and come back down."

I nod. "Take your time, we'll make some popcorn."

I pop a bag into the microwave and head to the living room.

"Hey," I grab Jackson's waist and twist him with a tickle. He wiggles in my arms. "Tell me something. How was your day?"

"It was so fun. We got to paint, and I stacked Harry Potter books and then Charlie let me set up the reading buddies table."

"Nice. What about Tessa? Did you look out for her like daddy would have?"

"No, I was nice to her." He wiggles free and hops on the couch.

Fuck.

Here I thought I'd been raising my kid to be a gentleman. But apparently, my actions speak louder than words.

"So...nothing happened? Everyone else was nice to her too? Anything that might have upset her?"

He considers it for a moment, then shakes his head.

Paranoid. I'm paranoid. And my kid is left to deal with it.

I ruffle his hair.

"Okay, I'm ready for movie night. What are we watching?"

We both turn to Tessa coming down the stairs. Her hair is tied up loosely over her head. Strands of red curls framing her face. She's in pale pink pajama pants and a white tank top.

And fuck, she looks like the one thing that's been missing on movie nights.

Her skin is freshly washed, possibly moisturized and it's almost like she got her second wind.

The microwave dings, snapping me back to reality, and I move to the kitchen without a word.

"We're watching Jumanji," my son raves. "Are you in?"

"I'm so in."

I return with a large bowl of popcorn as Tessa grabs the faded family throw, wrapping it around her shoulders and settling into the couch.

It was my mother's. Dad used to wrap Jackson in it when he was a baby, insisting it was better than those useless swaddles. It's not the first time I've seen her use it to her comfort and I'm surprised at how much I appreciate it. Especially since anyone outside our family has always been turned off by the ragged old blanket.

I clear my throat, sitting on the long side of the L-shape couch. "I'd ask you if you're comfortable, but you look it."

She grins sleepily. "Thank you."

We're barely twenty minutes into the movie, and I'm not sure Tessa is going to make it. Her eyes flutter closed every few seconds. I could practically feel the weight of them.

I should tell her to go upstairs. That her "shift" ended hours ago, but I don't want to. Something about her here with us, even asleep, feels...complete.

When her eyelids finally fall, I guide her gently onto the pillows in the corner. The throw still wrapped around her shoulders as she falls sideways onto them.

Jackson peers over and I shrug. "More popcorn for us."

He seems sad for a moment, and I'm on alert. "Hey, what's the matter?"

"She was tired. She...she fell asleep in the car."

I nod absently, reaching for another blanket, and freeze, twisting my neck to look at him. "What did you say?"

He hesitates.

"Jackson?"

"She asked me not to say anything."

Something sharp hits my chest, but I keep my tone even. "Right, but we don't do that anymore, right? We don't lie to Daddy about important things."

He nods.

"We were in traffic and she kept closing her eyes. We almost hit another car. I think she fell asleep."

I release a breath and pull him against my side. "You alright?" I rasp.

He nods but I can tell he feels guilty. "Thanks for letting me know, buddy."

I cover Tessa's legs with the other blanket and lower the volume as we finish the movie.

Later, I tuck him in and change into a sleep shirt and shorts before returning downstairs.

She hasn't moved. The family room is dark, the only light illuminating her face are the porch lights we always keep on.

I set a pillow across from her on the couch and sit against it, staring like a therapist observing his patient.

Trying to understand her.

She put my kid in danger today. And God knows who else around her.

Who the hell wakes up at four in the morning each day?

Enough is enough. If she's going to have my kid in her care, she's getting some goddamn sleep.

Even if I have to lose some myself to ensure it.

That is if I don't fire her for making my kid lie to me.

I hear little steps coming down. "Dad?"

I sit up. "Hey, what's going on? Thought you were asleep."

He's got his dolphin light when he comes around to me. "Tessa bought me this today."

"Charlie brought you that a few weeks ago."

"I know. But Tessa told me she's afraid of the dark too." He places the dolphin light next to her. "Now we're nightlight buddies."

I rub his back. "That's really sweet of you."

"And she doesn't like to sleep with closed doors. So good idea to let her stay down here." He looks down at her with a small smile. "Told you he'll keep you safe."

I swallow a hard lump in my throat. All I ever wanted was for him to feel that. That I'd always keep him safe and loved. It took Tessa coming around for him to let me know that he does. I stand. "Come on, let's get you back upstairs."

"I'm okay, Dad. You stay here."

"You sure?"

He nods and says goodnight.

I don't know how long I stay up looking at her, wondering what the hell I'm going to do with the information she tried to hide.

But eventually, my eyelids fall heavy and I give in.

Faint whimpering in the darkness reaches my ears. My eyes fly open finding Tessa still asleep but disturbed. Her lips part with a breathy "No."

I'm over to the edge of the couch in a flash. "Tess."

Her eyes are shut, her body restless as she shifts in place, moving backward like she's stuck. "No."

I put a hand on her arm, wary of scaring her awake. "Tessa." It's a whisper, but I'm ready to shake her until she's alert and knows she's safe.

Her breathing accelerates and she jolts with a sharp gasp, sucking air into her lungs like she's been stabbed.

Her head snaps to me and she screams. I grab her face between my hands. "It's okay. It's alright. It's me. You're okay."

Tessa's breaths come rapid and heavy. Her chest, forehead, and neck are damp. "Indie."

"Yes, it's me." I swipe back loose strands of her hair.

She nods and then covers her face. "Oh my God, I'm sorry. What time is it?"

"Not time to wake up yet. Go back to sleep."

She lowers her hands, staring at me like I'm crazy. "What? No. I can't."

"Tessa. It's the middle of the night."

"No." She looks away, curling into herself. "I won't fall asleep. I've tried."

"Stay here." I lift the old throw over her shoulders and push to my feet, returning a few minutes later with warm chamomile tea. Tessa's knees are pulled up to her chin, watching me warily. "Drink this."

She takes the mug, staring at it.

"Don't worry, poisoning is your thing, not mine."

She glances around awkwardly. "Sorry I fell asleep here. Did I wake you?"

"No." I watch her take a sip, treading carefully. "Bad dream?"

"Yeah." Her gaze flicks to the plush dolphin with the nose light.

"Lie down."

She hesitates.

"I'm not asking. You need rest. More than four hours." There's an unmistakable edge in my voice. And I'm no longer reluctant to use it with her.

Her eyes lock with mine, and she bites the corner of her lip. "I'll try."

I give her a curt nod. "I'll be here." Taking her mug, I settle back across from her and sip slowly.

For someone who claimed it was impossible, Tessa's asleep within minutes.

And stays asleep for another few hours.

Between studying her features and drinking what's left of the cold tea, I've been trying to come up with an appropriate way to deal with what happened last night. The danger she put my kid in.

The lie.

Nothing but *'What the hell does she dream about?'* consumes my mind.

This isn't new.

Something in the way she rose. There was no panic in her eyes—just a weary acceptance that expressed familiarity.

This wasn't the first time she'd been haunted in her sleep. Whatever that was, Tessa *lives* with it.

I press my finger to my mouth, shushing Jackson when he comes down close to eight o'clock.

He sees Tessa sound asleep on the couch, and I wink at him.

"Dad, it worked. Must be the dolphin."

I spread butter on toast and set it next to his banana. "Must be."

"Are you going to work today?"

"Of course."

"Can Tessa and I come? She's been asking for a tour."

"I'm going to be too busy for that, buddy, maybe some other—"

"Good morning."

Her raspy voice cuts through the air, pulling my gaze. She steps into the kitchen tentatively. Her hair tousled, falling in waves around her shoulders, framing that freckled face. I try not to notice the way it glows in the soft morning light.

Quietly, she moves to the coffee pot, filling the mug I prepared for myself. I can't look away as she takes a slow sip, humming softly.

"Morning."

Looking me in the eyes for the first time since coming home last night, she tucks her hair behind her ear. "Thank you for letting me sleep in."

"You're welcome."

She turns to Jackson with a warm, genuine smile. I can't remember the last time he got one of those besides from immediate family.

"Thanks for Willy, Wiggles."

"You named him? It sounds like mine. I love it."

She laughs, and there's appreciation in her eyes that makes me forget I'm mad at her.

"Jackson wanted to give you a tour of the ranch today," I say stiffly, giving my son credit for his thoughtfulness. "Unfortunately, we're all—"

"Really?" Her eyes go wide with excitement. "Oh, I won't bother anyone. I don't even need an official tour guide. Jackson could totally show me the ropes."

I suck in a slow breath. "I can't just have you walking around. Wouldn't be safe if the animals got loose. You two could get lost. What if it starts raining?"

"We won't wander, will we, kid?"

Jackson cheers. "I know everything about the ranch. I hang out with Dad all the time when school's out."

I sigh. "Fine." I whip out my phone. "Roger will supervise."

"Supervise?" Tess jerks.

I don't need to explain myself. "Yes. I'll see if Roger can give you a short tour and still stay close to the pasture." I step out of the room to make the call and get ready to head out.

When I return minutes later, Tessa's prepared a small plate for herself. Berries, cheese and a scrambled egg.

"Better appetite this morning?"

She frowns, looking at the plate as if she didn't realize what she was doing. "Huh. Yeah, I'm kind of famished."

The idea that the nightmares and nausea may be linked is sending my protective curiosity spiraling.

I hate that I don't know what's going on with her.

Because she's taking care of my kid—obviously. There's no other reason to care.

None.

"We can have breakfast together, Curly."

She takes a seat next to my kid. "Curly?"

"Yeah. You like it? Wiggles and Curly. Ranch Adventures."

Tessa frowns. "Why not Curly and Wiggles?"

Jackson rolls his eyes. "Fine. Women."

My lips are a tight thin line. I won't be swayed by their blooming friendship.

"Be ready in an hour. I'll come back and walk you two over." I point to my kid with a stern look. And I know he reads me loud and clear. "No wandering off unless Roger is with you."

They nod once, simultaneously, and I shake my head as I step out into the heat.

12

Tessa

Jackson kicks at a loose rock, watching it tumble down the dusty path before looking up at me. His oversized cowboy hat, which keeps slipping over his eyes, adds a little extra swagger to his stance.

I tried to dress the part. Dark pair of denim shorts and an orange button-down tied at the waist. It's comfortable and weather-appropriate.

His grumpy dad left us sitting on a bench by the barn and told us to wait for Roger before heading to someplace called the Wrangler Room.

He was a little extra short with me this morning. Jaw tight, words clipped and barely looking at me for longer than three seconds.

My chest is still tight over what happened last night. Guilt will surely eat me alive.

After nearly losing mine, I put another life in danger. And then made him lie about it.

I need to figure out a way to undo the damage. I might not believe it myself, but the kid should probably feel like he's safe with me. That I'd never do anything to hurt him.

Not intentionally.

"Are my boots okay?" I flip my foot backward like a ballerina, balancing on the other.

"They'll work. They're a little pretty, though. Hope it doesn't rain. That's how I ruined some of my shoes out here."

I poke his little chest. "Then we'll take them off and run for it."

He laughs and I take the moment to explore with my eyes. Rolling hills stretch in every direction. I see cabins in the distance, mountains behind them, and another structure further away. I don't mind a good hike every now and then, but how's one to see it all on foot? "It's… big."

"Couple thousand acres," Roger says, stepping out from the barn. He's an elderly cowboy with heavily tanned skin. His frame is small, but those arms look strong enough to lift cattle. "Where y'all want to start?"

"Let's show her the horses," Jackson cheers.

Roger frowns like the kid's lost his mind. "The stables are all the way on the other side. There's plenty to see and do before that. You like apples, miss? Couple weeks we'll be busy for apple picking season, but we've got a few tiny ones growing over by the orchard. Come on, I'll show ya." He starts walking, and Jackson and I shrug.

"I like tiny apples," I say, not that it mattered. I take Jackson's hand. "Do me a favor kid, steer me clear of any manure and sh—stuff."

We don't walk far before reaching the orchard, a sweet and flowery-scented land that's fenced in. I hold my hand over my eyes, following them through the small gate. "Are these edible yet?" I stretch out my hands, rustling my fingers between small trees.

"Not those," Roger says in front of me. "But these here are." He stops in front of a fuller tree with several luscious apples hanging from their branches. Then pulls a mesh bag from the side of his belt.

Jackson doesn't waste any time. He's like a pro, picking off ripe apples and tossing them into the bag.

Roger subtly inspects each one and smiles down at the boy with pride. "Good job, buddy."

Absently, I pick at a leaf, rubbing the smooth texture between my fingers, watching this happy kid do one of the many things he does best. Melt my heart.

I don't envy that his childhood is surrounded by dependable grownups who will teach and protect him. But I do wonder what that's like. And if I ever have kids, will I have the means to do the same?

About one hour into an uneventful tour and way past the feeling of being babysat, I'm ready to take this kid home. When I mentioned I wanted a tour, I hoped it would be a little less touristy and a bit more personal.

Even Jackson looks bored. And he's always raving about the ranch. And some creek.

As if reading my mind, he tugs my hand while Roger explains livestock care and feeding. "I wish Dad gave you the tour. He's a lot more fun."

Doubtful.

We're in the feeding shed, where buckets are stacked next to other feeding supplies for the smaller pasture. Apparently, after this, Roger plans on taking us to the larger one—and to be frank—I'm not quite sure how much more of this I can take.

"Hey, why don't we head home? Looks like it's going to rain soon anyway." I look up at the grey clouds. "We could have popsicles and watch cartoons?"

Jackson's deep in thought, staring off into the distance, then turns his head up to me, a mischievous spark lighting his face. "I've got a better idea."

"Better than popsicles and cartoons?"

He nods, then whispers. "Follow my lead."

I narrow my eyes, keeping my voice low. "Wiggles, are we about to go rogue?"

He shrugs. "I am. You're just stuck with me."

I think I *love* this kid.

While I'm in my head, unsure if I should be proud or concerned that I'm a bad influence, Jackson drops my hand and is on the move, tiptoeing his way around the shed behind Roger.

When the man stands, I circle in front of him. "Wait. Show me that again. So you just fill these little buckets with anything?"

"Depends on who we're feedin'. This here's for the goats."

I nod with interest, chancing a glance behind the old man. And oh...no, I really wish I'd asked what he was planning.

Jackson winds his little foot and kicks the stack of empty buckets. They clatter to the ground, bouncing and rolling in every direction. The sound echoes off the walls, startling livestock, causing a commotion.

Roger's on his feet and out of the shed. "Stay here," he shouts over the noise, closing the gate behind him.

"What did you do?" I hiss at the kid.

Jackson giggles as he races to the gate, pulling it open, then waving me over. "Let's go."

"Where?"

"Hurry!" He pulls me along.

Jackson and I bolt across the pasture, leaving behind a frazzled cowboy.

I wince. I'm in so much trouble for that.

But it's all worth it when I look at this little boy's face once we're in the clear. He's absolutely glowing with joy.

Worth it.

"Kid, that was genius."

He tilts back his hat. "I got you covered."

We disappear over the hill and it's nothing but clean, crisp grass.

I stop for a breath. "What now?"

He glances back. "The creek."

I follow his little feet as they zigzag between trees, ducking under low hanging branches.

My heart races, but in a good way. A thrilling way as we venture freely toward someplace less... predictable. Much like my life.

"You sure this is a shortcut?" I call, my boots kicking up dirt.

"Pretty sure!" Jackson calls back over his shoulder, still running ahead. "Dad never takes this way to the creek. He'll never find us once Roger calls him."

I laugh—and that is not a good sign. I shouldn't find this funny. But I do. Especially after his overprotective dad basically had someone 'watch the nanny' when Jackson and I were perfectly capable of...

"Hey, Jackson, maybe we shouldn't stray too far. I can't see over the hills anymore."

"No, no. I think it's this way."

"Okay, but then we should turn around. Find Roger before he finds your dad."

"Here's the creek," Jackson cries. "Dad's only brought me here on Willow, but look, we found it." He sits on a rock in the shade of the trees.

He looks quite proud of himself.

"Willow?"

"One of our horses. My favorite. Dad's too, I think."

"Pretty name." I lower myself onto a rock next to him as we watch the water. "I've never been on a horse. Wild animals are not my thing."

"Horses aren't wild. Well, not our horses. They live and work on the ranch. They're *domesticated*."

I ruffle his hair. I've pictured myself on a horse before. I've also pictured said horse tossing off the bad seed that landed on him. I'd quicker plant myself on a rollercoaster. They have seatbelts and can't smell fear.

A ripple in the water freezes my thoughts. It's followed by another and several more.

"Uh-oh." Cold shivers run down my arms and I pull to my feet, blinking up at the sky.

Jackson sits up. "We...should probably..."

"Run!" I yell, grabbing his hand and sprinting back toward the grove of trees.

Before long, the rain comes down fast, soaking us in seconds.

I look for the clear path we had taken earlier –but it seems to have disappeared. We both spin in circles as panic creeps in my voice. "Where's the trail?"

"Umm..." He points forward. "That way." Then moves his arm. "Or...was it that way?" His eyes are wide. "Are we lost?"

I take a deep breath, kneeling in front of him and securing his hat. "Of course not. We're close. Let's go with your first guess, huh? I think you might be right."

I push to my feet and tug him along toward the trees. "That will give us some coverage."

Thunder rumbles in the distance, and I tuck Jackson beside me. We're breathing hard and soaked through. When the rain slows to a drizzle, I turn to him. "Wait here. I'm going to see if I can find our path."

Stepping out, I squint to see behind the fog. Nothing. To my left, I hear a faint, rhythmic thudding. It comes in irregular bursts, but there's no doubt that whatever it is, it's making the ground tremble.

13

Tessa

Jackson sees him first, running out from under the trees. "Roger!"

I sigh with relief. "Never thought I'd be happy to see *that* guy," I mumble.

"There ya are." Roger hops off a beautiful dark horse that's getting a little too close for my comfort.

A second horse emerges from the fog, and my chest tightens when I see the cowboy riding it. Levi isn't as laid-back of a rider as Roger seems to be.

Nope. This is one angry boss heading my way. Each strike of his stallion's hooves splashes through puddles as he aims toward us.

He stops a few feet from where I'm standing. His scowl like nothing I've seen before. And I've seen this man angry plenty.

I step back, turning to the less intimidating of the two men rescuing us. "Hey, Rog. What uh...what happened? We turned around, and you were gone."

He smirks. "Pretty sure that's my line, Red."

Red? I frown with disgust. "Well, thanks for coming. But we're fine," I chirp like I had it all under control.

Roger glances at his boss. "Not for long." He extends a hand to Jackson. "Come on, Champ, let's get you dry."

"I can get him dry myself." I move to step between them but jump back as Roger's horse inches toward me. "Just uh...point us in the right direction, and we'll be back in no time."

Levi hops off his horse. His blue eyes darken as he closes the distance. I'm prepared for this. But then he turns the same glare at his son. And that, I was not prepared for.

My boots drag me in front of him and I put a hand on his chest. "Indie, you've got to teach this kid to live a little. It took a whole lot of arm twisting to get him to run off with me today."

"Tessa," the kid whispers behind me.

Levi takes another step, crowding my space. "Move."

Well, I tried. I step aside.

Levi lifts Jackson onto Rogers's dark horse and secures him. "When you get home, I want you to hop in the shower, alright? Roger will take you back there."

"What about Tessa?" I give the kid a grin as he looks my way.

"She'll be back soon."

Roger hops behind the kid, and they take off, disappearing behind the low fog.

The buckles on Levi's boots clatter with each step as he stalks back toward me. My boots are muddy, my clothes ruined, and if I weren't already shivering from my wet skin and hair, the look on Levi's face would do the trick.

I glance around me. "So, is this where you bury your nannies?" I perk my brows. "Or am I your first?"

I blink up when the rain picks up again. Levi curses and shifts direction, grabbing the reins. "Come here."

I back up. "Um, no. I'll just follow you. It's fine."

Levi hops on expertly and extends his hand. "You're getting on my horse. And then you and I are going to have a little chat about your employment."

"As tempting as that is..." I start down the same path they came from and call out over the rain. "I'll pass."

I don't make it far before I'm pulled off my feet. Levi's strong arm scoops me up by my waist. I screech as I swing my leg over for some balance on the moving horse.

"Hold on to me."

He doesn't need to ask twice. My flailing arms wrap around his body, and holy crap, the upper strength of this man. I'm no Charlie. I've got at least a foot on her and slightly more body fat, but man, this cowboy made me feel like a toothpick just now.

"Your horse doesn't like me." If the way it glanced back and nearly wiggled me off was any indication.

"She was just startled. Horses need to be prepped for two riders. She didn't expect it." He flexes his arm and rolls his shoulder back.

Maybe I'm not that light after all.

I pull tighter against him, tucking my face between his shoulder blades to shield myself from the sharp drops falling from the sky. Removing his hat, he reaches back and places it over my head.

Indie's hat.

Our horse finds a steady, even pace, and I relax, soaking up the breeze, the thrill. And the man I can hold close for as long as he'll let me.

I reach up to adjust and hold the hat in place. I wonder if I can keep it after he fires me today.

Levi settles the horse back in her stall, then adds a fresh stack of hay. He pets her nose and mutters something that sounds like a praise.

I wonder if that's Willow.

The rain stopped, and I'm less shivery as the summer heat slowly returns. Especially with the blanket Levi wrapped around me when we got to the stables. The one he grabbed from behind a cabin door labeled the *Wrangler Room*.

Blue eyes turn to me, but instead of backing away, I move toward him. "Before you start—"

Gripping my waist with both hands, he lifts and sits me on a wooden table near the haystack and leans in. "Give me one good reason why I shouldn't fire you for making my kid lie to me last night."

I blink and swallow hard.

Shoot. Wasn't expecting that.

My lips part to respond, and his gaze drops to them. "I don't have one."

"The correct answer is there is no good reason."

"I didn't realize it was a pop quiz."

His jaw ticks and it's clear he's waiting for me to explain. When my eyes start to burn, I give in. I meet his heated glare with one of my own. "I made a mistake. I told you Jackson's safe with me. He's not."

He pulls back, crossing his arms over his chest.

"I crashed." I shake my head vigorously. "Not the car. Crashed as in my body just shut down. It was a long day, I was tired and I..."

"Tess..." He doesn't need to hear the end of that as much as I don't want to say it out loud.

"I dozed off, I should have pulled over or called you or something, but—"

"Tessa."

I meet his eyes, surprised to find them soft. "You were right—okay? Is that what you wanted to hear?"

"It happens."

"It's not like I—wait, what?"

"I know you were tired. It happens. No one was hurt."

"I don't understand. You just threatened to fire me. You should. Levi, I could have—"

"You *didn't*."

"Then why are you mad?"

His jaw sets and his scowl is back. "You asked him to lie to me."

Oh. "That wasn't cool, was it?" I bite my lip, drawing his irritated gaze to it.

"No, Tess. It wasn't. Look, I know you're no saint. You're new at this. Asking a kid to lie to his parents is a big no. Asking Jackson to lie to *me*? That's a downright felony in my book."

I throw my hands in the air. "Then put me away, Sheriff. Oh, that's right. You don't have a badge. You don't make the law. You just walk around town with a chip on your shoulder."

"Only when you're around," he mutters.

I shove his chest but it's rock solid. "Then don't have me around. And it was a little creepy, you watching me sleep this morning."

"Explains why you slept like a baby."

"And for your information, I was going to tell you about the car incident. I just wanted you to hear it from me."

"Right, because you're so good with words." He runs a hand over his face like he doesn't know what to do with me.

"You don't have to like me," I growl, pressing a finger to his chest. "It's enough that your kid does. And I happen to really like him. Which is important. Probably."

He stares at me, and I'm not certain that he's entirely with me.

"So yeah, if Wiggles and I want to keep secrets, that's our prerogative. Weren't you ever a kid? Parents are meant to be lied to."

"Not *this* parent," he roars, making me flinch back.

He turns away, seeming to settle himself. "Jackson's mom isn't allowed to see him. Not without me or some other supervision. For years without my knowledge, she'd sneak in a visit with him, would pull him out of school for a day, and make him tell me all kinds of lies."

He runs a hand through his hair, and I resist the urge to catch it in mine.

"I'm not getting into it right now, but she's done enough damage with that kid for me to ever let her near him again."

"I'm so sorry." My apology is breathy and broken, and I'm not even sure what it's for. What he's been through or how I made it worse.

He crosses to the opposite side of the stalls, and while I thought I'd be relieved for the space, I miss the closeness.

"I didn't like grilling him. I didn't like looking at him like he might be hiding something from me. It took us a while to get there, but we trust each other now. I trust that he'll always come to me and he trusts that I'll always be there when he does. So yeah, it's important, Tessa."

There's a stabbing pain in my chest. Like I'd destroyed something so precious for these two. Like I'm no better than her. I didn't realize until now that I wanted to be everything she wasn't for Jackson.

Sucking in a breath, I drop my head with a small nod. "No lies. Got it."

14

Levi

Tessa's damp hair falls around her face and I just...*stare* at her.

The breathy...raspy way she complies. That overly abused bottom lip is pulled between her teeth again and my chest pulls.

Goddamn this woman. Downright dangerous the way she has me raging out of control one minute and my cock twitching the next.

The way it seems to do when she's this close. Or when she's challenging me. Pushing me.

Like I didn't have enough when her breasts were planted against my back for the entire ride back to the stables.

A ragged breath shakes out of me.

Stepping close, I capture her jaw with both hands and lift her face. "Stop that," I bite out, tugging to save that bottom lip from between her teeth.

Too late. It's already raw and swollen.

She smells like grass and vanilla. Like we've mixed our scents into one. Except today, she was in *my* world. Covered in nature, she's as dirty as I get most days and I'm a caveman, hungry for his woman.

The mist in her eyes from just a moment ago is replaced with that familiar defiance. A fire.

"Does it bother you?"

"You have no idea," I rasp, the hard-on growing hazardously. A hazard to my self-control.

Because I'm having a hard time peeling away from her. And unless she asks, I don't see myself doing that.

"Indie." My nickname comes out in a lust-full breath. Her fingers graze my chest, but just barely. Like she's testing a metal knob in a building on fire.

I move one hand into her hair, twisting a lock around my finger. "Whiskey."

She frowns in question.

"Your eyes."

She holds my gaze in that heady way that tells me she's not only okay with this...

She's *waiting*.

My eyes drop to her full, tempting red lips.

"Better hurry, I'm on the clock."

With a grin I can't help, I crush her mouth with mine. Her soft, full, sweet mouth.

Tessa grips my shirt as she opens for me. A moan I didn't know I craved rips from her throat. It makes me slide my fingers behind her neck and flush my body against hers.

Damn the hard-on she'll feel.

Damn the scruff of my chin scraping against her delicate skin. Our kiss is so desperate and hungry, if it doesn't leave marks, it wasn't enough.

Her hands snake up to my neck, grazing my jaw. Our tongues dance like we're competing for a gold medal.

It's too good. She's too fucking good.

I pull back with a sharp suck for breath and put distance between us.

I've done it too many times. Put distance between myself and anyone else who could hurt me. Who could hurt Jackson.

He doesn't need another free spirit walking away.

I don't need it.

Tessa shouldn't be any different. Tessa should be on the top of the list of women to stay away from.

But she's somehow snuck her way onto a different list.

A list of people I'd protect with my life.

"Please tell me what you're thinking," she asks in a desperate, breathy rasp I'm newly obsessed with.

That I'm two steps away from flipping you over and spanking you for the wreck you've made of me.

"You're on the clock."

She glares at me. "When am I off the clock?"

"Tessa. This can't happen."

She hops off the table. "Hate to break it to you, cowboy." She scans me with those amber eyes like she sees right through me. "It already has."

Tessa's energy all day has been uncompromising. Focused eyes, easy smile, and a heart fit for a small town.

After she left the stables, she went back to the house and made several jars of mint iced tea and corn muffins for the staff. They all welcomed her with open arms.

Especially after Roger spread the word on how the new nanny took the rap for Jackson running off to the creek again.

Priceless.

And fucking adorable.

I expected her to avoid me all day, but she just smiles and talks like we didn't cross that line.

And if we were keeping score—she's winning the 'acting like it never happened' game by a landslide.

After dinner, I leave Jackson with Tess and head to the Inn. She made some chicken dish and didn't cut any corners. Roasted vegetables, garlic sauce, garden salad and a side of French fries for Jackson.

Dad's clearing glasses from the bar when I walk in. "Hey, need some help here?"

Since Tessa vanished two months ago, Dad never bothered hiring anyone else. Summers are slow at the Inn, and if I know Dad, he hates dealing with new people about as much as I do.

"Hey." He looks behind me. "Where's the rest of the fam?"

"Jackson's watching a movie with his nanny."

"Oh come on, even I considered Tess part of the family when she started working here. And don't tell me you don't consider every cowboy on Hideaway Ranch part of yours."

"She's the nanny!" I remind him. "You and I both know she disappears with the drop of a hat."

He grumbles and reaches for my usual beer of choice, holding it up for me with a question.

"Maybe just one."

He glances over at the couple by the window to see if they're alright, then pops the lid off two bottles, coming around to join me.

"How's she doin'?"

"Fine, I guess." I take a swig.

He smacks my arm with the back of his hand like he's got news. "You know who was in here today? Remember Carol Hendly? Susy and Danny's kid. You believe she's in grad school already?"

My jaw tightens and I take another swig.

He chuckles. "She told me the strangest story." He shakes his head like he doesn't believe it. "She said she was at your house just last week for an interview. Was damn right confident in herself, too. Years of experience, reliable, good small-town gal. *Way* too young for you and certainly not interested in any relationship."

I set down my bottle and wait for the punchline.

"And yet mid-way through her interview…you followed *my* old bartender out into the driveway and *insisted* she was your new nanny." He chuckles and takes a sip. "Strangest thing."

"Jackson likes Tess."

Dad scratches his beard. "Jackson also likes worms."

"You got a point?"

"Tessa was doing the very thing you ask her to do every time she's back in town—*leaving*. Sounds to me like you were stopping her."

I suck my teeth. "I don't know, Dad. Maybe I'm under her spell."

He laughs. "That's the most sense you made since you walked in."

"I don't need to be under anyone's spell."

"No, of course not. Especially not a beautiful redhead."

I lock my jaw. "She's not Lilly."

"I know that. Do *you*?"

"You think my disdain for the woman is because she reminds me of my ex-wife?"

"If Tessa reminds you of your ex-wife, you don't know her at all."

"I don't need to know her."

I don't want to know her.

I shouldn't want to know what the hell she dreams about. Or who still haunts her.

"Well, she's going to be around at least until the end of the summer. You're going to want to know things."

I snap my head. "What kinds of things?"

He shrugs. "Like what's in Summer Hill? She didn't have a home, I know that. And why she keeps showing up then disappearing."

A horrid thought comes to mind. "You think this might be a Lonnie situation?"

One of the reasons my ex, Lonnie, and I broke up was the baggage we both came with. My trust issues. My overprotectiveness. Lonnie was on the run from an abusive relationship—still is. She had trust issues of her own. It was too much for both of us to deal with. And she wasn't the one.

"I think that before someone falls in love with her—say, Jackson—you might want to find out."

"If she hasn't told you, what makes you think she'd tell me?"

He shrugs. "I never asked. I only offered to help."

We're both quiet for a moment. Finishing my beer, I twist the empty bottle between my palms. "She has...nightmares. She fell asleep on the couch last night, and I watched her. I think...I think she gets them often."

Dad curses under his breath. Twisting his neck. "You think this disqualifies her? Because she's got problems?"

"No."

"Then why are you telling me?"

"Because her problems are my problems."

Dad's brows jump. "I wasn't expecting that." There's a beat before he adds, "Noah could help. If there's anything on record, he'll find it. You and I both know he's found plenty *off* the record, too."

I can't sit here and tell him I haven't thought of that. "What if Tessa wants to keep whatever it is private?"

He taps his bottle against the wooden bar. "Think privacy went out the window when she moved into your house."

I run a hand down my face and push off my seat. "Thanks for the beer."

"Want me to look into it?"

"No."

"Levi." His tone stops me in my tracks. "What if it's bad?"

He didn't see the fear in her eyes when she woke up. I *know* it's bad.

But so is betraying her trust.

It's after eleven when I walk up the steps to my front door and quietly enter. A dim light glows in the foyer, the living room, and beneath the kitchen cabinets.

It's clean and smells...piney.

I do my usual sweep to lock up, but the back doors and windows already are.

I turn off the foyer lights but leave the others before heading upstairs.

Tessa's bedroom door, right across from mine, is wide open. I'm about to knock and ask if everything's alright when I notice the room is empty. The bed is still made.

Where the hell? The gym is the next thing that comes to mind but the basement door was closed and the lights were out.

Panic grips me, and I rush toward Jackson's bedroom. His night light is on, but he's not in his bed.

Covering my ground before losing it, I check my bedroom. And freeze.

Jackson is tucked in the middle of my bed. Head on the single king-sized pillow. I hate pillows. And nothing screams "I like to sleep alone" than a single pillow on a bed. But right now, I wish I had it filled edge to edge for the comfort of these two heads.

Tessa is next to him. Her auburn head just barely lying on the pillow.

With soft steps, I close the distance, scanning the way her hair is spread wildly around her. How does it always look so fucking silky?

I'm tempted as fuck to move my kid to his bedroom and come back here for her.

But I need Jackson here.

If only to remind me that she's the fucking nanny.

I run my palm across the top of her head. "Hey."

Inhaling deeply, she flutters her lashes and accesses her space, then looks up at me. "Oh, right."

She sits up, stretching, then drops her chin to look at my son. "This kid is somethin' else, Indie."

You're somethin' else.

I follow her gaze. "He keep you up?"

She's all sleepy and gorgeous. "He was just worried you weren't home yet and wanted to wait up for you." She shrugs.

I chuckle. "Yeah, I used to sneak into my parent's bedroom when they were out late. Or when my dad was traveling, I'd pretend I was only sleeping on his side so mom wouldn't be afraid."

She looks up at me like she can't relate. I have the strangest urge to explain it to her. To have her look at this from my eyes. Coming into my bedroom with my kid fast asleep on my pillow. A beautiful woman next to him who took care of him while I was gone.

"Help me up, will ya?" She grabs my wrist and pulls herself up, moving in the opposite direction of where I want her.

She stumbles groggily, and I catch her by the waist, my mouth by her ear. "You don't have to leave."

Tessa's cocky grin is contagious. "It's cool. I've got a neat place just across the hall."

I laugh. "Oh yeah? Did you just move in?"

She nods, pushing against my chest playfully. "Rent free. Can't beat that."

Placing a hand on her lower back, I follow her. We're in the dark hallway between both rooms when I twist her to face me. I want to thank her for sticking up for Jackson today—even if my kid doesn't need protecting from me. I want to thank her for making him feel safe, taking care of my home, for dinner and just...being here.

Gentle, thoughtful words when it comes to anyone other than my son is foreign to me. So I just stare at her.

Her eyes meet mine. "I don't need a lecture on appropriate nanny behavior, Indie. I'm aware I screwed up on several counts today."

I blink. "Several?"

"The creek." Her eyes drop to my mouth. "The stables. Then falling asleep with your kid in your bed. I promise I'm not—"

"Tessa, you let my kid drag you on an adventure. I kissed *you* in the stables. And in there, with Jackson, it's exactly the kind of thing..."

"A nanny does?"

"Yeah."

That's much better than what I almost said.

The kind of thing he needs. That I want.

She nods like she's reassuring herself she's not in trouble. Then looks up at me tentatively, wincing almost.

"In that case, maybe I can get one 'rogue' comment in before the day's over?"

I roll my eyes. And it feels intimate. Being out here. Like we're sneaking around. Like we're sharing a secret.

"Go for it."

"That kiss has got me wondering what else cowboys do better."

My eyes stay locked on hers. Other than my heart landing in my throat and my cock jerking to attention, I can't react. But I don't need to because Tessa turns with that sleepy smirk and steps into her bedroom, closing the door a fraction of the way. "Night, Tess."

15

Tessa

My eyes shoot open but my head is still on the pillow. Pulling my hand to my chest, I frown at the steady beat of my heart.

Huh.

It's quiet and pitch black outside my window. I have a rough idea of the time, but still, I reach for the cell phone on my nightstand to check.

4:37 A.M.

I twist back, facing the ceiling. My guess this morning was off by thirty-seven minutes. But that's not what stuns me.

I didn't wake gasping for air.

My sleep shirt is dry. The sheets aren't sweat-stained.

The nightmare still plays on repeat, and even though I know history is not repeating itself, I still fear it.

But something was different tonight—just before I woke up...before that gun went off—a powerful intuition of security washed over me.

Like I somehow knew that on the other side of that wall of slumber—I was safe.

Which is strange considering my door is closed—a dumb live-in nanny rule. And I'm alone in a place where people...let's say, *tolerate* me.

And a place where they regret kissing me.

Pushing stupid thoughts out of my mind, I slide into my slippers, tie my hair in a loose bun, and wash up. I'm about to walk out into the hall before remembering the house rule.

Must be fully dressed.

Right.

I dig around for a pair of lounge pants, making a mental note to order some. The little boy shorts I have in place of pants around the house definitely fall under the unacceptable pile.

I settle for a pair of spandex leggings, then pull my oversized T-shirt over it. I check the time again.

Four minutes?

I walk to the door, calculating the hours and minutes until my nanny duties start, and jump when I pull it open.

Levi is standing across the narrow hall, leaning against his bedroom door with a grin wide enough to *not* belong to this grumpy cowboy.

"Mornin'."

I lower my hand from my chest. "Christ. What are you doing? Wait—have you moved all night?"

He laughs, pushing off the wall. "Of course, slept okay, too." He steps up to me. "You?"

I tense. "You—you want me to try and sleep more, don't you? Look, Levi—"

"Shh—you'll wake the kid. Come on."

"Wha—where?"

"Assuming you were just headin' downstairs?"

"Yes, but—"

He starts down the hall, moving with an impossible energy for this hour.

I follow him down the stairs tentatively, finding the lights I'd left on last night still illuminating the main room.

He moves to raise some more lights while I turn into the kitchen. I yelp at the sight of another body—a strange elderly man I've never seen before. Breath caught in my throat, I flip around and slam into Levi's chest. He captures me instantly. "Hey, it's okay. It's alright. Harry is a friend."

Frazzled, I look up at him, and he continues. "He's one of the cowboys on the early shift."

Still tangled up in him, I groan and cover my face. "I'm sorry."

Levi holds me tight against him, his voice low and soothing. "It's my fault. I should have told you someone was down here."

I twist in his arms to face the other man, scrunching my nose. "Hi, I'm...Tessa, the weird nanny."

He holds up his hands. "No worries, lady. I'm just reportin' for duty. Heard about you from the boys. Ain't nobody say anything about weird. Just pretty and—" He glances at Levi. "Well, that's it."

My cheeks heat, and I remind myself to get a grip as I slip away from Levi's protective hold. It's been a while since I had to give myself a little pep talk.

They don't know I'm here.

They're not going to find me.

I'm safe.

"Thank you. It's nice to meet you." I move toward the coffee machine. "Um...can I make you some coffee?"

"No need. Levi already took care of me." He holds up his mug.

"Right." I avoid glancing back at my boss to ask the obvious question right now and move to make myself a cup.

Levi is at my side in an instant, pushing my mug away. "Are you sure you're alright?" he whispers.

I pull the empty mug back. "Your staff must think I'm a freak."

"You had a normal reaction to someone in your space. There's nothing wrong with that." He pushes the empty mug back and hands me a forest-green tumbler. "Here. Filled to the brim. Two sugars."

Then turns to Harry. "We'll be back before he's up, but just in case, give me a ring, and we'll head this way."

Harry nods.

Levi turns back to me. "Put your boots on."

"Am I going somewhere?" I ask with a yawn.

"I'm taking Harry's morning shift at the ranch. And you're coming with me."

My eyes light. "Really?"

He scans me once and moves to the sofa, pulling on the afghan I've grown quite fond of. Then wraps it around my shoulders. "It's chilly in the mornings."

With our boots on, Levi stuffs the hot beverage back in my hands and moves to the sliding doors.

With a look back at Harry, I follow Levi out into the crisp summer morning.

It smells different this early in the day—an earthy aroma. Like the dampness of dew in the grass and hay from the barns mingled with wildflowers.

It's refreshing in a way that makes you wrinkle your nose but still appreciate nature.

"Yesterday, Roger and Jackson gave you their tour. But..." He takes my hand as if I need help stepping down to the field. "You don't really get ranch living until you've done the morning shift."

We take a small two-seater tractor to the other side of the ranch, parking in front of the Wrangler Room next door to the stables.

The door creaks open as we step inside. It's dark and about the size of one of the smaller barns Roger showed us yesterday. There's a wooden desk, a weathered sofa, supplies, and several boxes spread throughout.

He moves behind his desk. "I just need to check the weather and confirm the schedule. Then we'll start with the stables."

"You do this every morning?"

"Usually start with Hideaway Headquarters. The ranch office at the entrance."

"Why isn't your office there?"

"Too many people. Too many questions. I'd never get any work done. It's mostly for tourists. Group tours, weddings, photoshoots. Sales."

"Sales? Like what you grow?"

"Meat and dairy. Supplies. Livestock. Riding lessons."

"Sounds busy."

"Not always. But we do our best."

"*You* do your best." As far as I know, this is his ranch. He runs it alone.

"We're a team. Almost everyone here has been with me since the beginning. I value loyalty and commitment. It's hard to come by, so I treat them like partners."

My chest tugs.

He pushes off his chair and grabs a saddle off the wall. "Come on, let's start with the horses."

A strong scent of hay hits my senses when we step through the side door of his office and into the stables. Horses shift in their stalls as Levi lifts a tall rake.

"This here's a pitchfork." He gathers hay with ease, tossing it into the feeding troughs, his muscles working beneath his shirt. Hay rustles as he tosses stacks of it for each one.

I watch as one of the horses lowers its head, munching on fresh hay.

Barely winded after all that work, Levi moves beside me, taking a sip of my coffee, then handing it back. "They'll be safer to pet after breakfast." He grins, leading me out the gate. "In the meantime, we'll feed the chickens."

We walk a small distance in the dark, my hand in his. We reach the chicken coop and Levi hands me a basket. Warmth spreads through me as he praises them, lifting fresh eggs out of the coop. I bend my knees, holding the basket out for him.

He labels them and stores the basket away for pick up. I look around to see where he parked that tractor. "You plan to show me the rest on foot?"

"Course not." He takes my hand and brings me back to the stables. "Now that they're not hungry, you can pet one."

Yesterday's ride with Levi was one hell of a thrill—but it probably wasn't the horse as much as it was the cowboy riding her.

I roam my eyes over each one. Curious about the one Jackson was telling me about. "Which one's yours?"

He scoffs. "All of 'em. You mean like the one I keep?"

"Like the one you love."

His lips quirks like I'm being funny, but his eyes fall to the far left of the stables and he moves toward it. "We try not to fall in love with horses. But..." He strokes the chestnut mare with large brown eyes that we rode yesterday. "This is Willow. Been with us for a bit now. She's young but fully trained. We use her for lessons and ranch work until she's sold."

The beautiful horse leans into his touch—as I imagine any female would want to. "Why would you sell her? Why not keep her for the ranch if she's useful?"

"No such thing as 'not for sale,'" he says like it's a way of life. "If a guest or tourist takes her for a ride and makes an offer, we consider it."

"What are the factors?"

"We screen every buyer to ensure our horses end up in good hands." He strokes her nose again. "I'd need to know where she's goin', the buyer's experience and knowledge. And if our horse is suitable for whatever their plans."

I reach out, mimicking Levi's caress. He drops his hand when Willow's nostrils flare slightly, her big eyes watching the newbie with curiosity.

"She's taking in your scent."

I stiffen. "Think she'll like it?"

"Can't imagine anyone not."

I lock my eyes with his for a brief moment, offering a flirtatious smirk. As if on cue, Willow leans into my touch with a snort that makes me feel like my hands are welcome. With her permission, I trace the contours of her face and hair. "She *is* beautiful," I tell him.

I wrap the blanket around my shoulders and step back, not overstaying my welcome but keeping my eyes on the beauty.

"Want the rest of your tour on her saddle?"

"Oh no. I pet. I don't ride."

He smirks. "That's too bad."

He steps past me to open the stall.

"What? That I prefer to pet instead of ride?"

Levi cocks his head, prepping Willow's saddle. "Where I'm from, we call that a tease."

"Are we still talkin' about the horse?"

He laughs as he hops on with practiced ease. "Yes, Tessa. We are."

I stroke her again, considering. My eyes flick to his. "So, I'd sit behind you?"

He shrugs, looking over my shoulder. "I'd prefer to be behind you. Safety measure." His eyes fall to my mouth when I pull my lip between my teeth.

"Alright." I wrap the afghan tighter around my shoulders.

Levi hops off. His strong hand catches and holds mine. "Step on this and swing your leg over her back."

"Oh, you mean I get to get on without being manhandled? Sweet." I follow the seemingly simple step and settle my ass over the leather. "Cozy."

Levi strokes her again and whispers something that sounds like, "Don't embarrass me, girl."

I laugh as he hops on behind me. "Too late for that, Cowboy."

We ride slowly along the ranch as he points things out to me. Like a talking map, he calls out every landmark and feature. Including his favorite view of the sunrise. The pride in his voice is almost soothing.

All the while, I'm resisting the urge to lean into the heat of his body behind me. It's hard. And I need a distraction—stat.

"Now that we're in the middle of nowhere and you're too good of a guy to leave me stranded, can I ask about Jackson's mom?"

He sighs. "Nothing to tell except what you already know."

"I know she's not allowed to see Jackson."

"She is very much allowed. Always has been. Just not alone."

"Besides making him lie to you, what did she do? I mean...before?"

He pulls on the reins. When I stiffen, he pulls me against his front.

"Lilly and I were married too young."

I want to tell him that I know about Aiden disappearing for days, sometimes weeks on end, shortly after their mom died. Leaving Levi, the only one over eighteen, to look after his brothers. I wonder if Lilly came around that time.

"Was she a high school sweetheart or something?"

"Or something."

I nod and keep my eyes straight ahead.

"She was my outlet during a time I didn't know what to do with myself. My...responsibilities tripled overnight and..." He pauses. "She was the only thing that kept me feeling my age, I guess."

"So what was the problem?"

"Ironically, she never grew up. Not even after Jackson was born." He helps me shift the horse in the other direction. "Guess I should have seen that comin'."

"How?"

"She was a free spirit. Left home years before then. Responsibilities and family meant nothing to her. Every time I tried to tell her I had to get back, check on my brothers, or prepare dinner, she'd convince me to stay. Insisted on teaching them survival rather than sacrificing my time with her."

"So...she was possessive?"

"She was destructive. Selfish." I feel his head dip down to my neck. "Unpredictable."

I can take a hint. "Can't deny that about myself."

"Unpredictable is fine. Favorable sometimes. Abandonment is not."

"She left you."

"I wish she did. It would have been easier. She...did the same thing I was doing when I met her. Checked in on me and Jackson, played mom and housewife like it was work rather than life, then..."

"Then what?"

I feel him shrug behind me. "Found her own outlet. Someone she felt free with."

I grow cold. "I'm so sorry."

"I didn't mind it. *That* part I should have predicted. But Jackson needed a mom. I could see the question in his eyes. The sadness. It was before he could form words that she kept disappearing." He pauses.

"Thankfully, I had my brothers and Dad to help while I worked on building this place. A future for us."

"You've done amazing with him." My voice cracks, and he leans in, his stubbled face brushing behind my ear.

"You alright?"

I nod. My heart feels heavy for both of them, but there's no good reason for it because they're just fine. "Thanks for sharing."

His voice shifts to something more resigned. "You're his nanny. You should know where he's coming from."

"Can I ask why the supervised visits?"

"That was difficult to get. Once I gained full custody, I didn't allow as many house visits because it gave Jackson empty promises. She kept telling him she'd be back soon. Promised him we'd be a family. After a few times of watching him wait by the door for her to never show, I took her back to court to set limits on her visits and what she's allowed to say."

"Poor kid."

"I don't feel sorry for him anymore. Especially after their last few visits."

"What's different about them now?"

He considers it for a moment. "She's more like a distant relative he's forced to see once a month. He doesn't trust her. He knows she's his mother and has an idea of why she's not with us, but once we're out of there, he's his old self again."

"Out of where?"

"The town bakery. I don't let her in our house. And we don't meet at the Inn because I don't want to associate that place with something he doesn't enjoy doing."

A breath is released from my lungs. I'm no mother but I'll never take Levi letting me into his home for granted. I'll be everything I can for that little boy for the rest of the summer.

He can trust me. They both can.

And I'd never make a promise I didn't intend to keep.

I'd never make a promise, *period*.

After sunrise, we bring the horse back to the stables and ride back to the house on the tractor. Harry is in the same seat we left him, but now there's breakfast on the counter. All made up of items from the fridge and cupboards that the cowboy seems to have pulled together.

Jackson is cozy on the couch, watching a vicious-looking cartoon and eating a bowl of cereal.

"Oh no, I'm late for work," I mumble, pulling the afghan off.

Levi catches it from behind my shoulders, his breath on my neck. "Knew you'd be trouble."

I quiver from the heat—the possibilities of it.

The clouds outside the windows turn dark as thunder rolls in the distance. Levi switches on the floor lamp in the corner, casting a warm glow that gives the room a cozy summer morning vibe.

"Second time this week," Harry says, sipping on his coffee.

Levi moves to the sliding doors. "Looks like we just made it."

I settle on the couch next to Jackson, fighting playfully for the blanket he's under. He responds by snuggling next to me and offering the other end of it. "Boy, you give in easily. Gotta fight for what's yours, man."

He shrugs. "I don't mind sharing with you."

"Ahh, you were raised with manners." I quirk my lip. "Well, I wasn't." I launch for the remote in his other hand and he giggles, holding it for dear life.

"No. Mine."

I tickle his side, and he drops it straight into my hand. "Okay, okay. But no old shows like Daddy watches."

I turn at the mention of his father, finding Levi holding a coffee mug and staring at us. I'm trying to find that familiar scowl when I do something that annoys him.

But he's unreadable. Then he turns to his son, pointing his finger. "Knight Rider is not old."

My jaw drops. "First of all, it's *ancient*. Second, you have *Knight Rider*?" I point the remote to the television eagerly. "Where? Bessie watches it, and I've become obsessed."

Levi takes the remote from me, his fingers somehow skillfully avoiding mine when he swipes it. His jaw is tight. The scowl slowly reappears as he flips through the streaming shows until he finds the familiar series.

His eyes sweep past us. "We're going to head out. Text if you need me." He instructs no one in particular, but I'm assuming he means me.

I frown, shifting.

Does he regret telling me about Jackson's mom? Maybe I got too comfortable? Should I be working, working? Like on my feet?

He did say cleaning wasn't part of the job, although it does help keep me distracted when no one's around.

"See any lightning?" Harry asks as Levi moves to a nearby storage closet for a pair of rubber boots.

"Not yet."

"Daddy." Jackson runs to his dad, throwing his arms around him.

"Sorry buddy, I can't take you out there with me today. You might get a little dirty, and we need to move fast."

"Oh no, I was just going to hug you now because you're going to be filthy later. I'm good." He races back like he's been out in the cold too long and snuggles under the covers.

"Right. Later." He and Harry walk out the door.

Despite not being totally comfortable with the affection or proximity, I could never turn the kid away as he leaps himself back to my side.

"You just let me know when you're settled, Wiggles."

He smiles and shifts on the side of my ribcage.

I laugh. "Jesus, kid."

I catch a glimpse of Levi with one foot inside the tractor just outside. Hard, untrusting eyes linger on us before he hops in and drives off.

I sigh.

I'll never make that man happy.

16

Tessa

I'm running out of things to do with this kid.

It rained all day yesterday, so staying in made sense.

But I can't exactly have a repeat of the same day. The kid needs friends, a park, the frozen yogurt shop. Or even the community pool. Hell, I could sure go for a dip, myself.

But we can't *walk* to those places.

And I haven't driven since the night I put Jackson at risk.

"I know!" Wiggles calls out. "Let's make more cookies."

I laugh. "Again?"

Yesterday, we whipped up Bessie's special chocolate chip cookies, the ones she makes with a generous layering of powdered sugar.

Levi's grumpy scowl was firmly in place when he got back from the ranch just before dinner and found evidence of our sugar shenanigans on the counter. Wiggles drew a picture of a horse and wanted his daddy to see it.

"Please? I'll be super careful not to get any on the floor." He smiles brightly.

I narrow my eyes at him. "Fine. But first, let's put on some sunscreen and take a walk through the ranch."

"Again?"

"This time, we're going to go to Pepper and Chase's place. She said they have ice pops."

His eyes widen. "I'm. So. In." He races up the stairs, insisting that he'll have *two* or no deal on all this walking.

If I didn't know any better, I'd say that kid was trying to get me fired.

Not that I need help in that department.

I didn't leave my room when I woke up this morning. I stared at the ceiling and wondered what the hell I did to this grumpy cowboy yesterday morning to make him go all one-eighty on me.

I finally ruled out asking about Jackson's mom.

He willingly answered and I didn't get any negative vibes after that conversation.

I finally settled on what it is.

It's me.

I'm being clingy. First, we made out, then I run into his arms because some stranger was in my kit—his—*his* kitchen.

Then I hop on his horse and ask about his ex?

It's me. I'm totally doing the one thing this man made very clear he doesn't want.

It took every bit of energy not to hop out of bed, head downstairs, and do what I do best.

Do.

Clean, cook, bake, work out—anything.

But I don't want to keep being a problem he has to deal with in the mornings.

That's not what he signed up for.

And I won't be anyone's burden.

Levi

Chase kicks the fridge shut, three beers in hand. "Let's sit outside."

I take one of the beers while Noah takes the other, lowering his glasses and inspecting the label.

"Would you prefer a nice rosé instead?"

My younger brother glares back at me. "There's nothing wrong with having a nice rosé, and no." He looks at Chase. "How old is this?"

Chase rolls his eyes, takes a swig, and steps out into the backyard.

"It's fucking beer," I tell him. "It doesn't go bad."

"Does too go bad. Sure, not as fast as say, milk, but it can still go stale from storage, even in cold temperatures."

"Why are we out here again? I've been sweating my balls off all day," I growl.

Chase glances inside. "Pepper just got all this outdoor furniture and she wants people using it. She's apparently big on *entertaining*."

"Isn't that a deal breaker?" I laugh. "You're not exactly a people person."

Noah grins and takes a swig of his stale beer. "No, but he's a Pepper person."

Chase lowers himself onto a patio chair. "Just sit and act like you're comfortable, alright?"

"She's not going to come out here with lemonade, is she?" I joke, thinking of Tessa's easy smile and refreshing iced tea she makes for my staff.

"Fuck you," the brunette from inside calls.

I flash her a wide grin. "Oh hey, Pepper. Patio looks great."

"Jackass. No wonder you're single." She turns back inside the house with a smirk.

"Oh yeah, how's your new nanny?" Noah asks. And I don't touch on why he thinks of Tessa at the mention of my being single.

"Just fine," I lie.

My brothers stare at me. Fuck, Dad's trained them. "She's fine. Jackson adores her."

"And you tolerate her," Chase continues for me.

The implication pisses me off because Tessa is a heck of a lot more than *tolerable*.

She's confusing.

Maddening.

Beautiful.

I don't confirm or deny his assumption.

"Heard you're asking Dad questions about her."

My gaze snaps to Noah. "What?"

"Like where she's from, what he knows about her."

I glare at him until he breaks. "He asked me to look into her."

I sit up. "What do you mean *look into her*?"

"You know, like a background check."

"You can't do that without someone's permission," I growl.

Noah's brows shoot to the sky. "Like...yours?"

"Like hers, dumbass." Noah's no dumbass. He's the smartest attorney I know. Dad was right. If there's something on this woman out there. He'll find it.

"Relax. I didn't find anything."

I blink. "Nothing? Not even where she went to school, jobs?"

"Sure, there was some job history. But that's it."

"So, she's clean?"

Noah stares at me like I'm a client he's trying to intimidate. "Too clean."

I roll my eyes. "You bored or something?"

Noah glances at Chase. "There's a...slight gap in her history."

I swallow the hoppy liquid. Everyone takes time off working occasionally. But something about Noah's tone makes me ask. "How much of a gap?"

"All of it."

"What do you mean all of it?"

"Three years ago. Just before her first appearance in Hideaway Springs. There was no trace of her. Anywhere."

I flick my gaze to Chase and something about his expression tells me this isn't the first he's hearing of this. They've *discussed* this.

Without me. "Elaborate."

"Either Tessa Banks is three years old. Or that's not her real name."

"You watch too many law shows."

He shrugs and sits back. "Suit yourself. It's not my kid she's watching."

"That's enough," Chase snaps. He's always been a fan of Tessa. But that's because they're both town outcasts.

Chase by choice.

Tessa because...well, because I made her one.

"She's only here for four more weeks. I'm not going to ask her if she lied about her name. What difference does it make?"

"You don't want to know?" Noah probes.

Hell yeah, I want to know. I want to know why she wakes up from what's clearly the same nightmare every morning before dawn. I want to know why she disappeared all those times only to come back when she needed a job.

Why she was desperate enough to come knocking on my door...

Why she looks lost.

I don't want to notice that last part about her, but I do. It's hard not to.

It's hard not to want to wrap her in my arms when something scares her. Or be there when she wakes up so I can assure her she's safe.

She didn't come out this morning.

I set my own alarm and waited downstairs. When it was clear she was avoiding me, I spent the rest of it in the gym until it was time to head to the ranch.

Noah's eyes flick to Chase. "Maybe Pepper knows something. Or...can ask?"

Our newlywed brother shakes his head. "I'm not asking her to do that."

Noah turns to me. "Lonnie?"

I mimic Chase. "Lonnie would never sell out another woman."

Noah winces. "Right. Sorry."

My ex may not be trusting, and would be the first to warn me about a suspicious female in my life. But if Tessa's running scared from something, Lonnie would take her secret to the grave.

Regardless of who she's keeping it from.

"Doesn't matter. Tessa's only here until the school year starts. That's less than a month away." I remind myself. Like that inevitable date is coming all too quickly.

I hear the sliding doors open behind me with Pepper's voice. "Look who's here."

"Dad!" I twist in my seat, catching my kid as he races up to me with red lips and a cherry ice pop in his hand.

"Hey, buddy. What are you doing here?" I look behind him, finding Tessa stepping tentatively onto the patio.

Her eyes find mine, and I take her in. Her curls hang down around her shoulders. Full red glossy lips shimmer in the sunlight. She's in those white denim shorts and plaid shirt again. Her shoulders rise as she pushes her hands in her front pockets.

Breaking eye contact, she flicks them back to her friend. "Could've warned me my boss was here."

The anxiousness in her tone makes my dick twitch in my pants.

The fuck is wrong with me?

Pepper waves her off. "Oh, please. You can't take these guys seriously. Can I get you a beer?"

Her response comes quickly. "No. No. Water, please."

"Dad, Dad. I'mma have a blue one next," he tells me. "Tessa says it's okay."

I flick her a small grin. "Did she?"

"Not if he keeps rattin' me out."

Jackson turns back to me, eyes wide. "You heard nothing."

Tessa covers her face, laughing, and follows Pepper back inside.

"Hey, Jackson. Come here." Chase pulls my kid to stand in front of him. "You like Tessa?"

He nods like my brother just offered him a new PlayStation. "She makes my food special. And she plays without checking her phone all the time," he adds with an exasperated sigh.

Noah leans in. "Yeah, but what do you *know* about her? Besides making your plate pretty and playing games with you?"

Jackson considers the question like it's a spelling bee. "I know that she likes a clean and organized kitchen. I know that she wakes up early because she likes the morning sky. Oh, and that she doesn't like doors."

Noah's brows shoot up again. "She doesn't like *doors*?" He looks at Chase as if to say, 'Are you hearing this?'.

Jackson jerks back like he's offended for her. And it makes me a little proud. "She says they scare her."

"When did she tell you that?" I ask.

My kid turns back to me. "When I told her I don't like the dark and that's why I have my nightlight. She told me she doesn't like the dark either. Or doors." His eyes widen in surprise. "Nature calls." He races inside.

I take a swig of my beer. Wishing it was something stronger.

"Maybe she *is* three years old," Chase chuckles, clearly amused.

Pepper drags Tessa back onto the patio. Pepper with her beer and my nanny with a glass of water. "So? What do you think? It's super cute in the dark with the tree lights."

"I love it. It's very you. Can't wait to see it at night."

"What nights do you have off? I'll call Charlie. We'll have a girl's night."

"And where the hell am I supposed to go?" Chase argues.

"I hear there's a lovely little Inn in town." She bats her lashes, and now it's my turn to laugh at him.

"Um...I don't know," Tessa answers.

I tap her arm gently with the back of my hand. "You can have any night you want. I really only need you with Jackson during the days."

Noah leans back in his seat. "That's true. It's not like *you* ever have plans."

I ignore the dig and focus on Tess. "Really, it sounds like fun. Just let me know."

Tessa doesn't respond, but Pepper jumps from her seat. "Eek, I'll call Charlie. Oh, and maybe Lonnie."

Noah's brows jump again, as if an opportunity presented itself.

I shoot him a warning glare.

Jackson pops his head back out. His lips now suspiciously purple and a blue popsicle in his hand. "Tess, now can we go to the park by the school?"

Tess stiffens. "Oh...um...you know...it's going to get dark soon. We'll go somewhere tomorrow."

Jackson sighs and heads back in. I straighten my spine trying to remember the last place they went. The last time Jackson talked about where they've been. It hasn't been in days.

That can't be right.

Tessa stands. "I'm going to go make sure he's not sneaking in a third popsicle..."

"Hey, Chase, can I leave Jackson here for a bit? Need to take care of something."

Chase's eyes flick to Tessa inside. "Take your time..."

"If I'm not back in two hours, bring him back to the house." Ignoring both my brother's stares, I follow her inside.

"Hey, Tess," I call softly, feeling like she tenses when I'm around.

She twirls like she expected me. "Hey. Sorry, we ran out of Italian ice at the house, and Pepper said she had some..."

I open my mouth, but she cuts me off. "He had lunch. Chicken salad, and I cut his juice with water."

I catch her wrists. "Tessa." She freezes at my touch, her eyes dropping to where we're connected. "It's fine. I was actually going to ask if you could run a quick errand with me in town."

"Oh. Okay, let me just grab him."

I tighten my grip. "No. Just you and me." I scan her outfit. One of the three I've seen her wear in the past week and a half she's been here. "I need to get some new clothes for Jackson. Could use your help."

"Sounds good." She checks her watch. "You think we can leave him with Pepper and Chase?"

"Already taken care of." I lead her out of the house and toward the driver's seat of my truck.

She stiffens. "What are you doing?"

"Well, I certainly can't drive. I've been drinking."

Her chest moves up and down as I open the door for her. But she recovers quickly, leaning against the car. "You're telling me you never drink and drive? I've seen you leave the Inn well after I've served you two to three beers."

I try to think of another reason before I realize I don't have to. I close the gap between us. "Tessa, get in the damn car."

She glances back at it. "It's too big for me."

I lean in with a smirk. "Oh, I think you can take it."

Her eyes heat, and I can almost feel her panties melting as she shifts with a hard swallow.

With a huff, she straightens and settles into the driver's seat. "Alright. But I'm not paying for any damages."

I close the door and hop around the other side.

The truck roars to life as she turns the key and sits back. Wrapping her hands around the steering wheel, she takes a breath, her breasts perking in a distracting way.

"Good." I tease. "Think you can drive it?"

"Think you can be quiet over there? I've got this." She narrows her eyes, checking the rear-view mirror. "Now, if I could just hit the pedal hard enough, I can cause optimal damage to the bed of this thing by hitting that tree back there at forty miles per hour."

I buckle my seatbelt, calling her bluff. "Ready when you are."

She backs out of the driveway carefully, barely breathing. Her knuckles harden around the wheel and I put my hand over hers, steering it left.

Tessa keeps her eyes on the road as she cruises through town. I quietly give her directions to Crest Lane, it's the more expensive part of town where the boutique and fancy restaurants are. "Okay, so I've been a little nervous getting behind the wheel lately. You don't need to be a rocket scientist to figure it out." She finds a metered parking spot and pulls over.

"Tess, you need to let it go. It was a long day. It could have happened to anyone."

She stares ahead. "I had your kid in my car."

I pull her hands off the wheel, making her look at me. "He's okay."

She sniffles sharply and pulls her hand away, unbuckling her seatbelt. "I'd rather be in the passenger's seat."

"Fine." Leaning over, I scoop her up, making her squeal and settle her onto my lap. "There, you're in the passenger's seat."

She wiggles over me with that raspy laugh I've come to love. "I meant *after* you're out of it."

I shift my pants with a groan. "Baby, you've got to stop moving like that."

She freezes and glances down. "Sorry. Not about that—that was entirely your fault. I mean about everything else."

I grip her waist. "Tess. Don't be so nervous." I push her hair behind her ear. "You're doing fine with him."

Her eyes drop to my mouth. "I don't think straddling my boss falls in the 'doing fine' category." She swallows like she's fighting to keep from closing the small gap between our lips.

I'm ready to close that gap. Fuck boundaries, fuck everything. "What category is it under, Tessa?"

She whimpers like she's about to break too, and I wish she would. Fuck I wish she would crush my mouth with hers and rock these hips over me, slicing the tension building between us for the past week. "I think...it's in the category of 'not looking for a real-life love story'."

Fuck.

I release a breath. Because she's one hundred percent correct. "You're right." I push open the door and twist her until she's seated comfortably on the leather seat while I slip out. "I'm sorry." I'm still holding her hand when I lean into her, despite who might be watching nearby. "I'm taking you into these boutiques. You're picking out several new outfits, new boots and anything else you might need for your stay here."

She opens her mouth to protest.

"And if you argue with me, I'm making you drive home."

She folds her arms. "That's supposed to scare me? It's your funeral, buddy."

"Alright." I peer down the street, considering something that would make it her funeral. "I'll ban coffee in my house."

Her eyes widen, and she hops out. "I could use a new pair of boots."

17

Tessa

LEVI LEAVES MY SHOPPING bags by the den when we walk into the house.

I hear Jackson's favorite cartoon playing in the other room as Chase comes around from the living room and into the hall. "*I'll only be an hour, tops.*"

"I said two," Levi argues as he passes his brother with a grunt to check on his son.

Chase eyes the bags on the floor and a small grin forms on his pretty face. With a perked brow, he puts his arm around my shoulder as we walk toward the kitchen. "Could this mean you're staying past your term?"

I glance at Levi. "No. But did your brother enjoy playing with dolls when he was younger? Cause he sure enjoyed dressin' me today."

He flicks off the television, and I follow his gaze to a sleepy little boy on the couch.

"You picked out her *clothes*?" Chase teases.

"Well, she wasn't doing it," Levi says defensively. "Besides, it wasn't hard."

"Oh, this is *gold* for Pepper." He clasps his hands and moves backward toward the patio. "Alright, I'm heading home to my wife. She sent dinner. It's on the counter. The kid ate. I don't do the bath thing—that's all you. Goodnight."

Levi walks him out and I move to Jackson in the living room, feeling guilty for abandoning him tonight.

I swipe his hair from his face, wondering how many times he must have felt second. Second to Levi's work. Second to the slew of nannies this man has had that were clearly more interested in their boss.

That kind of misplaced attention could do a number on a child. But hell, does he have a bright spirit.

It's no wonder at all. Jackson's surrounded by love. It's natural for him to give it and expect it in return.

I sit beside him, blowing softly against his sweaty forehead. I don't know if I'm in a position to undress him, but he's definitely overdressed for sleep.

I pull the throw blanket off him and stand to set it aside, finding Levi watching me —his hands in his pockets.

He's not scowling this time.

He's...thoughtful.

I let Levi take over, carrying Jackson upstairs while I set the table for us. Pepper had sent back some fancy eggplant dish I can tell was from a recipe book but clearly missing or replaced ingredients.

Levi returns, finding me lightly spooning and tasting the lopsided dish. "Oh good, I'll wait a few minutes to see if you drop dead before trying some."

I laugh. "It's not that bad and I'm going to tell her you said that. Here." I take a forkful of the warmed meal. "Try."

He grunts, making a face before opening for me, and I shove the eggplant in his mouth. "Mmm. Not... terrible."

I nod, moving back to the stove. "I'm going to add some garlic salt. Oh no...*fresh* garlic. Sauteed."

He steps behind me, watching me as I toss pieces of garlic into the hot oiled pan. "Where'd you learn to cook?"

"Bessie."

"How do you know Bessie?"

I stiffen but continue to stir. "She was my boss at the diner I worked at."

"In Summer Hill?"

I frown, pausing mid-stir.

"Something wrong?"

I spin, locking our eyes. "How do you know where I live?"

There's a beat before he answers. "Area code."

"Oh, right." I blink, turning back to the stove. "I um...think this is good to go." I shut off the burner and move about the kitchen like I've got a house full of guests.

Levi's the picture of calm as he pours the wine. It's almost maddening until he grips my waist, spinning me to face him. "I'm sorry."

My head shakes. "You didn't do anything. I'm just tired, on edge, I guess."

"I respect your privacy. I've asked my last question. For now, okay?" His tone is so gentle, it's almost foreign.

I nod. "Okay."

His easy grin settles me somehow.

He pulls a stool out for me before settling himself on the one beside me.

Throughout dinner, we play the game of accidental knee brushing, touching, leaning, and laughing.

Levi clears our plates and empty wine glasses.

I wait for him at the bottom of the stairs as he locks all the doors and does a final sweep of the floor. He keeps low lights on in nearly every room. Almost the same way I had it the night he left me to go to the Inn.

I don't like dark places. He's learned this about me. He's accepted it without judgment.

He steps in front of me. His voice soft. "Ready?"

I glance up and nod. Feeling uneasy and ashamed. I've let my fears, insecurities and trauma affect this whole house. Because of me, he's been waking earlier. Because of me, he's changed his nightly routine. Because of me, his son isn't having the best summer I could give him.

He lifts my chin. "Did I forget something?"

"I'm sorry about the last few days with Jackson. I'm going to take him out tomorrow. And every day. It was selfish of me to keep him home."

"It wasn't selfish. It was cautious. It's a normal reaction." He steps closer, cupping my face and lifting it to his. "Tessa, I want you to come to me. With anything you need. A night off. A problem with Jackson. A problem with you. If there's something on your mind or if you need anything at all. Just ask."

I search his eyes. "Anything?"

"Anything."

"Can I sleep in the den?"

He lowers his hands and steps back. "Baby, we've been over this. You can't live in the den. There's no privacy. There's no doo—"

His words cut off but I have my answer. It's a stupid request and I shouldn't have asked again. I nod and drop my head.

"Alright," he rasps.

I look up. "Really?"

He nods, but there's hesitation. Concern.

"I promise, you never have to worry about him walking in on me half naked. Or even naked. I'll be super careful about that."

He looks into my eyes like he's not hearing me. "What happened to you?" he asks, already breaking his own promise.

Pools hit my eyes, and I draw back, hitting the wall. "I don't like confined spaces. Jesus, Cowboy, paranoid much?"

The irony.

He catches my wrist before I can turn away and the touch makes it even harder to resist him. To not press myself into his warm, safe, chest. To not yearn for that husky voice telling me all the ways he'd wreck me if I broke my walls.

"I don't like lies, Tess, but I'll let you lie all you want if it keeps you from walking away right now."

Like that.

"You could make an ice queen melt with that mouth."

"Are you an ice queen?"

I laugh with a snort. "Pepper's the ice queen. I'm a bowl of mashed potatoes."

He doesn't find the humor as he threads his fingers with mine. "I like potatoes."

I smirk and he uses the opening to pull me close. "I like you," he clarifies before sweeping his tongue over my lips, parting them.

I wrap my arms around him, opening, whimpering as our tongues meet again. His body is strong, powerful, gentle and secure; I want it to consume me.

I moan when his hands slide up my short shorts, calloused fingers gripping my flesh. "Levi. God, yes."

His hips roll forward and I feel how much he wants it too. I'm ready for him to carry me upstairs, shut the door and keep me wrapped up in his arms. I want him to fuck me in ways I've denied wanting him to for the last three years.

I—

Feel cold.

Levi tears his lips from mine and pulls back, raking his fingers through his hair.

"Shit."

I'm breathless and afraid of the inevitable answer this hot, brooding cowboy is going to give me when I ask. "What's wrong?"

I hold my breath. Waiting for the *we can't...this is wrong...I shouldn't have led you on...*

He shakes his head, then closes the gap between us again, holding my face like he can't *not* touch me. "I'm sorry," he grits out. "It's been a while since...I've done this."

"Oh." My eyes stretch. Was Lilly the last woman he'd been with? How long ago was that?

Reading my expression, he sweeps a thumb over my cheek, a grin playing on his lips. "That's not what I meant, beautiful."

"Okay..."

"You're not just...I want to do this right. Cook for you. Maybe a little whiskey, candles."

I nearly melt into a puddle.

But that's not my image. That's not who I am. I've melted for a man before and it got me a bullet above my ass.

I grip his shoulders and twist us so that he's against the wall and press myself into him. "Indie. Look, I'm sold on the whole gentleman thing, okay? I don't need wining and dining."

I lift onto my toes to kiss him but he flips me back over. "I'm not selling anything, baby. But I am a gentleman, and you're getting dinner tomorrow."

I bite the corner of my lip, and he tugs on it with his teeth. "Quit it."

His eyes are dark and jaw set. He's so intense. So bossy. And this small space beneath the stairwell is so intimate my core heats.

"You didn't let me finish." He pins me with those eyes. "Dinner tomorrow. Dessert tonight."

His lips crash over mine, and I moan into his mouth. His large hands hook the back of my thighs and lift me as I wrap my arms and legs around him. Our kiss is desperate, passionate, like we're famished for each other.

Like we haven't kissed before.

Or never will again.

The thought makes me moan harder into his mouth, and he shushes me before carrying me up the stairs.

Silently, I accept that this might be a one-time thing, but God, I hope it's enough. Because just his arms around me is something I think I'm already addicted to.

I nip against that hard jaw and the side of his neck.

"What did I tell you about being indecent in the halls, Whiskey?" he teases before drifting me into his bedroom. It's big. Airy with large windows and a balcony overlooking his ranch.

He sets me on my feet, leaving me lightheaded and watches me for a moment. It's tender and attentive. He leans in for a soft kiss. "You trust me, Tess?"

The question throws me off but the answer is easy. "I do, Indie."

His arm secures my waist as he grips the edge of the door. "Okay if I close this?"

Warmth spreads through me and I grin. "Yeah. It's okay."

Levi closes the door and moves his fingers over the lock.

Panic rushes through my veins. "Leave it unlocked," I call before I can think.

His hand shoots up and he steps back. For a brief second, he almost seems mad at himself for even considering it. "Of course."

Way to go, Tess.

I tense and turn away. "Sorry, you're right. There's a child—and I'm—"

He catches my hand. "That kid could sleep through an earthquake. He hasn't come into my room in the middle of the night since he was five. We'll leave it unlocked."

"Please don't ask," I whisper.

His eyes are dead serious when he responds. "I won't."

I nod again, staring at the door as if to reassure myself I'm okay. I pull my shirt over my head, leaving my white lace bra on display. "Put your hands on me again," I practically beg.

Levi sheds his shirt like a lifeguard on duty and lifts me. His body is warm against mine, and I cling to the skin-to-skin contact as if he's Superman holding me fifty feet above the ground, and I'm deathly afraid of heights. He carries me to the massive bed in the center of the room and sets me over it.

I tug on his belt, desperate to set the erection I felt all the way up here free.

He catches my wrists and I look up at him with a breathy laugh. "Sorry. It's been over three years for me, so if I'm too eager or a little resistant, you know why."

"Three...years," he repeats, like that number means something to him. I hold my breath before he finally nods. "We'll go as fast or slow as you want. You set the pace."

With my bottom lip between my teeth again, I smile up at him and lean back on my elbows.

"How do you want me, Tess?"

I sit up, flashing him a flirty smile. "My choice?"

"Tonight, it's yours. Tomorrow it's mine."

A shiver of excitement runs down my spine, along with an ease of knowing I'll have him again.

"I want you all night." Of this, I'm sure. The next thing takes a little courage as I undo his buckle slower this time and the button of my white shorts. "I want you to fuck me with your tongue. Then finish me with your cock. I want it slow, and I want it hard. No shortcuts."

"Fuck. That was going to be mine."

I giggle as he hooks his fingers into my shorts and slides them down my legs. "You're so goddamn beautiful. You're bringing me to my knees already, baby."

Levi's mouth is on my throat and he works his way down my body with soft kisses and tiny nibbles. I'm so high off this brooding man, I'm floating in space.

He lowers the cup of my bra and hisses. I gasp when he tugs on a hardened nipple with his lips.

My panties will be soaked through before he even gets below my belly button.

He must feel my impatience. "Regretting asking me to go slow, Rogue?"

"Gravely."

He chuckles and slides his hands under my ass. "These are sexy. You been wearin' these around my house?"

I writhe. "Off, Indie. Take them off."

He stands. "If you say so." He steps out of his pants, and I scan him from the bed. Heavens, he's fucking perfect. A flawlessly carved mountain of a man.

And tonight...and apparently tomorrow, he's mine.

Levi's on his knees on the floor. I moan as hands as rugged as the man they belong to slide my panties down my legs. "Fuck, sweetness. You're soaked."

I let him pull me closer, sliding my knees apart. I'm desperate for his mouth. For the penetration of his tongue. I lift off the bed to feel him... to watch him.

When his tongue sweeps through my slit, I cry out. He moans as he pulls on my clit, sucking slow, then fast. It's warm and rough at the same time. The scruff of his beard will leave my skin raw and I welcome it.

"Christ, Indie." I bend my knees and arch my back, my fingers sliding into his hair.

"Fuck, Levi. Yes. Oh my god."

He pulls back with a breath. "Ride me, baby. Ride me like I'm your cowboy."

I hesitate, and he responds by teasing me with his lips barely grazing my flesh.

I lift off the bed, spreading wider for him, moving my hips, and riding his mouth hard as he pumps his tongue into me.

I'm so close. But I've never come this way before. This is the part where it trickles away. It's why I asked him to finish me with his cock.

"Now. Levi. Fuck me now."

But he doesn't stop. He's devouring me. I'm delirious. My breath catches, and I'm on the edge as he pulls my orgasm out of me. It's impossible and yet—

"Oh, oh god." Stars, I see stars. My thighs tremble. Every muscle below my belly tightens and my mouth drops silent for a second before I pull the pillow over my face and scream, jerking against him as he licks me clean.

A rumble of a laugh comes from Levi as he rises off the floor and lifts the pillow from my face.

I'm breathing hard, watching his gorgeous chest rise and fall as he grins down at me.

I swipe the pillow with what little strength I have right now and whack him with it. "What happened to my choice…"

He presses his lips to mine. "I went rogue."

I drop the pillow to my side with an impossible grin as he moves over me. "You alright?"

"I could have woken the livestock." I glance at the door. "…or worse."

He drags me over the pillow, hovering that strong, masculine body over me. "Seems fair." His heated gaze sweeps my face. "You didn't exactly come with a warning yourself."

I reach up to kiss him deeply, desperate to have his body pressed against mine again. My fingers work his briefs down.

And holy hell. His erection is rock-hard, long, and thick. I lick my lips.

"Like what you see?" He teases and it's so playful, I love this side to him. It's what I imagine he must have been before things like responsibilities and an ex-wife fucked with him.

I lift my eyes to his. "I'm getting you a new mug."

He bursts out a laugh and kisses my neck. "What's it gonna say, Whiskey?" he asks as he unstraps my bra.

My response is caught in my throat when I watch him devour me with those deep blue eyes. "God, you're perfect, Tess."

I bite my lip.

As long as I don't turn around, everything will be fine.

"I'll surprise you," I finally answer, dazed by his fingers tracing down my side.

"Love how responsive you are. Can't wait to be inside you."

I'm so ready for him to fill me to the brim, it's not even funny.

Foil tears and he slips on a condom that seems to sheath all of him somehow.

This is all so intoxicating. The last time I had sex—too long ago—lasted minutes and was in the backseat of my ex's car.

It wasn't my first time, but I don't think anyone's completely broken me into taking all of what Levi is preparing to give me.

He lowers himself to me, his words gruff but gentle. "I've already been inside you. You can take all of me, Whiskey Eyes. I promise."

I relax at how in tune he is with me. I open my eyes, meeting his with a smirk. "You're nailin' this gentleman thing, Cowboy."

"Good. Because I'm not about to fuck you like one."

He jerks my hips and sinks down.

I gasp, taking him in. The sensation arousing me so intensely. He doesn't ease. He *thrusts*. He treats me like a woman. Not a girl.

And I own it.

I breathe evenly, my body relaxing as I inhale him inch by inch.

"You're taking me so good, Tessa."

"Deeper, Indie. Fuck me like the town troublemaker deserves."

Heat flashes in his eyes and a guttural sound erupts from his throat as he pounds into me. "Fuck, Whiskey."

I've only ever had it rough. I never liked it. But I'm reveling in this. In him. In being his tonight. Being fucked senseless by this grumpy, broody man.

My fingers wrap around his ass, and I rock against him, feeling full but needing more.

We're in heaven. He's a freaking god and I'm his goddess. Every muscle in my body tightens. Every burning need quenched.

"So fucking perfect, baby." He repeats the endearment that should melt my heart.

But all it does is remind me how little he knows me because I am anything but.

"Levi," I whimper, my insides burning to explode.

"That's it, baby. Come with me."

My thighs shake as he pulls out almost all the way, thrusting back in.

I rise off the bed as another orgasm hits me hard. Levi crushes my mouth with his, muffling his rough groan and my cry as he jerks himself empty inside me.

"Holy fuck," I whisper on a gasp.

His big hands cradle my head that's still lifted off the pillow. "Took the words right out of my mouth, baby." Hazy blue eyes search mine. "You good?"

"You said we're doing this again?" I ask, still seeing stars.

"Fuck yeah."

I smile in his arms. "Then, yeah. I'm good."

18

Levi

It's not the first time I'm watching the clock as a woman stays asleep in my bed.

But it's the first time I revel in the fact that she *stays* asleep. It's nearly six a.m. and Tessa's soft silky tresses are spread wildly over my pillow. Her eyes peacefully closed, and I hope to God she's not in dreamland.

I don't want her having any dreams. I'd much rather she get a fucking break while she sleeps.

An empty mind is a peaceful mind and something tells me it's been a long while since Tessa Banks had any peace.

We whispered late into the night. I had every intention of having her go back to her...den. But every time she tried to leave, I'd pull her back against my chest.

She also kept covering up as if I hadn't seen all of her. Tasted all of her.

Come to think of it, there is one part of her body I didn't get a good look at last night.

And it's my favorite thing to look at when she's walking away.

I'm careful not to disturb her as I slowly lower the sheet down her back. Taking in her smooth skin, the perfect curve of her—

The hell?

A deep red, round scar catches my eye. My stomach tightens as I zero in on it. That *can't* be what I think it is.

The alarm goes off and I curse, pulling the sheet back over her.

Tessa moans as she stretches, soft curves turning into me. She gasps sharply when she opens her eyes. "Indie." Her eyes sweep her covered, nude body. "Hi."

"Mornin'." My response is tight as I glare down at her.

She scans her surroundings tentatively. "I didn't mean to spend the night."

"I did."

If I don't get a grip, she'll pick up on the edge in my tone.

Her eyes look out into the light-colored blue sky with a shy smile. "Morning."

I release the sheet and move my hand to the side of her face. "You look good rested, Whiskey."

Her warm body stretches into me again. I breathe her in, my cock jerking to life instantly.

How the fuck does she have this effect on me after what I just saw?

Tessa jolts, wrapping the sheet around her waist. "Oh no. You have work. *I* have work." She sits up. "Breakfast. I can make you something before you go."

Grabbing her clothes from various sides of the bed, she clutches the sheet that's bound around her like a mummy and moves to the door, opening it softly. "I'll wash this and bring it back later," she whispers.

I open my mouth to assure her it's not necessary, but she's gone.

I feel like a jackass being angry with Tessa. Hell I'm as angry now as I've been every time I'd walked into a room and she'd be there. Every time I heard about the town outlaw or the town rogue causing trouble again.

I drag my hand down my face. If I'm honest, I'm probably angrier with myself for being so goddamn attracted to the wrong person.

Again.

But nothing about Tessa feels wrong. Not since the day I met her and certainly not what we did last night.

What the fuck happened to you, Whiskey?

I spend the morning doing mindless work in the field just to keep from walking back to the house to check on her.

Then when I see her in the barn, bringing over fresh iced tea and biscuits for the cowboys, I ride back to the Wrangler Room and lock the door.

The ranch website needs updating with available products and livestock. And the Barley family sent a friendly reminder to confirm the ranch is closed for their daughter's wedding reception.

It's an uncommon event for Hideaway Ranch, but certainly profitable.

Out of town folks typically rent the space for engagement photos. It's been happening more and more lately. Maybe cowboy romance is a thing, and I missed the memo.

Gritting my teeth, I push off my desk where a pile of vendor invoices still wait to be paid.

Shit. I need to clear my head and take care of those.

It's not that I don't have the money. Hideaway Ranch is the most profitable establishment in town. I've just never been a paper and computer guy.

That's all Noah.

And Noah certainly does his part in sending me reminders. When he gets calls asking him to write a legal letter to the ranch.

I review each bill and send the front office a note of approval to get these paid asap.

I still feel off. Like I'm missing something. Like I'm not doing enough.

Tessa's been on my mind all day. Last night was fucking perfect. We were in sync more than just physically. We fit. *She* fits.

I promised her a repeat because I knew before I touched her one night wasn't going to be enough. But I can't just ignore what I saw. And I won't scare her by asking more questions.

Not yet.

Stalking out of the Wrangler Room, I jog around to the stables. I need to go for a ride.

"Howdy, Cowboy," a familiar voice calls as I bring Willow back to her stall.

I pat her twice and whisper, "Thanks, girl."

I hang the saddle and turn to one of my closest friends. And a woman who drove me bonkers for nearly a year when we were dating.

"Hey, Lon."

"Got any apples?" She swings her empty basket.

"Yeah, Harry's got a bag full waitin' for ya." I lean over to kiss her cheek.

There was a time when I couldn't even do that without her flinching.

Five years ago, Lonnie was in a toxic, abusive relationship. Physical abuse.

I was the first man she trusted after changing her name and moving to Colorado. But with a young kid, I came with my own baggage, and things didn't work out for us. Call it bad timing or just two pieces that don't fit.

She's still one of my best friends.

"When you gonna take me for a ride on one of these?"

"They're *horses* and anytime. Just let me know and I'll set it up with one of my guys."

She rolls her eyes. "I really hope you've got better game than that or you'll never get laid again."

I dust my hands off on my pockets with a smile, happy to see her. If I'm honest, she's been on my mind too. Just a little differently. "Come by the house for a drink?"

She jerks at the sudden interest to spend more time with her. Usually, it's small talk as I toss her a bag of apples and tell her to get off my lawn.

Especially during work hours.

"What's up?" she asks once we're in my kitchen. I offer her a glass of Tessa's iced tea with mint and lemons floatin' around inside.

"Mmm...yummy. You made this?"

"Tessa."

"Oh. How's that workin' out? Aiden tells me she bullied you into hiring her." She crackles a laugh.

"She didn't—you been talkin' to my dad?"

"No. What? Maybe. So the town rogue is now on your payroll?"

"For the summer."

She nods and watches me carefully. Then something near the sink catches her eye. "Aww, it's the mug I got you."

"Tessa likes it. I think she uses it just to fuck with me." I chuckle.

Lonnie sets it down. "Did you tell her it's from an ex?"

"Yes."

"Ooh...pretty *and* secure. I like her."

"Lon, I gotta ask you something."

She slams the table like she'd just won a bet. "I knew it. You want to bang the nanny. Yes, it's totally cool. No one will judge. Go for it."

"I already did."

She stares at me, her face sobering. "What's wrong?"

"I don't know anything about her. I thought I was okay with that, but I want to know who she is. Where she's from."

She nods. "Anyone you can ask?"

I shake my head. "Think there was a name change. She doesn't seem to exist before three years ago. Around the time she first showed up in Hideaway Springs."

Lonnie's eyes flash—and it's likely because this sounds very familiar to her. "You think she was abused?"

"She has nightmares. She barely sleeps at night. I'm concerned."

Lonnie's face pales. "Does she flinch when you touch her?"

"No. It wasn't like you and me."

She nods.

"I don't know who else to talk to. I don't want to ask the police to look into her. I mean, there's background check stuff, but that wasn't part of the deal."

"Look, I've been around her enough to know that woman is running scared and she's got secrets. Do me a favor and keep your dist—"

"There was a bullet wound in her back—just above her hip."

Lonnie freezes. "Are you sure?"

"I know what a bullet hole looks like, Lon."

"Alright, alright, easy, Cowboy."

I release a steady breath, flexing my arms against the edge of the counter. "I want to ask her about it."

"Why? So she could open up to you and be out of here by the end of summer? Yeah, I saw your ad. Don't make her vulnerable to you only to show her out come September."

My jaw is tight as I clench my teeth. "I fucking hate it when you're right."

"You've got major control issues, dude. Just because you want to know doesn't mean you have the right to."

I glare at her.

She grins comically. "I'll see myself out."

19

Tessa

MY HEART POUNDS IN my chest as I step out of the shower. Daylight. I was with him—in his bed. Naked. In broad daylight.

What was I thinking falling asleep in his arms?

Oh, that's right. I wasn't thinking. Not with my head anyway.

I was thinking with the buzz in my stomach, the ache in my chest that wanted *more* of Levi. *This* side of him. The sweet and funny side that kept distracting me from leaving so I could "accidentally" spend the night.

But it was stupid. He could have seen it. He almost *did*.

I'm pretty sure he didn't. He was so easy with me when I turned into him. His eyes were soft, not horrified.

So, I guess it was worth it.

It was the first time in nearly a year since I'd slept through the night. The last time must have been my first night in Hideaway Inn when I drove all night, knocked on every business I hadn't ruined somehow, and asked for a job.

Aiden hired me on the spot. Knowing my history in town and just not giving a shit, he said, "*The way I see it, I need a waitress, and you need a job.*" Then tossed me an apron and welcomed me behind the bar.

I'd promised myself it was going to be one night. But hell, I slept so damn good after a long day, I was tempted for another.

That's what it's come to. Sleep is my drug and I can't get enough of it. I'd do anything for it. Except maybe sell my blood. I've lost enough of that.

I'm in a plain white t-shirt and sleep shorts as I head downstairs. Levi put Jackson to bed an hour ago and just before he went up with him, he told me to meet him down here later.

He's in the kitchen pouring two glasses of red wine. His face unreadable. And maybe a little tired.

"Long day?" I ask, forcing a grin to mask my nerves.

He sets the bottle down and comes around the counter to me. His hands stretch as he grabs hold of my waist. "You have no idea."

"Indie."

"Whiskey."

"Last night was...amazing," I say honestly, my face twisting anxiously.

"Don't say but."

"But I can't stay in your room again."

His scowl says he agrees, but when his eyes flick to mine, his words are completely different. "Why not?"

My lashes fall as I consider how to answer. "It wouldn't be right."

"Neither is sleeping with your kid's nanny." He frames my face with his hands. "Tessa, look at me."

He's so goddamn gorgeous.

And right now, he's looking back at me like he's thinking the same thing about me. "I'd never make you do anything you don't want to do. But I'm not the type to ask a woman to leave after having her in my bed."

"You wouldn't be—"

"And I *liked* holding you all night. I plan on doing it again tonight if it's alright with you."

Warmth spreads through me and my core pulses. I glance at the wine. "Am I off the clock?"

He turns, reaching for the glasses, and that's when I notice the spread. Crackers, cheese, grapes, a honeycomb, and other delicious gourmet assortments on a massive board.

"Are you wining and dining me after we just had dinner?"

"It was two hours ago and we'll be here for a while." He wraps an arm around me.

"Hmm...what would we talk about?"

His face sobers. "Anything you want."

The back door knocks, and I sprint back like a firefly.

Levi checks the clock on the kitchen wall. "The fuck?" Running a hand through his hair, he stalks to the door and pulls it open, allowing in two very chatty girls and their grumpy men behind them.

Chase, Pepper, Noah, and Charlie pile into the house rowdy and intrusive despite their whispering.

Levi growls a reminder that he's got a kid sleeping upstairs before asking them to get what they came for and get out.

"What's up your ass?" Chase mutters, opening up the fridge and reaching for a beer.

"Can I get anyone else anything?" I offer, feeling flustered and caught off guard.

"No," Levi says flatly. "You're off the clock and they're *leaving*."

Charlie perks her little blonde head between us. "Pepper and I were coming over to steal Tess away for a bit, but then the *guys* thought we'd make a thing of it and just hang out here instead."

I smile. I never had this. Family and friends popping in on you unexpectedly to whisk you off into the night for fun.

I scan myself briefly. I've stripped my make-up for the evening, and I'm practically in sleep clothes.

"Oh, you look so comfy. Now I want to change," Pepper whines.

I push my hair behind my ears. Comfy. Is comfy the new *"you look tired"*?

"I'm not walkin' back to the cottage, Pinky. You're fine," Chase calls, picking up a cube of cheddar from the board Levi put together. "Y'all have people over or somethin'?"

The way he asks almost makes it sound like Levi and I are a couple, like we host parties at our home.

I catch Levi's tired glance. "Or somethin'," he mutters.

I carry the board to the living room and join them on the couch. Things were probably about to get pretty hot in here with Levi, but this...his brothers, my friends, a late-night snack and drinks...is *warm*. It fills my heart in a way I can't explain. In a way I know I may never have again. And if only for a little, I want to pretend I'm one of them. Pretend I belong.

"Are nicknames a thing with all you boys? Noah, what's yours for Charlie?"

Grump number two glances at his girlfriend but doesn't respond.

"Well about an hour ago, it was *drama queen*," Charlie snaps in his direction.

"Whoa." I sink to the back of the couch, feeling like I am starting—or rather, continuing—a war.

"Clearly, I was way off," Noah says dryly, rolling his eyes.

"Proof that you don't know me at all!" Charlie flips her hair back and stalks to the kitchen.

Noah pushes off the couch. "Look, can we just drop it? I said I'll fix it tomorrow."

Charlie shakes her head, grabs the wine glass that belonged to me a few moments ago, and stalks out the back door. "Don't bother."

I jump off the couch as Noah starts after her and hold my hand flat against his hard chest. Damn these boys have good genes. "Hold it, four-eyes."

"Tessa, move." There's a warning in his voice and it almost makes me laugh.

"Watch your tone," Levi growls.

Lover-boy looks over my shoulder. "I don't want her out there alone."

Pepper looks at Chase expectantly, and he sighs dramatically. "I'm on it."

I press Noah toward the couch. "What happened?"

When he gives me a look that says *I don't have to explain anything to you*, Pepper joins me, crossing her arms next to me like we're—quite literally—Charlie's Angels.

The grumpy nerd runs a hand through his silky hair. "Charlie and Bruce—one of the contractors for her bookstore—got into a little bit of a disagreement today."

"Oh boy," Levi mutters from the kitchen.

"She wants an open and airy space where people can roam with coffee, books, and a seating area. Bruce complained about practicality and electrical outlets being hidden and whatnot."

"Where do *you* come in?" I demand.

He jerks like it's obvious. "He's got a point. Her vision is just not practical for—"

"Where do *you* come in?" I repeat slower. "As in, what did you *say*?"

"I don't remember...I just very calmly told her to consider what he was saying."

Pepper and I continue to glare.

"She got upset, said he's not the one who's going to walk in there every day and look at something they didn't envision because some lazy contractor took the easy and practical route."

"And?" Pepper pressed.

"And I...said she was overreacting."

"I believe the words were *drama queen*," I correct.

He sighs. "Anyway, she went all *Charlie* on me and rambled until I kissed her to shut her up—then she slapped me—again."

Levi snickers.

"Sounds like you didn't support her. You didn't have her back. That makes you a jerk and you need to apologize."

"You don't think I did? I hate fighting with her. When we both calmed down, I said *'I'm sorry if I upset you'*."

Pepper and I groan simultaneously.

"What?"

Pepper holds up her hand, her fingers spread. I point to each one as I go through the list. One, never use the word *if* when apologizing. Two, always recite specific occurrences where you went wrong. Three, tell her she was right and *why*. Four, repeat step two. Five, give her one hell of an orgasm to make up for being a dick."

Pepper drops her hand.

Noah's eyes shift from me to his new sister-in-law. "That's not a thing. How is that a thing?"

I take a step closer. "I'll bet you my summer salary if you do all those things, you'll be her hero again."

He considers it. "What about the contractor?"

"Oh, you're handling the contractor regardless." Levi jumps in, handing me a fresh glass of wine. "That bookstore is part of mine and Chase's investment and we did it for Charlie, not for some disrespectful jackass."

Noah rises off the couch, scratching his chin. "What was three again?"

Levi laughs, slapping his brother's shoulder. "When in doubt, bro, skip to number five and repeat."

"Sorry," I mumble when I collide with him for the third time in the kitchen as we clean up.

He grabs my waist, holding me in place. "You're impossible."

"What did I do now?" I ask playfully.

"You're tempting me to leave evidence that we had a party without Jackson and take you upstairs right now."

I giggle and wrangle myself free, missing his warmth around me. "Come on, there's not much left."

I feel him grinning at me. "You handled my brother like a badass."

"I cringed when he said 'if' because that's basically calling your woman crazy and trying to settle her. It factually implies you have no fucking clue what you did to upset her, and therefore, your apology doesn't count."

He whistles. "Remind me never to get on your bad side."

I spin, narrowing my eyes. "You wouldn't grovel."

He cocks his head. "You're right. I don't grovel. I'd be on my knees." He winks.

Heat floods my cheeks.

He grins and crosses to me. "Have I done anything to upset you lately?"

"As a matter of fact, you have."

His expression sobers, like we're not playing anymore. "I haven't been very nice to you."

I grip the edge of the counter behind me for support as I back up. "That's putting it lightly."

He brushes my face with the back of his hand. "I'm sorry I yelled at you at Jackson's birthday last year."

Anger roars in the pit of my stomach when I remember the look on Jackson's face when his old nanny was yelling at him. "That bitch had it comin'."

He laughs. "Maybe. Still, you could have come to me for an alternate solution."

"Where's the fun in that?"

"You said something to me that day—something I'll never forget." He steps into my space, lifting my chin. "When I asked you which kid she was yelling at, you said—"

"The one with your eyes."

"You defended my kid, knowing he was mine—"

"*Because* he was yours, Indie," I whisper, my eyes dropping to where his mouth hovers over mine.

"Then I owe you one hell of a number five," he breathes.

Heat rushes through every bone in my body.

"Come up with me, Whiskey."

"I...want to, but..."

"Don't spend the night then. I'll carry you down to the den myself later, I promise."

I hum in a daze as he kisses my neck. "I can walk myself back down to the den."

"Not after I'm through with you."

20
Levi

"Wнат's it gonna be, Indie?" Tessa asks, a mixture of nerves and anticipation flooding those amber eyes.

My hands snake around to grip her bare, perfect ass. It didn't take us long to get undressed. For me, it was a quick shower. For her, it was my simple command to be naked by the time I was done.

The lights were practically all the way down when I came out, but I didn't question it. Seeing her sitting naked and pretty on my bed is enough to shut up any man.

"Hmm...my choice, isn't it?" I tease with a sinful grin.

She nods. It's casual and a little flirtatious, but I don't miss the hard swallow as she glances down at herself.

What are you hiding? I want to ask without the intention of letting her answer. Because I'll follow it with. *Because you're goddamn perfect and I want to see all of you.*

I shake my head. "No. It's yours again tonight."

Her brows twitch. "That's not fair."

I smirk. "I've got you—after being an ass to you for no good reason. I think it's pretty fair."

She stands and bites her lip. "I want—" She closes her eyes and takes a breath. "I want you behind me, but—"

I flip her around and just as quickly, she flips back, burying her head against my chest. I give it a beat before dipping my head to hers. "Baby, what is it?"

She hesitates and I feel like an idiot.

Right.

Moving to the wall, I lower the lights all the way and make my way back to her with only the moonlight illuminating my bedroom.

She relaxes in my arms and I lower her onto the bed, kissing all her unwarranted nerves away. "Anything you need, just say it. Do you want the covers?"

She considers it, then shakes her head.

"Good." I dip my fingers into her heat. "You're perfect, Tessa. I'll take you any way you want me to." I rub her center. "So long as this stays wet for me."

She squirms. "Now. Please, Levi, before I lose my mind."

I flip her on the bed, lifting her ass. It's faint, the hole that's healed on her lower back. Looks more like a shadow or a mole if I really focus on it. But I look away, knowing she wouldn't want me to.

My fingers slide back into her. She whimpers, her hips rocking for more. I slip in another. "Fuck, I won't last long once I'm inside you, baby. You're so sexy. So beautiful."

"Fuck me, Indie. Hard." Her voice is muffled in the pillow, but her need is loud and clear.

I enter her slowly, then give her a good thrust. I'm hard as a rock, gripping her hips, riding her the way she desires. Her moans and groans mixed with mine drive me wild.

She's a dream.

A goddamn dream that's been in front of me all along and I've been too damn stubborn to see it.

To see past the resemblance.

She moves her ass, taking me all the way with each roll of her hips. I'm going to explode so hard. And it's now that I realize...

"Fuck. I'm not wearing a condom."

"No. Don't stop. Please." She grinds against me, taking more of my bare cock inside her.

I don't stop. I pump faster and harder. I don't deny her a single beat of my pulse. I don't hesitate. I indulge her. I give and I take and I ride my fierce woman.

Wrapping an arm around her, I rub her swollen clit making her cry into the pillow.

My thighs shake, blood rushing through my veins, and I curse as I explode, emptying inside her.

Fuck.

I won't soon recover from the power this woman has over me. There's no damn question in my mind. She owns me.

I pull out gently, wrapping her in my arms. A lazy grin meets mine as she twists her head back. She doesn't look the least bit sorry for what we just did.

We don't say anything as I hold her warm body.

Tessa looks too fucking good to move. Those brown eyes fluttering closed every few minutes. Her arms and head protectively pressed into my chest.

How have I never noticed how much this woman lives in fear? The dark circles under her eyes I always thought were part of her charm—her badass charm.

I make a mental note to pay my father for the months she lived at the Inn.

Suddenly grateful for it.

Grateful for her being safe from whatever's been haunting her.

How am I supposed to carry her out of my bedroom and bring her down to the cold, open den? How does a man do that to a woman?

To *his* woman?

But a promise is a promise.

Even if it has a few tweaks.

Tessa's fast asleep in my bed when I return from the basement.

She stirs slightly as I slip my white T-shirt over her. I never want her waking feeling uncomfortable or…seen. I lift her into my arms and carry her across the hall to her bedroom.

Safe. Close.

The way I always want her.

I just hope she doesn't hate me for it.

Tessa

I stretch, moaning awake from a deep sleep. Dawn cracks through the window.

Wait. Window?

I snap my head up, scanning the space around me.

I'm in my bedroom.

Not in the den. My heart falls at his broken promise, but I take a breath and will myself to be okay with it.

Swinging my legs off the bed, I stand.

Then freeze.

The door. It's *gone*.

I step over cautiously, inspecting it. Half deciding that I'm dreaming. But this is very real. The door's been taken off its hinges. Levi's door is also open. I tiptoe across the narrow hall to peek inside.

He's sound asleep. One leg resting over the covers. God, he's sexy.

Last night was sexy. Every touch, every breath, every delicious thrust had me coming apart at the seams. I can't believe I didn't make him stop when he realized he was bare.

And God, if I'm lucky enough to have him again, I don't want it any other way.

The reminder of last night makes me glance down at myself. I'm wearing his T-shirt.

It smells like the trees.

I take in the space with a new appreciation for where I'm staying for the rest of the summer.

This is better than the den. And it's close to him.

This cowboy knows me better than I know myself.

Heartstrings start tugging, and pretty soon, there will be no use ignoring them. In shutting them out.

They'll keep coming back. Stronger. Louder.

Until I admit.

I've fallen for Levi Reeves.

21

Levi

Tessa's in a floral skirt today—one I picked out for her at the boutique because I thought she'd burst out laughing. But she just grabbed the hanger, held it against her waist to inspect, then gave me a curt nod.

I like her in those plaid shirts and short denim shorts. But hell, I like this look too. Especially when those full pink lips and whiskey-colored eyes are stretched in smiles and laughter.

She and Jackson set up a mid-afternoon refreshment stand outside the house, serving iced tea and muffins. Her wavy curls are tied back and hang over one shoulder. She's a vision as she mingles with the cowboys.

Her hand goes over her eyes, blocking the sun as she focuses on something in the distance.

Following her gaze, my eyes land on the riding arena.

One of our younger cowboys, Max, is giving another riding lesson to Lizzie Thoreau. It's her third lesson with Willow. My bet is they'll be making an offer for her soon.

I swallow the hard lump in my throat.

At sixteen, Lizzie's a natural rider. Her parents have been bringing her to the ranch for years. They've got a small farm nearby. Willow would be happy there.

I force the rigid thought out of my mind. Nothing on my ranch is "not for sale." And Willow's a pretty penny. Could get the outer gates replaced or something.

But fuck, this ache in my chest is stubborn.

Swallowing hard, I turn the tractor and head to the ranch gift shop.

Judging by the hint of redness glowing beneath her cheekbones, Tessa could use a nice cowboy hat.

On my way back, I hand off the tractor to Max and tell him I'll return Willow to the stables. After a pitstop, of course.

Tessa beams when I ride up to their little stand.

"Hey, boss." She pours what remains of the iced tea into a paper cup. "Just in time, we're about to close up shop and head inside."

Boss.

I don't like it.

Maybe it's because I want to be more than her boss. Maybe it's because I prefer "Indie" or "Cowboy" or hell anything but *boss*.

Or maybe it's a reminder that she's on my payroll. That this is a temp job. She's not choosing to be here. With me. With Jackson.

I hop off Willow, giving her a pat before pulling the gift bag from the saddle horn. "Got you something."

"For me?" She shrugs at Jackson before digging into the bag. A small gasp escapes as she pulls on the fine straw hat with red trim around the base. She puts it on. "Howdy."

I chuckle and hop back on my horse. "You fit right in."

She smirks and picks up the empty pitcher and muffin tin. "Come on, Wiggles." She dips her hat at Mason and Harry. "Same time tomorrow, boys."

I watch them head up the porch steps to the house, then cock my head. "You boys need somethin' to do?"

They exchange a look and squint back at me. "We were just wonderin'...that your girl?"

My gaze flicks back to the windows, where I vaguely see her moving about the house with my boy.

"No," I answer firmly before giving Willow's left rein a tug. "That's my woman."

Tessa and Jackson are at the bookstore yet again. With its grand opening just three weeks away, they've spent the last few days helping with preparations.

I've been tied up at the ranch, but word is Charlie's in a real tizzy. Fussing over every little thing to make sure that bookstore opens up just right.

Tess sure has got her hands full these days between my adventure-seeking kid and Shelf-zilla. That's Tessa's new name for her.

I'd like to think she's found some peace here on my ranch. In my house. But exhaustion is probably the real reason for her restful nights.

She's been in my bed almost every night. If not with the lights off, then with the covers on.

She never stays.

I've never been one to force a woman to spend the night. But it's damn hard to accept a no when I'm well aware of what holds her back.

She's anxious about the nightmares that could come back.

The bullet scar.

And whatever else she's keeping from me that's haunting her.

One thing's for sure. When the summer is up, I'm not letting her leave without knowing she's safe.

That is, if I'm able to let her go at all.

If I'm having a hard time walking her across the hall, there's almost zero chance I'm letting her walk out the front door.

A car rolls up the driveway, snapping me out of my thoughts.

I recognize Noah's bright-light SUV and toss the towel on the counter before moving to the door. As part of a new routine, I keep it locked at all times.

Noah, Chase, and Jackson step inside while my eyes sweep behind them. "Forget someone?"

They slip off their shoes like they're staying and head to the kitchen. "Smells *good*," Chase drawls.

Noah spins, snapping his finger like he forgot to mention something. "The girls asked Tessa to hang back with them. Said they had more work to do."

Chase shuts the fridge. "Yeah, right. If I know my wife—and the bottle of margarita mix she brought along—I'd say they're not gettin' much *work* done,"

Noah takes two beers from him and passes me one. "Your girl's a bad influence, Levi. If I get a call from the Sheriff's office, you're bailing them out *and* paying for any damages."

"First, *if* they're out wrecking the town, how is Pepper and Charlie dragging Tessa along *her* fault? Second"—I smack his arm, cocking my head toward my kid—"she's not my girl."

Noah winces and mouths an apology.

Chase pulls the lid off the pot. "You cook?"

"I always cook."

"Not like *this*." He scans the counter, smelling the pepper steak dish. "Is that fresh garlic?"

I set an extra plate for the table and shove my brother out of the way. "Wash your hands and take Jackson with you."

"Come on, buddy. Let's wash up." Chase clasps his hands and points to the kitchen sink.

"But I washed at the store," he whines.

"Wash again," the three of us call back.

"What are they doing anyway?" I mutter, setting a pitcher of water on the table. Between the three of us, we'll go through it.

Chase especially. He follows a strict diet as an athlete, including a full glass of water before each meal.

Noah shrugs. "Who knows? We'll check the cameras on my iPad after dinner. Make sure they're okay."

"What cameras?"

"We had cams set up this week behind the cashier and a few other spots throughout. Just to keep an eye on things."

Jackson takes his seat after washing up. I reach over to cut his meat.

"How much that cost us?" Chase asks. He's got every right to, given both he and I went in on this project Noah produced to fulfill his girl's passion for books and children.

"Doesn't matter," I tell him. "Any kind of security is alright with me. Are they well hidden? Who'd you use?"

"They are. I'll leave you the guy's card. He's in Denver. Top notch system. I did my research."

"I'm sure you did."

"Speaking of..." Noah glances at my kid. "Are you sure you don't want me to dig up more on your...new friend?"

"I already said no."

"That was when you thought she was leaving."

"Still is."

"Bullshit," Chase howls. Then covers his mouth when I shoot him a glare.

Jackson scarfs down the last bite. "Dad, I'm done."

I check his plate and look at the time. "Still got a half hour. Want to watch some TV?"

"No. It was a long day. I'm going to go to bed."

I set my fork down. "Good idea."

Chase waves me down. "I'll tuck him in. It's been a minute. Come on, kid. You still sleep with a nightlight? Because if it's lights out, I'm going to pass out before you."

"I'll give you my dolphin. I don't use it anymore."

News to me.

I catch my kid's wrist, turning him back to me. "Hey, I didn't know that. When'd you stop using your nightlight?"

He shrugs. "I'm good without it. The house is safe. Tessa reminds me every night. She also said if there was something scary in the house, I'm the first person she'd come to."

I smirk. "To rescue you?"

"No. To hide with me under my covers." He laughs.

Chase takes Jackson to bed while Noah and I clean up.

"The girls eat dinner?" I ask.

"Yeah, we ordered takeout before leaving." He turns up the iPad and moves to the living room.

"Okay, you guys," Tessa's voice comes on, and I freeze. "*Last one*, but then I really need to get ho—back to the house."

Pepper comes on next, a grin in her voice. "You were going to say *home*."

I shut off the water and move to sit next to Noah on the couch. Through the screen, I see them all seated on the floor behind the mini kitchen counter on the first level. Each with a margarita in hand.

Tessa shifts, sitting straighter against the back wall. "Sure, technically, I am living there. For a few more weeks."

"You just got here. You're leaving already?" Charlie pouts.

Tessa shrugs as if to say, *'What other choice do I have?'*.

I want to give her that choice. I want Jackson and I to be that one choice.

"Oh, we got you something." Charlie claps, twisting the mood. She does that well.

"That's right. Oh my god, I almost forgot." Pepper sits up, snatching a small gift bag from a nook under the counter.

From my distant, hazy view, I watch Tessa take it with something that looks like hesitation. It's a small box about the size of a phone case.

"Wait, this is...a phone? Like a real phone?"

Charlie nods happily. "We noticed yours sitting on the counter the other day was cracked. And that sucks. So we got you a new one and...bedazzled it."

Tessa twists it in her hand. "That's...wow. This...I'm not sure what this is," she breathes, making me swallow hard for her.

"It's a gift from your besties and you can't refuse it."

"Besties," she repeats like it's a foreign word.

Pepper waves a hand toward the box. "We didn't do any of the technical stuff, but I'd bet Jackson could get you all set up and running on it. That kid's going to be a tech genius."

She chuckles softly. "I bet he can. Thank you."

"Ooh, are we spying? Turn it up," Chase calls from behind us.

I push off my seat when I realize how right my little brother is. "Shut it off. It works. They're safe and still at the store."

Chase takes my seat next to Noah. I move about the living room, feeling uncomfortable. Voices are muffled as the conversation shifts.

Pepper's voice comes on. "Chase has got a huge—"

"Whoa, turn it down," Chase cuts in.

"Ego. I swear he thinks he's the king of the earth rather than just on the ice."

Chase chuckles. "She loves my ego."

Charlie's voice comes on next. "You guys are cute. Always thought so. But you're so right. Hard to believe that boy could love anyone more than himself."

"Chase? I think *Noah* is the real phenomena here," Pepper argues.

Noah shakes his head with an eye roll but watches the screen like he's waiting for his girl's rebuttal.

"The only thing Noah did that was not Noah-like is take in all my parents' belongings into his home, keeping them for me. Other than that, nothing surprised me. You guys forget we used to be best friends. He's got a tough exterior, but he's a softy when it comes to important things."

"When it comes to you," Noah mutters like we're not in the room.

"Guys. That's enough. Shut it off." My voice is firm, but they don't give two shits.

"What about you, Tessa?" Charlie asks.

Noah and Chase perk a brow in my direction. "Still want to shut it off?"

I don't reply. My hands are tight on my hips as I pace.

"Yeah, Tess," Pepper starts. "Don't tell me there's nothing going on with you and Levi. We've all seen it—and been seeing it since I came back to town."

That does it.

I move to sit on Noah's other side, watching the screen like a private investigator.

Tessa grins and it's too hazy to tell if she's blushing. "Okay. I won't."

The other girls erupt with cheer and giggles.

Tessa puts up a hand. "No, no. None of that. There's nothing going on. And whatever you're pickin' up is coming straight from me. Not him. He's focused on his kid, the farm and their future. He's not looking for a woman."

I wasn't looking for a woman. Till she showed up at my door.

Chase looks up from the screen, mocking me for my pet peeve. "She called Hideaway Ranch a *farm*. Let's lock her up now."

"Asshole," I mutter.

Pepper cocks her head. "So you got a thing for him?"

"I'm shuttin' this down." I reach over, but Chase snatches it from Noah first.

"Hold on, Cowboy. You might not be curious, but I am."

"They're having a *private* conversation. Or did you want to end up in the dog house again?"

Noah curses. "He's right. Chase, shut it off."

There's faint mumbling that neither of us catch until we all freeze at Tessa's words.

"He doesn't trust me and he's right not to."

Chase grins, scrunching his nose. "You're right. This is wrong. I'm shutting it down."

"Don't you dare," I grit. "Give it here."

Chase hands it over. There's not much to see since the screen is either frozen or the girls are quiet in response to what Tessa's admitted.

Charlie finally speaks, but it's low. "You can tell us anything."

I run a hand down my face. "I'm goin' to hell for this."

"Well, you know how I go a little rogue sometimes? The library fees, the traffic violations, the hardware store...even Jackson's old nanny."

"I didn't hear about the hardware store one." Pepper perks with interest.

Noah frowns, leaning in. "Yeah, me neither."

Tessa waves her tattooed arm like it's nothing. "Oh, I stole money from the cash register to pay the delivery boy the owner refused to settle up with. It was two years ago. He was a high school kid who ran Larry's deliveries for several weeks during the summer. I watched the man come up with excuses week after week to avoid paying him, until one day he fired the kid for being late and refused to pay altogether. The poor kid couldn't defend himself...so I did."

"How?" Charlie asks while Pepper lets it fly with a bunch of cuss words.

"Told the kid to wait up. Rang open the register, cleaned it out, and handed him all the cash. Then I turned to Larry and dared him to call the police."

"He wouldn't do it," Pepper says flatly.

"'Course not. He knew he was wrong." Tessa shrugs and laughs. "Tell ya this much, I sure as hell didn't get paid that week after he threw me out."

Chase looks at Noah, who sighs. "Yeah, I'll pay Larry a visit tomorrow."

"We both will," I seethe.

"Anyway," Tessa continues. "That's kind of my thing. I can't help it. I help people who the system, laws, rules or even grumpy store owners screw over. Including Jackson. He couldn't defend himself against that mean old lady. So I did it for him." She grins mischievously. "My way."

"You're my hero," Charlie breathes.

After a moment of silence, Pepper speaks up. "Tell us about the tattoo."

"Why?" Charlie asks, ignoring Pepper's subject change.

Tessa looks down, twining her fingers nervously and I worry that the girls are pushing it. "Because the system screwed me over. And I had no one to stick up for me."

Silence again.

"I'm sorry...what *system*?" Charlie boldly asks.

"Bureaucracy." She looks at Pepper. "Ironically, it's the reason behind my tattoo." She traces the snake around her arm. "I feel...confined...bound."

Charlie nods. "I don't suppose you'd elaborate?"

Tess looks up, blinking, and I know what she's thinking. She got carried away. "Nope."

Just when we think the conversation took a cold turn, the girls crowd Tessa, planting themselves on either side of her. They clink their glasses and gently lean in, resting their heads on her shoulders.

22

Tessa

I LEAN INTO LEVI'S chest as we watch the sunrise on Willow. His chest is firm, sturdy, secure. "I like this," I tell him softly. My thoughts slipping from my lips. I've been doing that a lot lately.

And so far, no one's made me regret my honesty.

Levi's arms wrap around me. He hums, brushing his nose against my neck. "Leaning against me?" He cocks his head to the sunrise. "Or that?"

"The whole package."

"Me too," he tells me. And it makes me feel like now is as good a time as any to say this. I take a breath. "Don't sell her. Willow. Keep her."

A heavy sigh releases from his chest. "Tess. Everything's got a price. That's how it works around here, how I keep it running, successful. I like her too. Jackson's already attached—it'll only get harder when—well, when she's no longer in her prime."

I'm quiet, and he chuckles behind me, his breath on my neck. "I think it's time we introduce you to some other horses."

"Not interested," I grumble, then relax back against his chest.

I've been waking at four a.m. again. The first night—after several nights without—was three days ago. When Frank texted me. It was followed by an immediate phone call. And for the first time in over three years...I pressed ignore and put it away.

The text didn't ask where I was. Just that I needed to come back.

I've only been here four weeks. My getaways are usually months. Never *weeks*.

He called again yesterday and today. But the message is clear. He needs to reach me.

Which can only mean one thing. I'm in trouble.

Sure, I've laid there, staring at the ceiling, thinking, *'Maybe this is good news'*.

But my gut tells me I'm not that lucky. It's never good news. They've been using me as a witness to come in at just the right moment, and I'm done being a sitting duck.

Frank promised me justice, but I'm no fool. My justice isn't coming. It should have been years ago when I identified Eric's killer and my shooter.

But it wasn't enough. His life and the threat to mine weren't enough.

"How are things with Jackson?" Levi asks, luring me back to the present.

"Oh, you mean the adventures of Curly and Wiggles?" My chest shakes with laughter against his. "We don't share our secrets."

"More lies?" he asks, a smirk in his tone behind me, his breath on the side of my face.

I reach my hand behind me, snaking my arm around his neck. "Not lies if they're none of your business, Indie."

He's quiet for a moment. "What if I want to make it my business?" His words are soft and almost a proposition.

I inhale the scent of grass. "Then maybe we'll share a detail or two."

He kisses my temple. "You ready to go on back?"

"No, but let's do it anyway. My boss might get a little grumpy if I'm late for work."

"Hiya, Tess. Did you bring by more muffins?" Maggie, the ranch manager in the front office rises from her chair with a chipper personality. She's a sweet older lady. A golden hue to her short blonde hair. A colorful silk scarf around her neck at all times. It's a different one each time and I make it a point to go into town at some point to pick one out for her.

Especially for the huge favor she's doing for me.

"Sure did," I announce as Jackson carries them in behind me.

"Oh my goodness, they smell warm." She pushes her glasses down to look at the kid. "Darlin', why don't you go put that in the kitchen for me."

We both watch him leave the room.

She motions me forward, whispering. "Levi is going to kill me for not clearing a sale with him."

I wince. "I know, Mag, I'm so sorry to put you in this position, but he'd shut it down. Practically already did the other day."

"Well, we won't give him the chance, now will we?"

I put my hands up. "I'll take full responsibility. He won't fire you."

She laughs and waves me off. "Oh, please. Levi doesn't fire anybody. That man's as loyal as they come."

My chest warms. Those heartstrings tugged again. As if I needed a reason to fall deeper.

She winces. "But Willow's pricey, you know? She's young and well trained." She scrolls down to the figure.

I don't even flinch.

"It's fine. You have a payment plan?"

"Of course. No one gets turned away for financial reasons. We'll work something out but..."

"It's another thing that Levi needs to approve?"

She purses her lips as her fingers move swiftly around the keyboard.

My heart thumps in my chest. There's no doubt in my mind that I want to buy Willow before anyone can take her from Jackson. But have I really thought this through? Six thousand dollars is a lot of money for someone who's got no place to board a horse if the original owner refuses to keep her after the sale.

I'm paranoid.

That's not Levi. I'm just on edge, doubting everything around me with each day that my fate remains a question.

"Oops," Maggie chirps. "Forgot that one step of clearing with the boss. Call it my old brain. You're... officially..." Her fingers race along the keyboard. "Screened and approved." She looks up at me. "What do you have for a deposit?"

I consider the amount that Levi's payroll has been depositing into my account. "I can put twenty percent down."

"That'll do." She types it in. "Transport date?"

"Oh...um..." Surely she understands I have no place to keep a horse. Much less *myself* in two weeks.

She pushes up her glasses. "I've got to put something in the system otherwise the sale is incomplete."

"Two weeks from tomorrow."

"You got it."

Jackson comes back out with a mouthful of blueberry muffin. "Aunt Maggie, I tried them for ya. Little light on the blueberries, but that's my fault. I popped a few when Tess wasn't looking."

She narrows her eyes. "That tracks."

"Thanks again, Mag. When would...*he* be notified?"

She glances at Jackson. "No later than one week prior to pick up. That one is a requirement. So he can prepare them." She looks at her calendar. "So...next Friday."

I swallow. "But she's officially..."

She grins, easing my anxiety. "Officially off the market."

I release a breath. "Thank you."

The early evening sun slants through the window of Jackson's room as he and I freshen the space up before the school year.

"How many of these hats do you wear?" I point to the stack of worn, faded cowboy hats.

"Just the two on top. Dad picks me up a new one every summer. But I'd rather wear a baseball hat like my friends."

I pause, turning to him. "Do you play?"

He shakes his head. "I wanted to, but I've never played, and my friends have been playing since they were like six. If I start now, they'll laugh at me."

My eyes move to where I saw a bat and glove near the dresser. "What's that then?"

"Those were Uncle Elliot's. I got a lot of his stuff after..."

My shoulders sag. I watch the boy who's always had a quiet strength about him. Wondering how much of it he keeps bottled inside. How much he's afraid to ask for what he wants.

I pick up the baseball and move to him on the bed, tossing the ball in the air. "Well, slugger." I catch it with the other hand. "I happen to be pretty good. Maybe we can practice and get you ready for tryouts?"

He scrunches his nose. "But you're a girl."

I nod. "Some think so, yes."

"Can you throw?"

"'Bout to throw you across the room." I launch for him, and he giggles and wiggles away from me.

"Okay, okay. I'll let you show me what you got." Then he watches me like he wants to say something but hesitates.

"What's on your mind?" I whisper, leaning in.

"You're cool. And real."

"Real? Do elaborate. Real pretty, real funny…"

"Just real. Like when Uncle Chase says, *keep it real*."

"Ah." I watch his hesitation and decide to go a little rogue as the nanny who should never, ever ask this question. "What was your mom like?"

His unchanging expression tells me he was already thinking about her.

Jackson stands and moves to a dusty shoebox under his nightstand. He sits on the floor, cross-legged and pulls it open. He digs through birthday cards and loose paper, then pulls out a photograph. He hands it to me without looking.

A slim woman with red hair cascading down her shoulders and deep brown eyes smiles into the camera.

"She's beautiful."

Jackson shrugs. "You're prettier."

His comment makes me look at the photo again, studying her features. There's a resemblance there. Not much on the eyes since mine have more of a golden hue, but the wild red hair, petite figure. Even the way she smirks.

I tuck this new information away. "I know she pops in every now and then," I say softly.

"I don't like it. She makes me uncomfortable."

I wince, remembering what Levi told me about the lies she'd make him tell. "I know."

"Grandpa says not to take it personally. He says everything she does is to mess with Dad, not me."

A knot forms in my chest. I'm not the maternal type, but something about his sadness makes me want to crouch down and tuck him under my arm. So I slide off the bed and do just that. "I think he's right."

A figure at the door catches my eye. A sweat-stained cowboy leans against the frame, arms crossed. Levi's hard eyes dip to the photo in my hand. His jaw works tightly.

I open my mouth to say God knows what, but he doesn't let me.

"When you two are about done, dinner's almost ready." He strides off and down the stairs.

23

Levi

The bar is crowded tonight, so I slide into an empty booth at the Inn. Dad's training Ethan behind the bar, but he's not as swift as Tessa was back there.

Always quick on her feet.

Dad passes me a bottle that matches his and sits across me. "What happened?"

"Just stopped by for a drink. And maybe an apple pie to go."

"Apple pie, huh? Tessa loves my apple pie. What'd you do?"

I take a swig and sigh. "I was a dick at dinner."

"Oh you mean one of the few times that woman eats during the day? Smooth move."

I glare at him, wary about the fact that Tess barely touched her food. "You're not helping."

"If you told me what set you off, maybe I will."

"Earlier tonight, Jackson showed her a photo of Lilly."

He grunts, rubbing the stubble on his jaw. Then folds his hands on the table and waits for me.

"I was headin' to his room and stopped short when I heard him say *you're prettier.*"

He nods once. "So he sees the resemblance."

"She did too."

He checks the bar and turns back to me. "You see it too. You saw it that first day you met her back at the station. It's why you kept running her out of town. Why you didn't like her spending time with Jackson when she worked here. Why you didn't trust her."

"She's nothing like Lilly," I rasp.

I see that now.

"Then what's the problem? Tell her you know she's nothing like her."

I swallow hard. "I can't."

"Why not?"

"Because facts are facts, Dad. You know Tess as well as I do—"

"Doubtful."

"She's flighty. She's got secrets. A past no one in this town knows. She's not here to stay. It didn't even occur to me that Jackson compares her to his mother."

Dad releases a heavy breath. "Yeah. I've been worried about that too." He twists the bottle in his hands. "Forget Jackson for a moment. What do *you* want? We all know something's going on with you and Tess. Have you asked her to stay?"

I shake my head.

"Maybe I should ask if *you* want her to stay."

"I know I'm not ready for her to go. That her six weeks are up in less than two, and I'm a wreck about it."

"Then stop wasting it here with me when you know damn well what you want." He stands with a grin. "I'll get that apple pie ready for ya. Go home to your woman."

Tessa covers her face with a pillow and cries out, jerking against my mouth, then goes limp on the bed. I climb up her soft skin, settling myself behind her naked body and pull her close to me under the sheets.

"You're getting pretty good at number five, Cowboy."

I chuckle softly. "I'm sorry about earlier, Tessa."

She frowns. Twisting to face me. "Uh-oh. You used my name."

"I like your name."

"You only use it when you're serious." She pouts.

"Well, I'm seriously sorry." I smile, running my fingers down her arm.

Her face falls as she strokes the hairs on my chest. "I overstepped asking about her today."

"You didn't. Okay, maybe for a part-time nanny, you might have overstepped."

Her eyes flash with hurt.

I hold up a finger. "But you and I both know you're not just his nanny. You're his friend. You're...*my* friend."

She giggles. "I'm your *special* friend." Then bites her bottom lip. "She is pretty."

"You heard my son. You're prettier."

"He was just being nice."

I stroke her hair. "You're nothing like her, Tess. You're beautiful inside and out."

"Is she why you didn't like me all these years?"

I suck in a deep breath. "The similarities were...very distracting."

Her eyes water. "Jackson's mother reminds me of my father. He left when I was a baby and would come back every so often for God knows what. Sex, money, a change of heart. Who knows. I know what you mean when you say Jackson doesn't care about her anymore. After a while, you just give up. They become a stranger you just hope will leave as soon as they come."

I lean in to kiss her forehead, grateful for the insight into her life.

"She left, too. When I was seventeen."

I frown as my mind races. "You lived alone? How?"

She smiles like it's a happy memory. "Until the house foreclosed. Then, I'd stay with friends, snuck into the Y...I survived."

"Where was this?"

"Chicago."

"A city girl."

She looks around. "City girl obsessed with small towns."

I chuckle. "Why's that?"

"Where else am I going to cause trouble and make sexy cowboys yell at me?"

I grin, sliding my hand down to her hips. "Now, how about the real reason?"

"I suppose it's the slow pace of life. The connections and community. It's more about big hearts around here than big pockets. The mountains aren't all that bad to look at either."

I chance another question. "Is that what Summer Hill is like?"

Her grin fades, and her eyes drop back to my chest. "It's nothing like here."

"Then what's keeping you from staying?"

Fear flashes in her eyes when they meet mine. And I want to make it go away. I'd take anything back to make it go away.

That's not who I am.

I confront.

I face problems head on instead of avoiding them.

But Tessa is a whole new ballgame.

One I'd play outside the rules to win.

So I backtrack.

"I meant all those times you came to Hideaway Springs. What kept you from staying? Besides the minor detail that a sexy cowboy tried to run you out of town."

She scoffs. "I don't know. Unfinished business, I guess. I've got Bessie and..." She trails off and looks up with a grin. "I can tell you one thing for certain. This is my favorite time spent in this town. I'm going to miss it."

For a short second, I'm angry with her for thinking I'm going to let her go, for planning to leave. Until I remember I never asked her to stay.

And I need to be certain she won't keep leaving us before I do.

"You still have two weeks."

She nods and sits up in bed, reaching for my T-shirt. It's what she does when she's about to slide out of bed and tiptoe across the hall to her room.

I catch her wrist. "You had a nightmare last night."

Glassy eyes flick to mine. And I can't hold back anymore. "Sleep with me tonight, Whiskey. I'm not sure I can handle another night hearing you scare yourself awake and not being by your side."

Her full lips part. The hesitation comes before the response, and I stop it.

"Please, Tess. I'm not asking what they are. I just want you close."

Pressing her lips together, she nods. "Okay." She tugs on the shirt anyway and I help her slip into it.

When she falls asleep, I close the drapes in my bedroom. I'll let her hide her scars before the morning sun. But sooner or later, she's going to tell me who did this to her.

And when she does, I'm going to bury that son of a bitch so deep, she'll forget he ever existed.

24

Levi

On Friday, I set the alarm later than usual. Tessa's been sleeping in my bed all week. And I wasn't about to ruin it with a six o'clock wake-up call.

In the dead of night, I'd feel her jerk awake, often with a soft gasp. I've been keeping still, playing asleep. Not wanting to be another thing she's gotta worry about owing an explanation to.

She doesn't want to be my burden. And I'd die before I became hers.

Her appetite was good this morning. I left her and Jackson a bit ago. They were having eggs, bacon, fruit and cheese.

This woman is spoiling my kid. He'd better not be expecting more than oatmeal or cereal come school days. It's all I'll have time for.

Before checking off morning chores, I stop at the office to catch up with my ranch manager.

"Mornin', Maggie." I walk in and pick up the mail from the wicker basket. "Anything good?"

She tenses slightly—odd for her. "Just the usual, boss."

I eye her. Something's off. "That a new scarf?"

"Oh yes." She smiles, running her fingers through the silk. "Tessa bought it for me."

The rumors about Tess and I have been spreading all over the ranch like a wildfire in a dry summer. And I'm not about to pour gasoline into the flames by commenting on that.

I clear my throat, shifting back to business. "Any more drama from the Barley family?"

"Now they're asking to move the reception to the far side for a better mountain view for their photos."

"Sure, why not?"

She lowers her glasses. "You're serious?"

I shrug. "You only get married once—hopefully—if they want the mountains, give 'em the mountains."

"We've already given them two horses for shots, no extra charge. Moved the date twice and agreed to provide entertainment for the children. I really thought you'd blow a fuse with this family by now."

I smile. "Lighten up, Maggie. The day will come and go and little Jessie Barley will have the best day of her life."

She grunts. "Well since you're in a good mood, here are the livestock sales from last week that need to be prepped."

"Ah, thanks." I take the stack of cards from her. "All cash?"

She pushes her glasses up the bridge of her nose. "One's on a payment plan."

"Sounds good. I'll run these by Harry and get them prepped for pick up. Thanks, Mag."

"Don't mention it."

I turn to the open door, flipping through the small stack. I approved four for pick up this week. I stop in dead my tracks when I count one too many in my pile.

And the name of the buyer on the extra card.

"Hey, Indie."

Tessa strolls into the stables late that afternoon. Her auburn hair is down and wild over her shoulders. Her plaid red and white shirt is tied at the waist.

But it's those goddamn short shorts that are going to make this so fucking hard.

Her rested eyes sparkle as she approaches. "You been hidin' out here all day. You alright?" She glances at Willow like she didn't just take her from us.

I set down the curry comb and stare her down. "Something you forget to tell me, Whiskey?"

Her gaze wanders, then flicks to the horse, eyes flashing with understanding. "What are you doing?"

"What's it look like I'm doing? I'm getting your new horse ready."

She steps closer cautiously. "Levi."

"What the hell are you going to do with a horse? Where are you going to keep her?"

"I—"

"You know I've still got the right to deny the sale. Return your deposit."

"You can't do that," she stammers.

"It wasn't an authorized sale," I yell. I've been hiding out between here and the Wrangler Room all day, trying to cool off, but it's been no use.

She rolls her shoulders back like I don't scare her. "Would it have been for the little girl I saw riding her three weeks in a row?"

My brows twitch.

"I told you not to sell her, Indie."

"You don't get to tell me what to do. How to run my ranch. If you fell in love with every animal on the land, I'd be out of business," I roar.

"Just the one. And I only love her because you do, Jackass."

I stare at her. "So what is this? Taking a piece of us with you?"

Her eyes are fiery. "Is Willow a piece of you?"

This hits a nerve, and I lose it. "You can't answer a question with a question, Tessa."

"I wasn't taking anything. I was going to leave her *here*. She's mine so you can't sell her. And stop calling me Tessa!"

"That's your *name*."

"You only call me that when you're mad," she shrieks, and it's adorable as hell.

"Oh, you don't like it when I'm mad? Then don't do this shit behind my back. First you make my son lie to me, now my staff?" I shout because I don't know how to deal with what she did for us. I shout because it's the only thing keeping me from going to her. I shout because I'm one week away from losing her.

Her eyes mist rapidly. Tessa steps back, blinking them away when her spine hits a stall door. She scares Anton—my rowdiest horse—and he snorts loudly behind her.

Tessa screams, the sound sharp and piercing. Eyes bulging, hands shaking, she leaps forward. I catch her and wrap her in my arms, pressing her head under my chin.

I glower at the uneasy horse as if he could read my warning.

I should settle him before he upsets the others, but I can't let go of her. She trembles in my arms, gasps against my shirt, catching her breath. And I don't know if it's from the scare or my words.

Either way, it's my fault.

Anton paws in the stall, settling himself.

I hold Tessa, stroking the back of her head. When her breathing comes back to normal. I move my hands to the sides of her tear-stained face.

"It's okay. He's calm now." Her eyes are glassy, distant. Like she's not with me. "Tessa?"

"It was so loud," she whimpers. "And…behind me…" She shakes her head vigorously. "I don't. Like it."

Fuck.

I pull her against me. There's no doubt in my mind that this is PTSD and I'm fucking responsible for the setback. For the tears I put in her eyes.

I lift her face and kiss my woman. Deep and soft.

Anger quickly replaced with gratitude for what she tried to do. "What am I going to do with you?" I ask softly.

She swipes her red eyes against my shirt and glares up. That stubborn fire calming me. "Yell at me some more? Call me a liar? Throw me out?"

I pull her tight against my chest. "Keep you. I'm keeping you."

"Levi." My name almost comes out as a warning. But I'm not ready to hear it.

She bought my horse. Mine and Jackson's.

"Tess, we don't have to talk right now—but you have to know I'm not letting you go. Not without a fight."

She smirks up at me. "Like the one we just had?"

"If that's what it takes."

She swallows, then drops her eyes to my mouth and smiles weakly. "Looking forward to it, Cowboy."

25

Tessa

"Can you help me with this?" I ask Levi as he adjusts a bolo tie with a blue stone over a black button-down shirt. I smile over my shoulder, liking the way it brings out his eyes. He's in dark blue jeans and opted for no cowboy hat tonight.

He scans me in my barely-on black mini dress like he's ready to devour me.

"The door is open," I remind him as he steps behind me, kissing my neck and zipping me up.

He smirks. "That's why I'm zipping it up, not down." He tugs my hair from over my shoulder and drops the waves loosely over my back. Hooking an arm around my waist, he spins me. "I want to take you dancing."

"We're a little busy with Charlie's opening tonight."

"Next weekend then?"

My smile fades and I know he notices. I don't know how much longer I can dodge Frank's calls.

His warnings.

Or how much longer I can keep lying to Levi. Hell, his whole family. Because these past few weeks, they've made me a part of it.

"Hi." Jackson hops into the bedroom.

I jump away from Levi, but he barely moves, only pulls his gaze off me to look at his kid.

"What's a soft opening?" he asks.

I release a breath. Partly for the innocent question, partly for the save. Levi turns to his kid. "It's like a grand opening but not exactly to the public. It's by invitation only."

"So it's special?"

"Yes," we both say.

"What will we do there?"

I know what's on my agenda.

Act normal.

Breathe.

Smile.

And pray it's not the last time I see all these people.

"Charlie and her new staff are going to show us around."

"Will there be food?"

Feeling like I might come out of my skin and needing to get away from the cowboy still expecting an answer, I swivel, hands on my hips. "Do you need help getting dressed, mister?"

Jackson juts his chin. "I just need to know how fancy this thing is, so I know how to dress."

Levi shakes his head, turning back to his tie.

I turn the kids shoulders. "Let's go see what we can find."

"Will I be the only kid there?" he continues as I drag him down the hall to his room.

Thank God for this kid and the crowd expected this evening. I'm not sure how much longer I can hold Levi back from asking questions before I talk to Frank.

Which means...I need to do it tonight.

An hour later, we step into Charlie's Web twenty minutes late. I spot Charlie right away. She looks like a fairy in her puffy lavender dress that lands just above her knees, with matching purple boots and cowgirl hat.

"Knew I should have worn my hat," Levi bitches in a low mumble.

I elbow him. "Tonight's not about *you*."

"You made it. Late," Noah snips, crossing to us from the welcome desk.

"Would've been here sooner if I found parking. You'd think an investor of the establishment would have a reserved spot," Levi grumbles again.

Oh dear. He's in a mood.

But I know my cowboy. He's dealing with it on his own, instead of putting the pressure on me for leaving his question unanswered.

And my heart swells for it.

"Tessa, good to see you." Noah's eyes dip to Levi's arm around my waist. He coughs. "Right this way."

My little blonde fairy looks our way too. Eyes twinkling with delight when Levi pulls me protectively against him as we work through the crowd.

"Yay, you're here." She claps her hands, then moves onto business. "Okay, you have to pick a character hat from the round table." She points to a box on a decked-out round table. "Then we're going to take pictures, have cocktails, and mingle. There will be children's reading and coloring upstairs. And we have all sorts of fun giveaways."

Levi cocks his head. "This is where she gives us a job to do."

Charlie plants her hands on her hips. "Your only job is to have a good time."

My phone buzzes in my purse and I flinch. Chills running down my spine.

Levi's arm loosens as he turns to me. "You alright?"

"Perfect," I answer a little too quickly.

His jaw is tight as he looks away and nods. "I'm going to grab us some drinks." He kisses my temple and I thank him.

For more than he knows.

Frank: *Last chance, T.*

The gall of this guy. I scan my surroundings and quickly type out a reply.

Tessa: *The fuck does that mean?*

Frank: *Good. You're not dead. Call me. Now.*

I move to stand behind Jackson, who's been trying on several hats from the round table. "Hey Wiggles, see if you can find me a cool Cat Woman mask, okay?" I grab a mint from the table. "I'll be right back."

I slip an earphone in one ear and sneak away to the low nook under the staircase.

Sucking in a deep breath, I go to my last missed call and dial.

It rings once.

"You trying to get me fired?" Frank's voice is both soothing and menacing.

Menacing for obvious reasons.

Soothing because he could have passed me along to any other member of his team that wouldn't have been so understanding to my being M.I.A. for several days after initial contact.

"What's the emergency? And what do you mean by *last chance*?"

"You need to come back to Summer Hill." He takes a breath. "Tonight."

"Wh—tonight? No. Absolutely not. I—"

"Tessa. That's what I meant by last chance. If you didn't call me back, you would have been unpleasantly surprised when our squad raids the party you're at."

My blood runs cold. "How do you know where I am?"

Silence.

"Frank," I whisper hiss. "Frank, you can't *force* me into witness protection. I refuse. End of—"

His tone is robotic. "A protective custody order has been issued. You are to be detained and remain in custody until—"

"Custody?"

"Teresa. Listen to me—"

"Don't call me that." I shiver at my given name. The best part about getting a new identity was the fact that I don't have to be called the name my mother and father called me.

"Just. Listen. This only happens when there is an immediate threat to your life."

"Did you have me followed? We agreed, it's better that no one knows—"

"Come on, Tess, we *always* know where you are. But this isn't about us. *They* found you, Tessa."

"That's impossible. How?"

"Check your phone."

My breathing is erratic and my vision starts to blur. This has to be another dream. Another horrid dream.

I wait for the message and open it with a gasp.

It's an image of *me*. At first, I can't tell where I am because they're all zoomed in, until I scroll through each one.

They're all *right here* in this bookstore.

"Tessa, are there surveillance cameras where you are?"

I step out from under the stairs and peek at every corner of the ceiling. My stomach drops.

"Tessa?"

"At least two," I whisper, my throat clogging.

"*That's* how they found you."

"How did this happen? And how do you know about it?"

"The Brunetti family knows you're not far, Tess. They know you're testifying. It doesn't take a rocket scientist to hire a geek to hack into every surveillance camera within a forty-mile radius," he shouts.

"How do you know it's not someone else?"

"I can't get into specifics with you—especially over the phone, but our cybercrime division detected illegal intrusion and repeated focus on your face through these cameras. Digital footprint is linked to other organized crime investigations. This is definitely our guy, Tess."

My heart pounds. Levi is holding two drinks, looking for me. Jackson is in a Phantom mask as he hops over to his dad, holding a black cat mask.

Levi shrugs in response to a question from his son and they both look around for me.

They're in danger. My new friends. Levi, Jackson. If they track me here...

Frank is right.

I need to get out now.

I duck under the stairs. "What do you need me to do?"

He sighs with relief. "I'm going to make this easy for you. We don't want a scene as much as you don't. My team will meet you outside of town and take you to a safe house. I'll be there and can share more info then."

"I need an hour."

"Not a minute more. I'll text you an address. You'll need to abandon your car there."

I want the floor to swallow me whole. But now's not the time to cower. I step out and make my way through the crowd.

Slapping a wide grin on my face, I whisk the mask out of Jackson's hand from behind him.

He spins. "There you are!"

I slip it on. "How do I look?"

"Mysterious," Levi says flatly. "Fitting."

I meet his blue eyes, still so soft when they look back at me. He hands me a drink and winks.

The patience of this man.

I take the small plastic cup and taste the sparkly beverage.

Now's not the time to ask for something stronger, Tess.

"I'll be upstairs. See you later," Jackson calls as he races off.

I nearly drop my cup with the urge to chase after him and wrap my arms around his little body. I want to tell him I love him and that I'd never ever leave him.

Not by choice.

Levi watches me and I wait for him to ask where I went or why I'm on edge. He takes a step closer, hooking his arm around my waist. "You look like...you could use a mini hotdog."

I laugh. It levitates me, how easy he can be with me when he senses my tension.

"Come on. Let's make some rounds and act like we want to be here."

"I *do* want to be here, but—"

"Tessa, you look like you want to crawl into a hole. Not socialize and laugh at people's bad jokes. I don't mean mine—I'm hilarious. I mean like Noah's or my dad's."

Another laugh and I lean into him, needing desperately to feel him.

After a moment, I slip off my mask. The minutes are ticking by. "I'm not feeling well. I think I'm going to get back to the house. Um...lie down."

Turns out there is something more painful than a bullet.
Lying to the man I love.
It physically pains me.

He takes my drink. "I'll take you."

"No. No. I'll be alright. This place is part of your investment. Charlie is like family. Probably will be soon." I step back. "You should be here. I'll be alright. I'll call an Uber." I bite my bottom lip.

Levi glares at me. "Tess, what's going on?"

"I'll take her." Aiden steps beside us, his strong presence cutting in. "To be fair, I was just on my way out myself. I'll drop her by the house."

Levi hesitating. Then nods. "Alright. I'll be home soon." He leans in to kiss my cheek and slips away.

I swallow hard, feeling like I'm about to fall apart.

Aiden catches my hand. "You good?"

I nod and let him lead me out of the store.

We're quiet in his car for most of the drive, until Aiden finally asks. "Who's Frank?"

My head snaps to him.

"I was sitting on the stairs just above you during your call."

"How much did you hear?"

"Not much. I heard his name and that you're going to be meeting him somewhere."

"It's not what you think."

"Doesn't matter what I think. What do you plan on telling my son? My grandson? Or are you going to leave a note like the one you left me just before the summer?"

Silence falls between us after I don't give him an answer.

Until I tell him the only thing I've been wanting to scream out all day. "Aiden, I'm in love with your son." My voice cracks. "And your grandson. I just..."

He swipes a tissue out of a box in the center console and hands it to me. "You in some kind of trouble?"

I nod. "But I'm taking care of it. I'll be back."

"Oh I think we all know that by now. Here's the thing, Tess—"

"This is different. I want to come back for good. If...they'll have me."

"That's going to be a pretty hard sell if you walk out now."

"Aiden..." I stop myself. If I say anymore, he'll warn Levi and they'll *both* be in trouble.

He sighs like he's caught between a rock and a hard place. Letting me go should not be a tough decision. Yet he acts like it is.

"Please don't say anything to him. Don't stop me. This...my situation is bigger than any of us and I will not bring them into it, Aiden. Please don't make me."

He stares ahead, swallowing hard. Then finally nods. "Okay."

Twenty minutes later, my phone dings with a cross street I don't recognize. Frank tells me this is where they agreed to pick me up. And if I'm not there by ten o'clock sharp, they're coming to the house.

I dig out my bag and start tossing my things into it. I'll only be able to fit the items I came with. Nothing more.

Except one thing. I cross to the nightstand and grab Willy. My night light dolphin. I'll need him.

"Going somewhere?"

My heart falls to the pit of my stomach. Levi stands at the threshold of my doorless bedroom, hands in pockets, eyes sharp, jaw tight.

"I'll be back."

He perks a brow and steps in. It's slow, uncommitted.

"I just need a few days."

"Few days? Why so sudden? Get called for jury duty?"

"Not exactly," I mutter, stuffing the dolphin into the little space I have left.

His voice is soft and almost desperate. "Stay, Tess. Tell me what's going on with you. You've got to let me in, baby." More slow steps, but I avoid looking at him.

I shake my head. "It's nothing. You're being dramatic. It's a quick visit back to my town. I'll be back."

My nerves are on overload right now and I'm afraid I'm running out of time. I'd say anything to get him to let me go.

He watches me as I zip up the bag. The little black dress I wore tonight flat on the bed. I'm in the same clothes I arrived in.

I put a hand to his chest. The words I desperately want to say are in my heart but my head knows it's not fair to him.

"I've got to go." I suck in a breath, walk around him and down the steps. Slipping my shoes back on, I sniffle and reach for the knob.

"If you walk out that door, don't come back." His cold tone echoes through the long hall.

My heart literally stops. I turn to face him. His expression icy.

"Jackson doesn't need that. I don't need it."

Dropping my things, I run to him, tears already streaming down my face as I wrap my arms around him. "Don't say that. *Please* don't say that." I sob into his neck. "I love that little boy, I'd never walk out on him."

There's a beat before he loosens his arms around my waist and gently pulls me off him. He nods his head to my bag by the door. "I find that really hard to believe right now."

I sniffle, determination coursing through my veins as I have the gall to look into his eyes. "Take it back, Indie."

"Give me a reason."

"*I'm* your reason. Take it *back*."

He cups my jaw gently, but nothing about his features are soft. "Okay. I take it back. But on one condition." He steps closer, his expression hard. "Tell me where you're going. Why now? And don't lie to me or the deal's off."

I don't even blink. I use my scapegoat.

"It's Bessie. I think she's in trouble."

He narrows his eyes. "Bessie's in trouble? Not you?"

I shake my head. "No." It's a breathy lie, but necessary.

He watches me for a moment. "Can I help?"

No one can help me.

"I've got this." I kiss his lips one more time and race to the front door.

"Tessa."

I turn. His hands are back in his pockets. Pulling his gaze off my bag, he meets my eyes. "If you're lying…"

"I know." My stomach clenches, and nausea strikes. "Deal's off."

26

Levi

FISTS CLENCHED, I PUSH off the counter and pace the length of the front hall. My vision is blurred. I can't think.

I thought when this day would come, I'd see Lilly walking out. I'd feel the same rage and disappointment.

But the woman didn't even cross my mind.

All I see is Tessa.

The hurt in her eyes when I threatened to end us. The goosebumps breaking out over her arms when she ran to me.

I can read a fucking room. She didn't want to leave.

She had to.

I lift my phone from my back pocket and dial.

Noah answers on the second ring. "Your kid's fine, jackass. Even won a few prizes. Think it was rigged. This has Tessa written all over it."

"Have you been drinking?"

"A few. Seven. Not my fault. Every time Charlie makes a speech, she hands me her drink." He burps. "I think I'm gonna be sick."

That makes two of us.

"Pull yourself together and come over. I need you."

"What's going on?"

"Tessa left. Bring your laptop."

He curses. "Give me an hour. We're just about done here."

"You okay to drive?"

"Dad will drive me."

I'm about to hang up when I realize what he said. "Dad? He left with Tessa a while ago."

"Came back. Lookin' for you."

Exactly one hour later, Dad, Noah and Jackson walk through the front door.

Jackson shows me all his prizes and party accessories Charlie let him keep. I try to keep a smile on my face, but it's damn hard knowing I'm going to break his little heart in the morning.

I sure as hell don't have the strength for it tonight.

Or the words. I'm not making him the promises Tessa made me. That she'll be back. That it's only a few days. That she's just helping a friend.

I don't know if I believe any of it.

But if she's lying, I will find out.

As usual, Dad saves the day and helps settle Jackson into bed.

I walk over to Noah, who's seated at the kitchen island. Fingers racing across the keyboard, pausing, then clicking away again.

"Find anything?"

My brother looks up, glaring at me through his glasses. "Yeah. Digging up info on someone who didn't exist three years ago usually takes about seven minutes."

I stare back. "Is that a no?"

He shakes his head. "Get me a glass of water. Need to sober up."

Thirty minutes later, dad comes down the stairs and straight into the living room.

"Kid's energy reminds me of you when you were that age. Wouldn't bet on him sleepin' in tomorrow though," he says, like I don't know my own kid.

I join him on the couch. Dropping my head into my hands, rubbing my temples. "Thanks."

"Anything I can do?"

"You could tell me the real reason you left with Tess earlier."

He glances back at Noah, who's laser-focused on his task. "I heard her on the phone."

"Tonight? When she disappeared?"

He nods. "Had front-row seats to one side of a conversation."

"What did you hear? Who did she call?"

He shrugs. "A guy named Frank."

"Frank," I mutter. "Helpful, thanks." I shove off my seat. "Swear it's like pullin' teeth with the two of you."

Noah sighs, shutting his laptop. "I'm not getting anywhere tonight. And frankly, I'm not sure how far I'll get with what I have."

I run a hand down my face. "Thanks for tryin'. Will you apologize to Charlie for me for duckin' out early?"

"Charlie doesn't accept indirect apologies."

"Of course she doesn't," I grunt and walk him out.

Dad's behind him and I don't press him to stay. I got a gut feeling he knows more than he's letting on. But it's late. Everyone's tired.

He pauses at the door. "Come by the Inn tomorrow with Jackson. I'll make us breakfast."

"I don't know, Dad. I might make something here and then take Jackson for a ride. Spend some time with him. Alone."

"I get it. Keep me posted."

I head upstairs. My legs lead me into Tessa's room. The guest room with no door. She hasn't slept here in over a week.

She used the bed to spread the new clothes I bought her. Since she refuses to use the damn wardrobe.

I open the nightstand drawer. It slides out easily. But it's not empty. There's a piece of paper stuck in the seams of the drawer.

It's her pros and cons list.

I skim down to the bottom of Tessa's Pro list.

#5. If Frank is right...six weeks is all I need.

Something else is going on here. And I feel like a damn fool.

I don't get a lick of sleep. Random facts race through my head. Shit that shouldn't be filling my mind as a single dad.

I should be planning what to do with Jackson this last week before school. Prepping the ranch for the fall season.

Reminding myself of the reason I never liked that woman.

How much she reminds me of my ex.

With that last thought planted in my head. I take a stab at sleep. But all I do is list out those random words in different order until they can form together.

Chicago.
Summer Hill.
Door.
Bullet hole.
The system???
Three years old.
Bessie.
Frank.
Hideaway Springs.

"So, she's ours now?" Jackson asks as we head back to the stables. It's our third morning in a row riding Willow to watch the sunrise. Then we'd walk home and try to recreate Tessa's breakfast spread to the T.

"Technically, she's Tessa's."

"But she's going to live with us?"

"Tess doesn't have any place to keep a horse, so she's boarding Willow here at the ranch."

He frowns, his head dropping in thought.

"You meant Tessa," I say, not having the heart to ignore his feelings.

He nods.

I hop off the horse and lift him down. "You know the plan for a nanny was only through the summer, right?"

He squints up at me. "Was the plan for a girlfriend only through the summer too?"

"Christ. How old are you?"

"I'll be ten in November."

My chest squeezes and I take his hand as we walk back to the house.

"When is she coming back?"

He hasn't asked me this since that first morning without her. And I wish I had a better answer.

"When she's done helpin' her friend out."

Another beat. "I need help. I start school on Monday. You need help, too."

"Buddy—" I nearly snap with irritation and catch myself with a deep breath. "I'm getting a little hungry. What do you say we go whip up some pancakes?"

Noah: *What are these words you sent me the other day?*

Levi: *Everything I know.*

Noah: *It doesn't make sense.*

Levi: *Make it make sense. It's all I've got.*

Noah: *Come by the office. We'll need two heads for this. Yours will have to do.*

At two in the afternoon, I leave Jackson with Dad at the Inn and head to Noah's law office.

Again, the man was too quiet for my liking. Tessa told him something and judging by the way he hasn't looked me in the eye, he's been sworn to secrecy.

Fine.

I don't need them to tell me what's going on.

I'll find out on my own.

What I do with it is another story.

Noah's wide-eyed without the espresso dad sent me here with, but he gladly takes it.

"Thanks."

I sit on a black leather chair across from him at his spotless glass desk. Noah leans back with a question in his eyes. "Bullet hole?"

My eyes dip to the list he's got in front of him. "I don't think she knows I've seen it."

He sighs, sitting up. "You sure this is what you want? Look for a woman who doesn't want to be found?"

"She said she's coming back."

"Of course she's coming back. When she needs another job or when she gets bored or whatever other reason, she keeps showin' up."

"City girl who loves small towns," I mutter, remembering Tessa's words to me one night when she told me where she's from.

"What?"

"Somethin' she said to me."

Noah shakes his head. "Loves small towns. Hates doors. And I thought I had the weird one."

He taps his pen on the glass table. "Do you remember her first time here?"

I scoff. I'll never forget it. She was a hell of a spitfire then. Had passion, beliefs. She looked...hell, maybe a decade younger. She's lost some of that since. It's like something's been sucking the life out of her these last few years. Like she's given up.

"Yeah. She was workin' at the Hideaway Police Station."

"Okay. Any chance Sheriff can tell us anything?"

A vague memory strikes. And I can't believe I didn't think of this before. "He knows something. When she messed with their computers and deleted all their violations, they were going to arrest her. But then Sheriff got a call, and they let her go. He wouldn't tell me why. Just walked away from me."

Noah's brows skyrocket. He picks up the phone and puts it on speaker.

"Sheriff Bradshaw's office."

"Paula, hi. Noah Reeves."

"Hey, Noah. Who's complaining to you about us now?"

"My brother."

"The hockey player?"

"No. The grumpy one."

"Oh. Well feel free to tell him to pay us a visit and we can settle this my way." There's a smirk in her voice.

I laugh. "Hey, Paula."

"You two playing games again. I'll get the Sheriff for ya. Hang tight."

Noah lifts his glasses and rubs the bridge of his nose. Then points to me and I nod, taking the cue.

"Reeves, what's going on?"

"I need information," I answer.

He grunts. "Police business information?"

"It's for a client, Sheriff," Noah says then looks to me.

"Three years ago, you got a call about one of your employees. Tessa Banks. I need to know who it was."

"Of course. Why don't I just give you all our system passwords and social security numbers while I'm at it."

I smile. "Because I didn't ask for that."

"Look, if it's a client we have in custody, and you're calling as an attorney, that's a different story. But we can't comment or provide information not privy to us, much less the public."

Noah's interest perks, and he sits up, grabbing a notepad with the list of random words I gave him. Then turns to the speaker. "I'm not asking for information on her case, Sheriff. I was just going to ask who contacted you from the FBI. I've got a few names here, Frank something, and…oh darn, where's that list…" Noah shrugs at me as he improvises.

Wyatt grunts. "Hold on a second."

I shoot my brother a look to find out what the hell he's up to, but he holds up a hand.

The sheriff comes back on the line. "Mercer. Agent's name was Frank Mercer. That's all I can tell you."

Ice creeps through my veins.

Damnit, Tessa. What's going on?

Noah lifts a red pen and circles the name.

I swallow the lump in my throat. "Thanks, Wyatt. Let's get lunch soon. My treat," I offer.

"Later."

Noah presses the red button on his desk phone. "I can't get into that system."

"Tell me you know someone who can." I can't just give up knowing she's in some kind of trouble.

Noah types. "Most cases are not public. But there are other ways. They usually investigate crimes that originate from public incidents." He looks up at me. "This could take a while. You got time?"

I pick up my iced coffee. "Not goin' anywhere."

It doesn't take Noah too many misses until he finds something that lifts me off my seat.

"Twenty-seven-year-old male Eric Johnson was shot cold with two bullets in the chest in a second-level apartment in Summer Hill." Noah glances up at me. "Girlfriend, *Teresa Bennett*, witnessed. The twenty-five-year-old female was hiding in a wardrobe when shots were fired. An attempted getaway from a locked door resulted in a bullet in her back. Bennett was found bleeding nearly to death in the apartment minutes after the final shot was heard. Two suspects got away."

He stops reading, eyes shifting to the list. He circles several other words. "Your list is starting to make sense."

"Still doesn't explain why she went back there," I rasp.

"Levi, they didn't kill her. She *survived*. If she got a call from this Frank, my guess is she's in witness protection. Which means one thing."

My blood runs cold. "They found her."

It should make me feel better. That she's safe.

"Or..."

"Or what?"

He pushes off his seat and starts to pace his office. "Tessa's been in and out of town, which means she refused protection but is still working with the FBI."

"For what?"

"Either they caught the guys and need a material witness, or she's in immediate danger and they're putting her in protective custody."

"They can't force that either."

"They can."

My chest is tight. My stomach sinking. "So she's out of options?"

"I didn't say that."

27

Tessa

On Friday morning, I wake to the sun. Which would normally be progress for me. But given that I was up until three in the morning anxiety ridden, I'm not any more rested than the night I got here.

The heavily guarded studio apartment I'm in is small, but I'm not complaining. It's somewhat clean, stacked with fresh groceries and coffee. The window has bars, which is fitting, and I'm not even mad about it.

I'm grateful, in fact. Dangerous men are looking for me. And there's no way they can get to me here.

That should give me peace. Help me sleep.

But it doesn't. Because the truth is, until they catch these men, I can't go back to *mine*.

My whole life has been a beaded necklace of sand and dirt. Levi and Jackson are the pearl I found in the center, holding me together.

I owe them my cooperation.

Irony aside, no one's ever protected me from the world's cruelty. But I can protect them.

By staying here.

I love them and I'll fight to get back to them, but not until it's safe.

There's a light rap on my door, followed by the guard's voice.

"Ms. Banks? Agent Mercer is here."

I inhale sharply. Anger coursing through me at the man who took my phone away the day I was brought in here.

"Let him in."

Arms crossed, I keep my back to Frank as he walks in and face the window. "Let me guess, you're workin' the case."

"Settle down. I brought fresh coffee and good news."

Dropping my shoulders, I cross to him and take the larger one.

"I want to talk to a judge. This has gone on long enough. You won't catch them all. It's impossible."

He sighs and points to the couch. "We don't need to anymore—I mean we do. But not where it concerns you. There was an arrest two days ago."

I glare at him since one arrest means nothing for my freedom.

"Vince Romano was found in an unmarked delivery truck in Hideaway Springs."

A wave of nausea hits me. It makes it hard to swallow the lump in my throat.

"He's in custody now. And he's talkin'."

"Talking?"

"That's the good news. He and Eddie were facing severe punishment from the organization, so they took a load of cash and inventory but had one final stop to make before disappearing."

"Me."

"Eddie still wants you dead."

"Why?"

"He's been heavily criticized for leaving you alive that day. And paid for it with a demotion—according to his partner. Got tired of being treated like a rookie and went rogue. That's what got him in trouble."

I shiver and take a sip of coffee.

"We're close, Tess. Real close. Once we get Eddie, you're free to go."

It doesn't seem real. "What about the others?"

"You won't be in danger anymore. You didn't see anyone else. They'll be our problem, not yours."

"We're supposed to believe some coward from that night that no one else will be looking to finish the job?"

"No offense, but you're not their priority. They're not taking a risk if you can't identify any of them."

I release a heavy breath. "In the meantime, I just sit here when there may or may not be someone looking for me? Eddie could be halfway across the country by now."

"Tess, this guy's no small-time criminal. And before he goes, he's looking to prove it. If he finds you, you're as good as gone."

"I know what he's capable of. I've got a bullet hole to prove it, Frank," I shout. "I asked you for a judge. I said I'd cooperate, but you haven't even given me a timeframe. A guarantee. Nothing. This is my life, my freedom. All you care about is getting your guy. Not how your incompetence is affecting *me*."

And who you're keeping me from.

He lowers his hands, gesturing for me to calm down. "You are entitled to a hearing. I've set it up with Judge Larry for later this afternoon. My partner Agent Andrews and I will be there."

I scoff. "So what, it's me against two FBI agents? Is there even a point?"

"It'll be someone outside the agency telling you that these things take time when done right." His voice is so calm I want to stab his throat.

I fold my arms as he continues. "Then we bring you back here until he's caught. He's got limited resources now that he's solo. If Eddie's lurking around, we'll find him. Soon."

Back here.

I blink back tears. "I'm tired of hiding."

"You've come this far, Tess. Just hang on. We're almost there."

I shake my head. "I've lost him," I whisper.

"Who?"

Sniffling, I drop onto the couch, ready to be left alone. "I'll see you this afternoon."

Frank glances at his watch and nods. "I'll pick you up at two."

"Why are we in a courtroom?" I whisper to Frank. "I thought this could be in his office...a little less...official."

He stands up straight, adjusting his suit. "Judge Larry doesn't hold hearings anywhere but a courtroom." He points to an empty wooden table in front of the benches. "You sit there. Andrews and I sit here."

I scan the space, unwarranted nerves hitting me because I already know how this dispute will end. "Right."

The judge walks in, barely examining the stiff people in the room before landing on me. His bored expression falls to the papers in front of him as he takes a seat. He doesn't even look up as he starts to speak.

"Agent...Andrews."

Frank's partner stands. "Your Honor."

"Tell me again why this witness has been held in protective custody for so long without testifying. What progress has been made in the case?"

"Correction, Your Honor, Ms. Bennett has been given the freedom to live her life with certain limitations."

The judge blinks, waiting for the answer to his question.

Andrews continues. "The individual responsible for the murder Ms. Bennett witnessed is part of a larger criminal network. We've successfully seized one suspect from that day, but one remains at large. Given the danger to Ms. Bennett, it's been deemed necessary to put her in protective custody."

My stomach sinks. I don't exactly have a good argument prepared. And I sure as hell don't think *you don't know how to do your job* is going to pan out.

"My notes say her testimony is vital to the case, but you haven't been able to secure the final suspect?"

"Correct. And exposing her now would put her in jeopardy."

The judge nods, clearly in agreement.

Great. I've lost him before I had a chance to speak.

I push off my seat. "This is unbelievable. Your Honor, it's been three years and I still have no—"

He barely looks at me. "Take a seat, ma'am."

"No!" I move to stand in front of the room. Call it cabin fever, delusion, or just the fact that people are here to listen, and I have something to say. "I'm tired of being a sitting duck. I feel like fish bait."

"Tessa, sit down," Frank grits a warning.

My face heats and adrenaline spikes. "This shit just can't be legal. You can't keep me trapped like this. I have rights."

Two guards approach me, but the judge raises his hand, stopping them. "Ms. Bennett, I understand your frustration, but do calm down, you'll have your—"

"No, you don't!" I shout. The main door swings open, and I imagine they've called for backup. But I don't let it stop me. "You have *no* idea what it's like to be treated like a criminal when all I did was witness something I wish I could forget!" The tension in the room rises, and the same two guards grab me from both sides.

"Let go of me," I grit, jerking from their grip.

"Manhandling your only witness, gentlemen?" A new voice cuts into the room. A familiar voice.

All eyes snap to the back of the room. My heart sinks so deep it takes my breath away. Noah moves down the aisle, sharp suited, approaching the stand.

But my eyes lock with *the other* man that entered the room. Dark jeans, tan shirt, tight jaw and that familiar scowl. Levi tears his gaze from me and takes a seat in the back row.

I swallow hard, Noah's voice muffled as I try to find my breath.

"Noah Reeves. Ms. Bennett's attorney."

I frown as Noah passes in front of me, facing Frank and his partner. "This is how you treat a woman who risked everything to give you the testimony you so desperately need?"

The room falls silent as Noah turns to the guards, his voice low. "Release her, now."

My arms are freed, and I stumble slightly, feeling lightheaded and mentally drained. Noah helps me to my seat then turns to the judge.

"Your Honor, my client has endured three years of this so-called investigation, yet here we are with no resolution in sight."

Frank stands. "Counsel, this is a federal case. Ms. Benett's testimony is crucial, and her safety—"

Noah looks bored with his response. "If I didn't know any better, I'd say her safety is being used as an excuse to keep her trapped into giving you what you need."

"Objection. With all due respect." Agent Andrew stands. "Ms. Bennet was shot. They won't hesitate to do it again."

My heart sinks. I can almost feel Levi's heated gaze behind me.

"When you catch him—whether it be tomorrow or six years from now—you call my office, and I'll personally bring her in to testify," Noah assures. "Until then, she'll be leaving with us."

Wait. What?

"No!" I shout, pushing off my chair. "No. I'm not going with them." I shake my head at the judge and snap back to the agents. "Frank, make them leave," I beg.

The same guard is at my side, restraining me from pushing forward.

Noah doesn't even blink. "Your Honor, my client is concerned for her family's safety. While the Hideaway Springs P.D. is providing a generous level of protection, I believe it is reasonable to expect that, since she is agreeing to testify, the agency should assign a 24-hour guard as well."

The judge perks a brow. "Her family?"

Noah points to the back of the room, and my chest clenches. "Her husband, Levi Reeves, my brother, ensures her safety. He and I will be your main point of contact. I can confirm their cooperation with the agency and—"

"Tessa?" Frank cuts in, a question in his tone.

"I'm sorry, do you have a question for my client?" Noah asks. He's the picture of calm as my heart rattles in my chest.

Frank glares at Noah. Gritting through his teeth. "Last I checked, she wasn't married."

The judge inspects a paper Noah handed him. "This certificate is recent." He dips his glasses to look at me. "My congratulations."

My gaze carries to the quiet cowboy in the back of the room.

Agent Andrews stands, buttoning his jacket. "While we may release her from custody under the protection of her spouse, we'd need to inspect the grounds and arrange a visit with the local police department."

Noah nods with a smirk. "Sheriff Bradshaw is expecting your call."

I shake my head at my *brother-in-law*. "Noah."

"This hearing is adjourned." Judge Larry strikes the gavel against the table.

Noah moves to collect his briefcase while the room erupts in chatter.

"No," I shout. "I have the right to refuse. Frank, *do* something."

The man I've trusted to protect me all these years steps forward abruptly, catching my arm. "If you don't calm down, your mental state will be in question and your testimony will mean nothing to—"

"Take your hands off my wife."

Frank drops my arm and walks off. I turn at his steely voice, pleading. "Levi, you can't take me with you. It's not safe. He's still out there."

Catching my hand, he turns to his brother. "Noah—"

"Yes. Get her in the car, I'll finish up here."

Levi pulls me through the crowd, and as much as I want to fight him—my stomach buzzes with how much I've *missed* him. The gruff exterior, his hard scowl, these hands, his voice. Everything.

I want to be wrapped up in it all.

When we're out in the hall, I throw myself around him. He's quick to catch me, but it's cold and distant. His arms loosen all too quickly and I'm back on the ground as he leads me toward the exit.

I brace my feet on the hard tile floor. "Levi, stop."

He spins back to me. His hands rake into my hair as he pulls himself close. "Are you alright?"

"Yes," I breathe. "But—"

"Whiskey, don't make me throw you over my shoulder."

There's an idea.

I shake my head. "No. You're not listening to me. It's too risky—"

Noah sweeps past us. "All set. Let's move."

We're in Noah's SUV before I can process what's happening. Levi gently settles me in the back seat and sits beside me. His arm around my shoulders. At this point, I'm not sure if it's a romantic gesture or if he thinks I'm a flight risk.

I've been so worked up for days, I can't even tell. My nights are either restless or sleepless. I'm tired, emotional, and on the verge of tears. "My things—" I murmur as my eyelids fall heavy. "Willy."

"I'll get you another one," Levi murmurs.

The humming of the car evens out as we roll onto the highway. I let myself curl into his warmth. He reaches over and pulls the afghan from the back, draping it over me as he lays my head onto his lap.

I'm somewhat conscious before falling asleep. This cryptic exchange between the brothers is the last thing I hear.

"Thank you."

"Don't thank me just yet," Noah answers.

28

Levi

The sun sets and the streetlamps on the road start to look familiar. Each one casts shadows across my face as Noah rolls through yet another town just above the speed limit.

Tessa's still asleep but restless on my lap. Jerking and whimpering. There's no doubt she felt the storm brewing inside of me back at the courthouse. And if I don't pull it together, I'm going to scare her again.

My hand trembles as I run my fingers through her hair. I'm so damn in love with this woman, I can hardly breathe.

I try to focus on the rhythmic rise and fall of her chest. But it's no use.

The worry for her safety has me twisted into something sharp and cold. She fucking threw herself around me and I just stood there.

Blaming myself for all kinds of shit. *Angry* at her for trying to protect me when it should be the other way around.

"You alright back there?"

"Yeah."

"We got there in time, bro. You saved the day."

"*You* saved the day."

I've been too busy making my own assumptions about this woman. Mentally scarred by my ex to see her clearly. Calling her every name in the book. Trying to run her out of town. When all she wanted was a home, some peace...a safe place to hide.

I run a hand down my face. "She's been suffering silently all this time."

"Don't go down that hole, Levi. You know she'll pick up on it." He turns the corner onto the ranch. "Then she'll think you're mad at her. And you don't want that. Women get all kinds of crazy when they think you're mad at them."

I scoff, remembering Tessa's reaction in the stables when I accused her of trying to take Willow from us.

His tone shifts. "And I didn't save the day." From my seat, I see him swallow hard. "I'm the reason Vince and Eddie found her."

I glance down at Tessa. My voice low. "What are you talking about?"

"When I was finishing up in the courtroom, Frank practically laughed at me when I assured him we'd keep her safe. He said that was hard to believe when my surveillance cameras were the reason they found her."

"Fuck." After a moment, I add, "It's not your fault. And don't even think about taking those down. We'll just be careful."

Guilt still gnaws at my brother by the time we roll into the driveway. Thank fuck we're home.

"You gonna be alright?" Noah asks. "I'm going to go check on Charlie."

"She okay?"

"I sent her a text on the drive over to close up and head to Pepper's. Might as well catch them all up."

"Thanks."

I lift Tessa into my arms. She moans softly but doesn't wake.

Dad's car is in the driveway. He holds the door open as I climb the porch steps and carry her through the threshold.

All I want is to keep her safe. She is. And for now, that has to be enough.

I settle her on the couch in her favorite corner. She barely stirs, her head turning onto a pillow.

"Damn. She's *out*." Dad observes.

I watch her. "Don't think she's slept in days."

He rests a hand on my shoulder. "Neither have you. Sit down. I made soup."

"I'm not hungry." I stalk away to the den, pacing in place.

Dad follows me. "Levi, calm down. She's home. She's safe."

"Do you know she didn't want to come here tonight? She practically begged that FBI agent not to let me take her."

He sighs. "I know. That's...why I didn't tell you that Tessa was in trouble. She left to protect you and Jackson."

"We'll be fine. All of us. I'm making sure of it."

He nods. "Is there something else?"

My gaze drifts to where she's resting in the other room. "She was scared. When she saw me, she was scared. Not relieved. Not happy. But scared."

He crosses his arms. "Why am I getting the feeling you think that's your fault?"

"Because of what I said to her before she left. It was selfish and immature. I used her feelings for me to threaten her."

He blows out a breath. "Alright, well...every Reeves man deserves one jackass moment. That was yours."

"I exceeded my limit with her long ago."

"And yet, here she is, head over heels for you."

My heart slices at the idea. I've already claimed myself hers forever. That marriage certificate is half valid with my signature. She's yet to hear my vows, but she will.

Starting with my vow to protect her.

"I want to pay you," I rasp. "For the time Tessa stayed at the Inn. I want to thank you and pay you for keeping her safe. Even if you didn't know it."

"Neither are necessary."

"It is to me," I snap, then start pacing again. "I've— I've been the man she dreads facing. The one who forces her to put up her defenses. Ever since I met her..."

"You don't know that."

"Yes, I do. She knocked on my door to interview with a pros and cons list already drafted for me."

He chuckles. "Oh, I have to see this."

I sigh, running a hand down my face. A laugh escaping. "God, I don't know how she does it."

"Ask her. When she wakes up, just talk. Tell her you see her strength. How lucky you and Jackson are to have her."

I nod.

"What did Noah say? What's our next step?" he asks.

"Frank will be in touch about a guard they'll relocate here. But we'll need our own for him to alternate with. Sheriff Bradshaw has a private meeting with his team tomorrow. A selected group he trusts to assign to this." I chuckle bitterly. "He said it's the most excitement he's had in over a decade."

"Jackson starts school Monday. He's going to wonder why Tess isn't taking him. And why she isn't leaving the house."

"We'll all take turns with Jackson. He'll barely notice. We'll make it work."

Dad nods. "You're not alone. And thanks to you, neither is she."

Tessa

I wake up in Levi's bedroom. On his bed.

Water is running in the master bath and I sit up on alert. I've been in and out of sleep. First, in the living room, where I was hearing muffled voices.

Then when I was lifted off the couch and brought upstairs.

I'm cold and a little weak.

The water shuts off.

"Hey." Levi steps out of the bath and comes to me, sweeping strands of curls from my face. His voice is gentle. Not like before.

I blink up at him. "Hi." I look around the room. "Are we alone?"

He smirks. "Is that okay?"

"I've been hearing voices all night."

He nods and strokes my head. "It's just us now. Dad and Noah left."

I groan. "God, they must think I'm so weak. I can't even fight my own battles."

Anger flashes in Levi's eyes but it fades quickly as he leans in and kisses my forehead. "I don't know if you heard this, but before my dad left, he said, *'I spent a lot of years in the ring. I thought I knew real strength. But after seeing hers, nothing could ever compare to the kind of fight she's had in her all along'."*

My eyes sting. I clear my throat, turning away from the compliment I don't deserve.

"You're still shivering." His hand brushes my arm briefly before he stands and moves to the door. "I've started a warm bath for you. Get in while I heat up some soup."

I nod, grateful for the breathing room when he's gone.

Slipping out of bed, I cross the hall to my bedroom for clean clothes, stopping short when I see the door has been replaced on its hinges.

Well, that didn't take long.

I turn the knob and step inside. Something is different. It feels empty. My clothes aren't on the bed where I left them. The drawers of the nightstand are empty. For a second, I think he might have moved them into the wardrobe but—it's gone.

"D'you lose something?"

I jump and turn at his voice. I glance at the empty space where the standing unit used to be. "You found the story."

He steps inside and takes my hand. Silently, he leads me back to his bedroom door and kisses my cheek. "Everything you need is in here. Be right back."

He's gone again before I can ask questions.

I step into the warm, soapy bath, letting it do its job. Calm me. Settle me.

Settled.

It doesn't feel real. There's still so much more weighing on me.

Like where we stand.

I can sense how angry Levi is. I know he's holding back on confronting me until I'm feeling better. But I'm more than ready to talk now. Not about what he read in that old article, but what it's done to me. What it can still do to me.

Why he *has* to let me leave his house.

I wrap a white towel around myself, feeling refreshed and alert. I step into his massive closet for a T-shirt and freeze. One side has all my new clothes. Oddly, they are well organized. The drawers are stacked with new, clean underwear and even socks.

I gasp at his voice. "Pepper takes credit for this."

"You're moving me in?"

He steps inside. "You're my wife. Of course, you're moving in."

I step back, my spine hitting the back wall. "It's not real."

"It may not be *valid*." He cages me in, raising my chin. "But it's very real, Tessa."

Like he can't help himself, his eyes throw fire again.

I swallow. "Levi, I—"

"How could you not tell me your life was in danger? How could you think I'd leave you in anyone's hands but mine?" His voice is as sharp as his blue eyes. His hand dips under my towel, finding my wet center instantly. Without warning, he parts my legs and slides his fingers inside me.

My lips part with a moan.

"That's not a real question. I don't want you to speak. Not yet, Tessa."

I whimper at his touch, his breath on the side of my face. And the bite in the way he says my name.

"That's right, I'm angry. And there are no horses in this room to save you."

Holy fuck, I'm dripping.

He pulls out slowly and rubs my clit, teasingly. I moan pleadingly, leaning into his touch. He shocks me with a deep thrust of those expert fingers. I gasp, arching my back. "I promised myself I'd be gentle, but why should I go easy on you when you scared the shit out of me?"

He strokes almost punishingly, and I welcome it, gripping his biceps, chasing my release. The son of a bitch pulls out again.

"You're mine to protect, Tessa. Do you hear me?"

"Yes, yes. Just please don't stop."

He plunges deep with each word. "My woman." *Thrust.* "My wife." *Thrust.* "My love."

I come hard on his fingers, screaming and trembling. I'm shattering with emotion. I don't even try to hold back my tears. I'll cry for this man if that's what it takes to show my affection.

His strokes turn slow and gentle, drawing out my orgasm as I press my palm to his chest, feeling his racing heartbeat.

His forehead drops to mine, his defenses crashing. "I love you," he breathes.

A wave of warmth washes over me.

"Stay. You're not alone anymore. You have me, a little boy who adores you. This ranch, my family, my heart. You have it all. *Don't* walk out on us again, Whiskey."

"I won't," I cry out. Sucking in a sharp breath, I bring my hands up to his face, the towel falling loose around my ankles. "I won't, I promise. I love you, Indie. With my whole heart, I want to be yours. I want to be your wife."

He releases a breath with a smile I've longed to see all day. Then crushes my lips with desperate kisses. "We'll make it official. Big wedding."

"Small."

"*Small* wedding," he laughs.

Tears stream down my face. "I'll never leave you or Jackson. You have all of me. All of my heart, all of my love."

He swipes his thumbs under my eyes, kissing my tear-stained face.

"I'm sorry I lied—"

He lifts my chin, his eyes flashing with guilt. "You didn't really think I'd hold it against you, did you, sweetheart?"

My stomach buzzes. "You should."

He drops his hand and sighs like he's prepared to hear something else I've been keeping from him. "And why's that?"

I grip his biceps and flip him against the wall. "Because." I tug on his drawstrings and drop to my knees. "Number five works both ways."

29

Tessa

Turns out house arrest ain't half bad.

School started for Wiggles two weeks ago, and I've been streaming Matlock while cooking up a storm for my boys.

At first my *husband* wouldn't let me out of the house even to bring the cowboys their afternoon refreshment. But he's eased up the last few days.

We signed an official marriage certificate with witnesses two days after I came home. Noah claimed the last one had the incorrect spelling of the bride's name...oops... and had the "corrected" one filed with the state of Colorado.

I slip on my cowboy hat and step outside with my tray.

"Oh, let me get that for ya, Tessa." Max picks up my tray and carries it down the back porch steps. He plants it on the small folding table already layered with a plastic tablecloth.

"Thanks, Max." I frown. "You didn't have to set me up. I could see your boss getting all cranky because I'm distracting his boys from workin'."

"He's the one who told me to do it."

"You tellin' on me, Max?" Levi rides up on Anton and hops off.

I jerk back from my least favorite horse. "I can set up my own table, you know?"

"Appreciate the help, buddy," Levi says with a smile on his face. He's been doing that a lot lately.

Being friendly with his staff.

"Season's changin', Tess. Gonna need to switch that up to warm cider soon." Max tips his hat and races down the field. "Catch ya later."

"But I don't know how to make cider," I mutter.

"Grocery store." Levi winks. "They'll never know."

"Baby, I've got nothin' but time on my hands. I'm going to learn to make it."

He wraps strong arms around me and dips his head with a soft kiss.

I groan. "Ugh. You smell like horse."

"You love the smell of horse."

I scowl at the beast behind him. "Not *that* one."

He laughs and brings him over. "That's does it. You two are going to learn to get along. Even if I have to leave you in a room to work out your differences."

I fold my arms and turn away. "Never."

Levi lifts my chin. "What's botherin' you? Why you so grouchy?"

"I'm *bored*. I miss Jackson." I run my hand up his arm. "I miss our sunrise mornings."

"It's gettin' a little chilly for that, Whiskey. Things are pretty busy now, but after the fall festival, we could have a new morning ritual."

"Like what?" I pout.

He wraps his arms around me from behind. "Like lighting up the fireplace. Workin' out together downstairs."

I twist my head back. "You callin' me fat?"

"What? No."

"I've just been bloated."

"We both like working out. It was just a suggestion, woman."

I'm on the verge of tears, and I don't understand it. All I know is this stupid horse—as beautiful and innocent as it may be—is making me ill.

"Can I leave these out here for the boys? I'm going to go start dinner earlier. I need to neutralize this smell with fresh herbs."

He grins like he knows something I don't. "Alright."

I turn to head up the steps, but he twists me back, pulling me against his warm chest. "Let's put Jackson to bed early tonight and watch a movie in bed."

"Hmm..." I stroke his chest. "Maybe some wine?"

He narrows his eyes. "Or...strawberries." He kisses the tip of my nose.

I purse my lips. But then again, that does sound pretty good. "Deal."

Charlie waves to me from the driver's seat of her SUV.

I wave back. "Morning. He'll be right out. Come on, Jackson. Your ride's here."

With his brick of a backpack, he races out the door. "See you later, Tessa. Don't watch any Knight Rider without me."

"You try staying home with nothin' to do," I call after him.

When they back out of the driveway, I turn a warm smile to my guard, Kenny. "Morning."

"Good morning, Mrs. Reeves." Kenny greets me stonily. He's not the one from Hideaway Springs P.D. And he didn't like being relocated one bit. He's been staying in one of our spare rooms upstairs.

"Can I get you a coffee or anything?"

He lifts his cup. "Already got one. Thank you."

I nod. "Maybe a chair?"

He stares ahead. "Thank you. No."

"Mmmkay." I salute him and step back into the house.

I pull my *Cowboys Do It Better* mug from the cupboard and pour myself some coffee.

Levi bursts through the basement door, drenched in sweat. He glances toward the front door. "Who was it this morning?"

"Charlie. She's actually doing a reading at the school, so it worked out."

"Thank goodness for book lovers."

"Agreed." I hold up my mug.

He glances at it, then moves to the cupboard, grabbing one for himself. "Hey, did you hear anything from Lonnie about her and my dad? Sounds like they're talking—a lot."

I narrow my eyes at him. "Do you think of your ex every time you see this mug?"

He coughs a laugh. "What? Of course not. Just... when you're holding it."

I roll my eyes and dump the rest into the sink. Then open the trash and drop it inside.

With a wide grin, he pulls me against him. "Okay, *that* was adorable. But I thought jealousy wasn't your thing?"

"It's not." I step back stubbornly. "It was cracked."

"No, it wasn't."

I open the trash bin again and toss the near-empty jam jar into. It lands with a crash. "Is now."

He breaks into laughter. "What is going on with you?"

"I don't know. I don't feel like myself. Maybe I'm just on edge. Eddie is still out there. He could be halfway across the country or in our bushes. What if all this security is for nothing? I've upended everyone's lives. Especially yours." My voice cracks and my eyes burn.

His expression smooths and his arms wrap around me again. "I know. Let's catch up with Frank and the Sheriff tomorrow. See how much longer we need to keep up precautions before we move on with our lives."

I nod and rest my head against his chest.

"You ready for breakfast?"

I consider it for a moment. My usual morning nausea hasn't improved the way my nightmares have over the last few weeks.

In fact, it's stronger and surprisingly leaves me craving food rather than averting it.

"I think so. Are you staying for a bit?"

"For the morning. Then I have a catch up with Maggie about the Barley wedding next week."

My eyes light up. "A Hideaway Ranch wedding?"

He narrows his gaze. "Yes. Sound like something you might want?"

I bite my bottom lip. "Maybe. Think they'll let me spy on them next week? To get some ideas?"

He inhales a deep breath. "The ranch is private and closed in. I don't see why not, but let me check in with Sheriff later."

I smile up at him, already excited about the idea of a ranch wedding. Even if we are keeping it small.

The next day isn't much different. The fall chill hit a little harder when I opened the front door to walk Jackson to Chase's car. He and Pepper were going to breakfast at the Inn then driving to Denver for the first pre-season practice.

At two in the afternoon, I'm curled up on the couch with the third thriller novel Charlie dropped off for me this week. I made the mistake of telling her I was bored. And she knew just the cure.

It's a crazy intense series, and I'm hooked.

I jump when my cell phone rings, snapping me back into reality. Goosebumps race along my arms.

Heavens. Where am I?

Oh right. Phone.

The screen shows a private number. Chase and Noah both call from a private number. For different reasons.

"Hello?" No answer. "Hello?" I shake my head and hang up, lifting the book back up from my lap.

A moment later, my phone dings with a text message. It's from an odd phone number that looks automated.

Hello. Jackson never made it to school today. Could you please let us know if he's home sick?

Heart racing, I sit up, my fingers typing back a quick reply.

Tessa: *He was dropped off this morning. He should be there.*

I quickly shoot a text to Chase. He immediately confirms he left him in the school yard.

School yard.

Those are safe, aren't they?

Oh God.

A lump forms in my throat and I rush to find the school's phone number and dial.

Someone answers right away.

"Hi, this is—"

"Please hold."

"No, wait—"

Hand shaking, I hang up and call again. The line is busy.

Fuck.

I text the number back.

Tessa: *We dropped him off. Please check again.*

No response.

I shove off the couch and pace the living room.

Maybe it's the thrillers I'm reading. Maybe it's the fact that a dangerous man is believed to be lurking around Hideaway Springs, waiting to make his move. Or maybe it's just paranoia, but I'm *shaking* with fear that someone took him.

Lilly.

My mind spirals.

Levi told me she's pulled him out of school before, what if it was her? They wouldn't release him to her, so she must have grabbed him from the yard before he even had a chance to go inside.

That's got to be it.

I'm trembling as I dial Levi's number. He'll drive to the school and check. It'll be fine.

"Hey, love," Maggie's sweet voice answers.

"Mag? Did I call the wrong number?"

"No sweets, the boss left his phone here. He's been a little on edge lately and forgetful."

"He has?" This is news to me. He's been so calm and laid back since I moved in.

My heart sinks.

Of course he's on edge. He's been holding it together for my sake. While simmering on the inside.

"Just the last week or so. Probably the season change and the events coming up."

Or me. It's probably me.

"Thank you, Maggie," I whisper, feeling like I've lost my voice.

Fuck it.

I grab Levi's car keys. Since I had to abandon mine outside of town the night Frank sent his team for me.

I step out the door. Kenny is in front of me in a flash, his impressive biceps bulging from under his black T-shirt.

"I need to…pick up my kid from school." I don't have the energy to explain what's really going on. He doesn't need to hear the Lilly drama.

"Levi is busy and they won't release him to anyone else."

He stares at the keys in my hands, then motions to the car. "I'll go with you."

I give a curt nod and head for the driver's seat.

Ten minutes later, I pull up to the front of the school. "Wait here. They won't let you in." And the last thing I want to show this private school is the continued family drama of Levi Reeves' new wife needing security detail.

He glances at my left hand then nods. "Go ahead. I'll be here."

I sigh with relief. "Be right back."

I slip out and race down the well-paved walkway to the main entrance. I hold up my driver license to the camera and hope it doesn't get picked up on any illegally monitored surveillance.

I'm buzzed in and race to the front office.

The middle-aged lady at the desk scans me skeptically. "You're...Tessa? We have you down as an authorized pick-up. Are you Jackson's nanny?"

I shake my head. Not bothering to correct her. "No—I got a call—a text that he wasn't in school today?" I start breathlessly. "His uncle dropped him off this morning. He was supposed to be in the yard. Are you su—"

"Ma'am," she shouts, holding up her hands. "Please keep your voice down."

Was I screaming?

"Jackson is here today. It must have been a mistake," she says softly with a smile I know is fake.

I sigh with relief. "Thank you. I just wanted to make sure. It's been—he's—thank you."

She nods and I swear, she thinks I'm insane. I'll just have to explain this one to my husband later. "May I...see the message?"

I nod and tap my pockets. "Oh. I left without my phone."

She stares at me.

I laugh nervously and swallow. "You're sure he's here?"

She nods. "I saw him today and no one leaves school grounds until pick up. Which is in thirty minutes if you'd like to wait."

I shake my head. "That's alright. I need to get back. Thank you."

Still shaking and feeling stupid, I walk back to the car.

What the hell was that text then?

I want to cry. I can't keep living like this. I slide into the driver's seat and glance at my guard.

Jesus, no wonder Kenny never wants to sit. The man is out cold, head leaning against the window.

"Please, don't get up," I mutter, buckling my seatbelt. "I'll drive."

"Sounds good to me." A lethal voice comes from behind me. One that's rottenly familiar. Followed by something cold pressed against my temple.

I freeze.

"Sleeping Beauty is going to wake up soon. We're going to toss him on the roadside. Drive."

My breaths come in sharp, ragged gasps, chest heaving with panic.

"Drive!" he roars.

I jolt and grip the steering wheel, barely giving it a beat before my gaze lifts to the rear-view mirror. His eyes meet mine there.

It's him.

Eddie Graves. Dark hair, tanned skin, hostile grey eyes.

"If he wakes up, I shoot him. Go."

I shift into drive and hit the gas.

My heart pounds against my chest as we drive through and then out of Hideaway Springs. In the rearview mirror I see him glancing at his phone, giving me directions from his GPS.

"Take a right, then get on the expressway."

Swallowing hard, I resist the urge to ask where he's taking us.

I'm not sure I want to know yet.

"Pull over."

I slow the car over onto a gravel road. There isn't another car in sight. I'm virtually alone with this man. He's going to kill me. Right here.

Eddie snakes a hand to my door and hits the unlock button. Then hops out the back seat.

Within seconds, his small frame yanks Kenny out from the passenger's seat and onto the dirt road. Then he slides into his place, slamming the door.

My heart pounds against my chest.

"Nice ride, Red. This one's a lot prettier than the last piece of junk you been driving around."

I swallow the lump in my throat. "How long have you been following me?"

"Too long."

What do you know, we agree on something.

He points the barrel at me. "Go."

I tremble, feeling as cold as a dead body as I merge back onto the highway.

"This was supposed to be easy," he mutters. "Vince and I were supposed to bring you back dead that night."

"Bring me where?"

"The Brunetti family warehouse. But they're going to find you somewhere else tonight. An old logging site. They'll find you dead in a shed on their grounds, and they'll know I did it."

I swallow hard. My vision hazy. "You're not going to hang around to take the credit?"

"Starting a new life. But not till I show 'em I always finish what I start."

"I don't suppose you've been staying at Hideaway Springs Inn all this time?"

"Been sleeping in your car ever since Vinny and I split up."

"My car?"

"The night you were picked up outside of town. You abandoned your piece of shit and hopped into a black SUV."

"You were there?"

"Vin and I followed you. As soon as you got in that car, I knew they were onto us. It was only a matter of time before they tracked the surveillance device back to its source."

"Which was...your truck?" I ask, trying to make sense of it. Not that it mattered anymore.

"I couldn't be in it when they did. So I took your car and told him I'd be in touch."

It scares me how smart he is.

Because he was right. Vince was caught a few days after I was brought back to the safehouse. Just like Eddie suspected.

"So what now?"

He waves the gun around. "Prove I don't shoot to miss, and then...game over."

I swallow hard. "No kidding."

He laughs. "You're funny. I like you." He glances at my left hand. The same one Kenny glanced at earlier. "Too bad you're married."

30

Levi

It's been a long day. But productive. We finally put a hard stop to any more changes for the Barley family wedding. And the following week will be the fall festival. Then we close out the season with a Harvest Moon Hayride on the last day of October.

I pick up my phone from the front office before heading back to the house.

Shit.

Several missed calls from Sheriff Bradshaw. Did I forget a meeting?

I dial him back on my walk. I barely get a word in before he starts howling. "Reeves. I thought we agreed your wife doesn't leave the house. Now you're taking her out of town?"

"The fuck are you talking about? Tessa's home."

"Our signal alerted us that she's off premises. Levi, we're dealing with the FBI here. I'd really like to not piss anyone off."

My stomach twists, and I pick up speed. "What signal?"

"Her wedding band. We've got a tracker on it."

I race up the steps to the house, bursting through my doors. She's usually in the kitchen at this time. "Tessa?"

I don't know why I call. I got a gut feeling she's not here. My feet are lightning as I move to the front door.

"Kenny's gone too. So is my truck."

Wyatt curses. "I've got to brief my team. Get a few cars on the road. They're over forty-five minutes out."

My stomach sinks. "I'll be there as soon as I can."

Dad sends me a text that he's got Jackson, as planned, and I call Noah to pick me up asap.

Feeling like I might come out of my skin until my brother gets here, I search for clues.

I curse when I find Tessa's phone on the counter. Swiping it open, I scan the call log. One from an unknown number but didn't last more than a few seconds.

Another call to the school that didn't last long either.

Then I look at her texts.

Scrolling past the exchange between her and Chase, I click on the unknown number.

The fuck is this?

"Shit."

I ring Dad the second I get in Noah's car to find out if anything was off at dismissal today. He didn't see anything out of the ordinary. "Except Ms. Miller said Jackson's nanny came by today to confirm he's in school. Everything alright?"

I curse again. "Tessa's missing. I'll call you back." I hang up as he calls my name. I don't have the stomach to go through details.

"Did you know about her wedding band?" I finally ask my brother.

Noah nods. "Yeah. I wasn't sure Tessa would like the idea of it. Thought I'd save you from having to lie to her."

"Getting sick and tired of people keeping things from me," I mutter.

He stays quiet on the longest drive across town. And I know what he's thinking.

If Eddie got to her, chances are he's not going to miss this time.

I grip the steering wheel tight, my knuckles going white. My heart still drumming erratically as I glance at the clock again. 6:03 p.m. He's had my wife for over three hours. I wasn't taking no for an answer when it came to following the tracker to wherever Eddie Graves is taking her. They've got a solid hour on the road ahead of us and reaching them seems impossible at this point.

Luckily, we're driving behind the three police cars they've got heading in that direction.

Noah wanted to drive, given the state I'm in, but I need to be in control.

"As far as we know, she's alive," Bradshaw told me as we were leaving. Apparently, the ring also has a pulse monitor. Tessa is still breathing.

It's the only thing keeping me moving.

That and the radio one of the officers handed me on our way out of the station. Chatter from each car ahead of us keeps me in the loop on what's going on. Phrases like "suspect vehicle", "moving eastbound", and "eyes on target" fill the dark void of my racing imagination.

"She called me," I mutter. "She called me for help and I didn't answer."

Noah stares ahead. "She called you to ask about Jackson. Not this."

"She risked her life for him. And I let her."

"That does it. Get out of the car."

"No. I'm not stopping." We drive in silence for a few minutes. "What did Frank say when you called him?"

"He spoke to Vince. Judging by the route, this is Eddie proving himself before disappearing for good."

"Any clue where he's taking her and why?"

"Vince says it could be one of two places that belong to the Brunetti family."

"Reeves, keep right. Comin' up on an unmarked exit. It looks like he's taking her through some backroads." Sheriff's voice is calm, measured.

I follow them to the next exit, trying to keep up but I'm losing focus. My mind swirling to dark places.

To the pain I felt when they told me my mother was gone. To the confusion and agony I suffered when Elliot died.

Frank's voice comes on the line, bringing me back to the present. "We're almost there. Coming from the other side. You got a visual yet?"

Officer Sharpe, a rookie I met a few times, responds firmly. "No. We'll keep you posted."

I want to scream. They've done nothing for her for three years, now they roll in and start making demands? I slam my fist over the dashboard and grit my teeth.

Noah's unfazed.

Another voice comes on the line. "How do you know this isn't a trap?"

Sheriff comes on the line. "You can hang back if you're scared, Agent Andrews, but we're going in."

I sigh with relief as Noah laughs beside me. "Asshole."

"Reeves, think he's taking her to some logging site. It's too far off the grid—dead zone for communication," Sheriff says.

"What does that mean?" I snap, my patience worn.

"Need you to stay back, I don't need to worry about another—"

I slam my foot on the gas. "Like hell. He's got my wife."

"Levi, I don't need another dumb move today. Hang. Back."

Shit.

I hit the brakes and throw my head back against the seat. Counting the seconds while the radio is silent.

"They're on the move."

My pulse spikes. "Do you see her? Is she hurt?"

Static.

A mixture of voices come through the speaker. And it's hard to tell if it's our local police or the FBI anymore.

"Fuck this." I hop out of the car. Noah jumps out too, but isn't stopping me. He swings around to the driver's seat of his car. "I'll keep it running."

Leaves crackle under my boots as I follow the team going in on foot. My advance startles Officer Sharpe. He whips around, gun drawn in a fluid motion. Every muscle tense as he aims in my direction.

I freeze, throwing my hands in the air.

"Mother—" he curses silently. "Scared the shit out of me, Levi."

This is the guy Sheriff handpicked? Really?

I shake my head, keeping my voice low. "I'm not staying behind."

Static on the radio again. Then voices. "I see her. She's restrained. He's taking her into the shed."

My stomach twists. Tessa. Trapped with the monster that put a bullet in her back.

Sharpe curses. "Stay behind me," he grits. Then lowers the speaker volume.

I nod. My eyes sharp, breath shallow and heart in my throat.

I hear a sharp crack of a door being forced open. It's followed by a burst of activity and shouts. I listen for her voice but it never comes.

A fucking horse can scare her silly but all this and she doesn't make a sound?

Sharpe turns up his speaker. "What's going on?"

Silence.

"Sheriff, Kingsley, come in."

This is ridiculous. Leaving the nervous officer behind, I race around to the shed, finding the cracked wood on the floor.

My blood runs cold. Tessa's on a wooden chair. She's stiff as a board with a gun held to her head by a psychopath.

I lock eyes with my woman. Then the man who has her.

He smirks. "Look at that, Red. More witnesses. What do you think boys, one bullet or two?"

"I repeat. Drop the gun. You're surrounded. You're not leaving here a free man," Sheriff's voice cuts into the silence as he stands with a gun pointed.

As much as I want this fucker dead, he's got my wife inches from his frame.

Eddie laughs. "I haven't been a free man for a long time." He flips the gun between his fingers. "But I always finish what I start."

Tessa swallows hard, and it takes everything I have not to run to her. From the corner of my eye, I watch Sharpe go around the side of the shed. The small windows are dusty and cloudy and there's no telling what this man thinks he's doing. But he's going the wrong way.

The distant thrum of a helicopter fills the air.

Eddie looks up. "Time's up." He points the gun sharply at my wife and my vision blurs.

A shot is fired, and the air is knocked out of my lungs. Tessa screams and it's a beautiful sound. One I needed to hear.

Eddie is on the floor, bleeding out. The squad breaks into action, and Sheriff is on his knees in front of the criminal. "There's a pulse. Who fired?"

"I did," Sharpe calls from outside the cracked window in the back of the shed.

Sheriff cocks a grin. "Nice shot, Rookie."

Fueled with adrenaline, I charge toward her.

"Indie," my woman cries as I free her from the ties around her wrists. They wrap around me, and I lift her into my arms.

"I've got you. You're safe."

She clings to me with all her strength, broken sobs into my neck. I pull her off knowing I'll be holding her all the way home. "Are you hurt?"

Tess shakes her head. It wobbles slightly before she collapses into my arms.

"Tessa?"

"Shock and exhaustion. I'll get you an escort to the nearest hospital," Sheriff offers like he's seen this before. FBI agents surround the area, inspecting every building on the premises.

"Thanks, Wyatt." I cock my head at the men in black uniforms. "We through with them?"

He shrugs. "As far as I know."

31

Tessa

"Hey, beautiful."

Levi's voice is the first I hear when I wake in the bright, sterile room.

It's so soothing, I may as well be waking up in heaven.

I'm hooked up to an IV. I wait for the sharp pain in my lower back. Dejavu from the last time I woke up in the hospital. But there's no pain. Nothing hurts. Except my head and my body from all the tension.

"Kenny," I rasp.

Levi hands me a plastic cup with water. "He's alright. He might be losing his job, but he's alright."

I shift uncomfortably and take a sip. "I'm so tired."

"They're hydrating you." His gaze lingers on my stomach. "Both of you."

I frown. "What?"

He smiles. "We're having a baby, Tess."

A breath puffs out of me. "Are...you sure?" My voice is barely above a whisper. Tears already welling in my eyes because I feel it—I've *been* feeling it.

He's the picture of calm as he flashes me a grin. "I am now."

My face pales, my hand moving to my stomach. "Is everything alright?"

"Baby is fine." He glances back. "Which is what the doctor told me after they examined you."

I drop my head back. Tears streaming down the side of my face. "I've been feeling so weird lately."

Laughter fills his eyes. "I know. I had my suspicions."

I watch him. "You did?"

"I've been so worried for you, Tess. Every restless night. Every meal averted. Your mood swings. Then with all this weighing over your shoulders..."

I reach to stroke his beard. He catches it, bringing it to his face. "You're about six weeks," he tells me. "Are you happy?"

I smile weakly, scrunching my nose. "Yeah. Yeah, I think so." I roll my eyes. "Who am I kidding?" I swipe a loose tear from my face. "I'm over the moon to have your baby, Cowboy."

He releases a breathy, relieved laugh. "Good." He grips my hand. "Because I want a big family with you, Whiskey."

I smile back. Then gasp. "Oh my God, Jackson."

"Dad's got him. He'll spend the night." He leans in. "And he *was* in school today. All day."

I cover my face, feeling humiliated. "I thought it was your ex-wife."

"I realized that." He swallows. "I'm sorry you have to deal with my drama."

I scoff. "Yeah. *Your* drama." I look around the hospital room. "How did you all find me, anyway?"

He rubs my ring finger. "This told us where you were. And that you were alive."

I release a heavy breath. "Well, look at that. Being your wife really saved my life."

"Frank wants you to wear it for a while. Make sure there is no one else we don't know about. And I'm getting you a new phone number. I don't like that he was able to reach you." He perks a brow. "I don't like that you responded to a cryptic message when you knew your life was in danger."

I wince. "I'm sorry. I panicked. It wasn't Kenny's fault. He shouldn't lose his job."

"His job was to keep you safe," he says tightly. "*My* job was to keep you safe."

I pout, hoping it gains me some sympathy because I'm pretty sure he's waiting for the right moment to yell at me for all this. "I don't make it easy."

He smooths the top of my head and grins. "I married the town rogue. I signed up for this."

Aiden

EPILOGUE
Three Months Later

For years, Christmas has been a shadow of what it once was. A reminder of who's missing.

Marybell. Then Elliot. It seemed like little by little, this house grew emptier. Not just with pieces of my heart missing, but my boys—hollow versions of the men they should have been.

Until now.

This year, I had a reason to go all out with the lights. Fix that old doorbell. Cook for a day and a half. Whip out the table extension. And finally, make pitchers of eggnog.

The house isn't entirely filled yet, but it's already buzzing with a new energy. One we only got a taste of last year when Chase and Pepper hosted.

The doorbell rings a third time this evening.

"I'll get it," I call back to the hockey couple and my other guest tonight in the kitchen. Swinging the door open, I let Charlie in. Noah is behind her, carrying gift bags, and what do you know—he's scowling.

Following his girlfriend inside, he gives me a curt nod. "Merry Christmas. Next year, we do this at our house."

I help him with the bags and move them under the tree. "Levi and Tess already called dibs on hosting next year."

Noah looks around for the couple. "Well, I beat them here so—"

Charlie smacks Noah's arm. "They're going to have a new baby. It'll just be easier than schlepping everything to someone else's house."

Noah shrugs. "She'll be like six months old and"—he holds his palms apart about two feet—"this big. How much stuff will that baby need?"

Charlie rolls her eyes. "I'm going to get a drink. I can already hear Pepper laughing in the kitchen, and I want in."

I smack my son's other arm. "Please stop giving that woman reasons not to marry you before you even propose."

He smirks. "Don't worry. Pepper and Tess taught me a neat trick."

"What trick?" I ask as he walks away from me.

I'm about to follow when the doorbell rings again. I don't need to open it. Jackson lets himself in, zooming past me with a 'hi grandpa' and racing toward the tree. My oldest son and his wife behind him.

"Hey." Tessa smiles. Holding up a foil-wrapped dish. "We brought pie." She glances down at the bags Levi is holding, muttering with a wink. "And a few other things."

I set the dish down, then take her coat and scarf. Her growing belly has become more apparent in the last few weeks. The last time we all got together was when they announced they were having a girl. "Staying warm? Is my son feeding you well?"

"Too much. Can I do anything to help?"

"Nope, we've got it." The voices come from behind us. Pepper, Charlie, and Lonnie parade into the dining room, putting the finishing touches on the extended table.

Levi steps into my space, keeping his eyes on the little brunette in the other room—my other guest tonight. "Oh hey, Lon," he calls, then scans me once.

Tessa grabs his arm. "Honey, help me put these under the tree."

She gives him a tug, but Levi's like a sword in the stone. "What's my ex doing here?"

"She has a name, and I *invited* her," I tell him flatly. Levi is very much aware that Lonnie doesn't have family here. And just because she's still hiding doesn't mean she should spend the holiday alone.

Or...any other evening we might have spent together. As *friends*. It's never been anything more. Neither one of us would cross that line.

He softens but still skeptical. "I appreciate that."

I grin back. "I didn't do it for you."

Tessa steps up to her husband. "There a problem, Indie?" She smiles. "Or do I have to break more dishes?"

He puts a hand on her belly, leaning down for a kiss. "All good, sweetheart." With one look back at me, he follows her into the family room.

"Who's the extra plate for?" Noah asks, scanning the table.

The doorbell rings again.

"Who could that be?" Pepper calls from the dining room.

I open the door, ready to tell this sweet older lady carrying a tray of something that smells amazing, that she's got the wrong address.

"Hi. I'm Bessie. I'm looking for—"

"Bessie," Tess calls from the sofa. "Aiden, this is my guest."

"Oh, of course." I push the door open. "Please come in. I hear you're the one behind Tessa's way around a kitchen."

"Depends. Has she burned anything recently?" She steps in like she's family and passes off the tray to me. "Do *not* put these in the fridge. Room temp until time for dessert, please."

"Got it." I close the door behind her.

Levi is the first to approach our new guest. "Bessie, nice to finally meet you. I'm Levi. We spoke on the phone back in the summer."

She shakes his hand the way I would. Firm with skepticism in her eyes. "You ask a lot of questions, Mr. Single-dad Rancher."

Levi laughs. "To be fair, it was an interview, and *you* called me."

"You got my girl here?"

"I've got *my* girl here."

She pushes him aside as Tessa stands. It's a quick hug before Bessie pulls back. "Look at you." She eyes her belly. "Sure don't look like he made you sleep with the horses."

Tessa laughs nervously, glancing at Levi, who's cocking his head in amusement.

"Alright," I start. "Dinner's getting cold, everyone. Let's sit."

Levi wraps an arm around his wife's shoulders, leaning in to tease her about something that's not meant for our ears. She giggles, burrowing her head in his chest.

Noah and Charlie have a similar exchange across the room, and it warms my heart to see everyone happy. Settled. *Living*.

"Hey." Lonnie pokes my side, making me smile down at her. "You sure it's okay I'm here?"

I nod. "I've got something for you."

Her eyes flash with wonder. At thirty-four, she doesn't feel sixteen years younger than me. The biggest reason I've yet to kiss this woman is my son. Inviting her tonight is my first step in approaching him for…consent? Blessing? Hell, I don't know. But Lonnie and I agreed. I need to cross that bridge first. And I've waited long enough.

"What is it?"

"We don't open presents on Christmas Eve."

She smirks and points behind me. "Tell that to him."

I turn around and find Jackson by the tree, tearing the corner of a large, wrapped box. "Jackson."

He jolts. "It's got my name on it."

There's a rumble of a laugh, but it's not from me. "Hey, you two," Levi says, stepping up to where we're standing at the archway.

I step back with a breath. "I know. We're coming."

Levi shrugs. "I was just going to say…" His eyes shift between the two of us, and he points up. "Mistletoe." Then walks away with a grin.

Thank you for reading *The Rogue.*

Want a bonus epilogue?

Visit https://BookHip.com/GZMFMJN for a down-the-road look into their future.

Get exclusive bonus content by signing up for my newsletter! You'll receive updates, sneak peeks, similar book recs, and more…

Thank You

Thank you so much for reading!!

I hope you enjoyed Levi and Tessa's story. I've been looking forward to diving into their happily ever after all year and I'm so happy to finally share it with you.

I would be so grateful for an honest review. They're so important for authors, and I read each one.

New to the Hideaway Springs Series?
Flip for a preview of Chase and Pepper's story in The Runaway

The Runaway

ROXANNE TULLY

CHAPTER 1

CHASE

"Don't you have practice or somethin'?" Dad asks as he tops off my mug. Something the owner of the Hideaway Springs Inn shouldn't be doing. Like he's using the refill as a subtle opportunity to ask why I'm hanging around the lobby bar of the Inn. Instead of heading back to my condo in Denver the minute our family meeting was over.

He pours leisurely, almost deliberately so. Like honey out of a jar.

He only bought this establishment a few years back with the noble intention of helping the previous owner out of a bind when the IRS came to collect. At least that's how it started.

The motivation behind *keeping* the ancient inn open and revamping it with a lobby bar and coffee lounge came after town officials threatened to shut it down.

After the scandal with Robert Woods' fraudulent business transactions and then the tragic death of him and his wife, the town became vigilant in avoiding anything that could tarnish its reputation in the media.

The only hotel—if you could call it that—in town being permanently shut down would adversely affect our small community. With there being no hotel for ten miles, our town would get fewer visits from tourists and out-of-town family members. And have zero emergency accommodations for local residents. Or worse—the chance that a bigger fish would make a home here. Which, while better for our economy, would lead to more buildings, traffic, pollution and social tension within our small community.

Besides, Dad's a lifer in Hideaway Springs. After spending twenty years as a professional boxer, he needs something to keep him busy.

"Don't you have someone else who does that around here?" I deadpan, glancing at the pitcher of coffee.

He glances back at Bethany, one of two waitresses he has on staff. "Yeah, well, with that fresh bruise on the side of your eye and the scowl you've had on since you walked in, you're a little less than approachable today."

I flex my jaw and glance at the innocent waitress. "Last week you complained that I was scaring off the *customers*, now it's the staff? And if you didn't want me here, then don't call me in for a family meeting that has nothing to do with me."

"Helping your older brother plan his son's birthday party has everything to do with all of us, now snap out of it."

I lean back in my booth with a sigh—debating on telling him I've decided to hire someone to take care of Elliot's place.

And then sell it.

Without sounding like a coward. A coward who still won't admit that his little brother's death is on his head. A tragedy I could have prevented.

Had I not been so damned desperate for Elliot to be his own person. And leave me to be mine.

Dad turns and scans the small crowd, checking if all his patrons are alright for the time being, then takes a seat across from me. His tone suddenly shifting.

"Hey, I could have gone another way with that." He chuckles lightheartedly. "Could have said she's too intimidated to talk to Chase Reeves, the Dallas Kings' team captain and the guy on this month's cover of *Sports Illustrated*."

"Last month's." But the correction doesn't come from me. It's from my brother Noah—the second oldest Reeves brother, who just strolled in like he owns the place. Okay, so maybe he owns part of it, but he had his own reasons for rooting himself in this town. Unlike Dad, I don't meddle in other people's business.

Same way I wish people wouldn't meddle in mine.

Dad rolls his eyes. "I was making a point."

"A point about what?" Noah pries. The attorney in him always asking questions he has no business asking.

"She's just busy, Dad, leave her alone," I say, ending the whole Bethany is too intimidated by me B.S.

"Hi, Noah." Bethany appears suddenly at our now very crowded table. "Can I get you anything?"

My brother looks up politely, offering a small smile. "Hey, Bee, I'm alright, thanks. Just forgot to grab an espresso before I left."

"I'll get that for you," she chirps.

Dad cocks his head toward his other son but keeps his eyes on me. "Approachable."

That's because Noah is in and out of here in three seconds on a typical afternoon and *Bee* was just being proactive. As the only affordable lawyer in town—he's always busy. So after a long day of working in the office on his high profile city cases, he heads home to work on pro bono cases for the town locals, stopping for a caffeine spike here at the inn.

"Dad, leave him alone. He's just pissy because his game's been off the last few weeks."

"Just the last three games and piss off before I call Bee back and tell her you want to try her *special* today."

"You know it wouldn't kill you to be nicer to the female population."

"I am nice." I lean back with a smirk. "When it counts."

Dad stands with a sigh. "That's my cue."

Noah kicks me under the table. "Why do you have to get like that in front of Dad?"

Ignoring him, I check the time. "I've got to get to practice." The Denver Kings arena is forty-five minutes from town. I won't hit traffic around here, but closer to the city, I'm looking at, at least a twenty-minute delay. Polishing off my coffee, I grab the keys to my Harley off the table.

Noah stands first. "You're comin' back for poker night tomorrow, right?" he asks. "Levi wants to go over the guest list too. Says there's a suspicious number of single moms coming this year."

I zone out for a minute, remembering my game schedule. "Tomorrow's Sunday? Yeah. I'm good for Sunday."

Bailing on game night isn't an option unless I have a direct conflict. It was Elliot's thing and we vowed to keep it alive. We just call it 'poker night' now.

"Crashin' at my place again?" He looks down at me in expectation...or maybe as a challenge.

"Yeah, maybe."

He and I both know I don't sleep at the cottage that Elliot left me. I can barely stand in that house for more than five minutes without reliving the last time I saw him in it. The night before his accident.

Two minutes after Noah leaves and I've double-checked which days I have games, I'm considering a second attempt at telling Dad about Elliot's place when a car door slams on the quiet street outside, followed by the sound of screeching tires. From my vantage point, I catch a glimpse of the yellow taxi from the big city race its way out of town.

Soon after, the bell to the front entrance chimes announcing a new patron, which means it's clearly not the right time to approach Dad about my plans for the burden that was left for me.

A relived sigh carries across the room. "Oh, thank *God*, this place is still open."

The voice. It's breathy and alive. Desperate and determined.

Familiar.

"Please, please, *please* tell me the Inn upstairs is still open."

An old vision creeps into my mind before I look up. Of the small-town girl with the easy smile, long wavy red hair that reminds you of an autumn sunset in Hideaway Springs; breezy, colorful...naturally beautiful.

"Still in business," Dad answers. "But I'm afraid—"

"Fabulous."

I turn to find the visitor at the counter. I only see the back of her bleached-blonde head, but there's no mistaking who it is.

Pepper Woods.

She's wearing crisp white running shoes and a pink velour sweatsuit. Her hair is loosely bobby-pinned in various places. Her cheeks are shimmery and rose-powdered. And I'm almost positive that's a veil poking out of her tan leather backpack.

"Pepper, is that you?" I hear Dad ask cautiously from behind the counter.

"Mr. Reeves? Oh my gosh. Yes—it's me. Well, I go by Penelope now. I knew *someone* would still be living in this town. You work here?"

He scoffs. "Sort of. Bought the place."

"Really? Why? I mean. That's great. I need a room. Any room."

"I'm sorry, Pep—Penelope. We're booked."

"Booked?" She laughs but in a panicky sort of way that piques my curiosity. A curiosity I buried a long time ago when it came to her. "How can this place be booked?"

Dad blinks and I cough a laugh.

This grabs her attention and she turns, looking for the source.

Big, tired eyes lock with mine and her lips part—but only slightly—as she sweeps her gaze over me. Then turns back to the only gentleman in this entire establishment.

"Look, I'm desperate. I'm sure you save something for you know…important people?" She winces at her own words.

I prop up my elbow as I lean back against the window in my seat, curious as fuck to see how Dad will handle *that* one.

I'm stroking my jaw and bottom lip with my thumb when Dad catches his immediate response with a light chuckle.

I know he's about to comment something like "We consider everyone who walks in here important, *Penelope*," but I beat him to it.

"Is that how it's done in Washington, Pepper?" I ask smugly.

She turns to me with a scowl. A slightly more prepared 'you again' scowl that *almost* makes me laugh. And there isn't much I find funny these days. "Not surprised to see you still here, Chase."

Well, well. Pepper Woods remembers my name.

"Is that a veil?" I ask, leaning back in my booth and glancing at the white lace dangling from her backpack.

She snaps her head down and pushes the exposed piece back through the open zipper. "Mr. Reeves," she starts again with fresh determination.

"Please, call me Aiden."

She shakes her head. "Mr. Reeves. Please. I need...*something*."

He considers it, but he and I both know there's nothing he can do. Not unless he has her crash on his couch—for however long she needs. "Look, Pepper. I...*understand* you might not have family in town, but...don't you have *friends* you can call?"

He sounds hopeful. He really does.

She chokes a laugh. "Friends. Yes. Yes, of course." She shrugs awkwardly. "Lots." Keeping her eyes on my dad, she pulls out her phone and holds it up. "I'll just ring any one 'em...right now."

Dad licks his bottom lip and briefly focuses on the dark marble of the bar, like he wishes there was something else he could offer her.

"Why don't you...have a seat and I'll get something for you from the kitchen."

She shakes her head absently. "No, thank you. I'm not hungry. Water...maybe?"

He motions Bethany over with the pitcher.

I watch as Pepper's chest moves up and down. Her eyes dazed as if she's wondering how she got here.

It's like a train wreck, and I can't look away.

Dad circles the bar and sits across from me. I sit up on alert because this isn't going anywhere good.

"Well, I gotta get—"

"Sit down," he hisses.

I drop back onto the bench, already knowing what he's going to say: *take her back to the city, sit with her until she finds someone in town.*

Pepper isn't going to find anyone in town. She left without looking back. Without saying her goodbyes. She followed her big city dreams to New York, somehow ended up in D.C. and got engaged to Troy Mayfield.

Now she's here shaking in her Adidas like someone is going to burst through that door looking for her.

Glancing at Pepper sitting alone at a corner roundtable, he leans in. "You and I both know she's not calling anyone."

"Your point?"

"She needs a place to stay. The only one I know is the cottage you're not occupying at the moment. There's a bed. Take her there. Just for a night."

"Are you fucking joking?"

"Keep your voice down. Look. I need to close in one hour. You've got practice. So unless you expect me to throw her out on the street, you need to take her back to Elliot's place." He whisper-screams that last part.

"No."

"What's it to you? You're staying in your condo in the city tonight anyway."

"Dad. Look at her. Yeah, she's a hot mess right now. But that girl is not sleeping in an old cottage. She's..."

"She's desperate," he says.

I shake my head because I know how this ends. She's going to fight me on going anywhere with me. Especially to some little old house with rusty old furniture, squeaky floors and probably plumbing issues.

He taps on the table as if he's given up on waiting for me to respond. "Beau. Didn't they used to date or something? *He* still lives here. I'll give him a call." Like he's serious, he moves back behind the bar and pulls up his box of business cards.

With a growl, I push off the table and meet him across the bar. "What are you doing?"

Dad doesn't look up. "He runs his dad's old auto shop not far from here. I've got his card somewhere."

I yank the shoebox away from him. "You don't just call up someone's ex and ask them to come pick up their girlfriend from eight years ago."

"You got any better ideas, Chase? She's *alone*. And wherever she came from—which let's be honest, we all know where that is—she ain't plannin' on goin' back."

I run my fingers through my hair. I can't think about this right now.

"I'm late for practice. Besides, I've got my bike and I don't have a sp—"

Dad pulls out a spare helmet from behind the bar. "For just such an occasion."

Shaking my head, I take the helmet and stride over to Pepper, setting it next to her water. "Put that on."

Her eyes lift to mine. "You can't be serious."

"You're out of options, Blondie."

"Penelope."

"Look, maybe that's what your politician husband calls you, but here, you're Pepper or Blondie or Pinky or whatever else I feel like callin' you. Now unless you plan on getting intimate with the street corner tonight, you're coming with me. There's an empty place you can stay tonight."

She looks up at me, horrified, but then stands with a curt nod, picking up the helmet. "You uh...you get the news here?"

"No. This is just some imaginary small town with no television or cell phones. Can we go now? I'm late."

I turn and head out the back, where my bike is parked. I don't wait for her to follow. It's bad enough I struggled to tear my eyes off her in the last ten minutes.

The sooner I drop her off, the better. She'll have boarding for the night, and my one good deed for the day is done.

I hop on and make my adjustments before revving the engine.

Pinky lifts the sleek white helmet from under her arm and with deliberate motions, slides it over her head like a puzzle piece. Her fingers work under her chin and the click of the fastening strap echoes through the quiet alley.

I give her a nod. "All set?"

"How far we going?" she asks, checking out my ride.

"About five minutes."

She sucks in a breath, avoiding my eyes as she nods. In a small, and somewhat shaky voice, she replies, "I guess."

I'm tempted to ask if she's ever been on one of these. Hell, I'm tempted to assure her she's safe with me in the driver's seat. But all that goes against everything I vowed to never do when it comes to Pepper.

I give my engine a roar and tell her to hop on.

With a backpack full of buried secrets over her shoulders, she steps on the footpeg and swings her leg over. I shift uneasily as she settles behind me, her body molding with mine like it belongs.

I shake it off and lift the helmet over my head.

"You insured?" she asks.

"Sure. For myself."

Pepper presses her front to my back even more, wrapping her arms around my waist and my vision nearly blurs. I've given plenty of girls rides on this thing, their arms around me as natural as a seat belt—I barely notice it.

But this—I *feel*.

Maybe it's her scent?

No. She smells like faded, expensive perfume and the back of a city cab. Far from alluring.

"Thought you were in a hurry," she calls behind me.

"Right."

I head toward Elliot's when I catch the sun setting over the mountains. That means it's close to six, which means even if I were to head straight to practice now, I'll be ten minutes late, at least. And I still need to get across town.

After last night's screw-up and the shiner I got during a throw-down, I can't afford to be late. Coach *will* have my ass.

When I turn the corner, I pull to a stop. "Shit."

"What's wrong?" Pepper's voice is muffled behind me under the helmet.

"Change of plans. You're coming with me."

Want more of Chase & Pepper's story?
Visit: https://geni.us/therunaway_hss
to keep reading ***The Runaway***

Books By Roxanne Tully
Romance Author

Blades of Heart Hockey Series
Three Forbidden Love Stories

The Roommate Deal
A fake relationship hockey romance

The Better Bully
An enemies-to-lovers college football romance

Sporting Goods
A single-parent hockey romance

Wrong Twin
A mistaken identity hockey romance

Roxanne grew up in New York City, where she studied play and screen writing. From an early age, she loved storytelling and knew she wanted to be a writer. While her genre was never limited, she now enjoys writing small-town and sports romances, creating strong, realistic heroines and swoony alpha heroes.

Website: https://www.roxannetully.com
Newsletter: https://geni.us/rtnewsletter

Follow me on **Instagram**
for teasers, excerpts and more on what's coming;
https://www.instagram.com/roxtully.author/

Acknowledgements

Being an author never gets easier. In fact, it gets harder because, for me, if you're doing it right, you challenge yourself with each story. You step out of your comfort zone. You introduce a new side to your creativity.

That's why the support I've had from my family, friends, readers and everyone I've met in the book community are so vital for me to keep going.

I'm extending a first and foremost huge thank you to my husband. For believing in me and cheering me on every single day on this journey. For keeping the kids busy with crafts while I craft. For silently refilling my tea when I'm so too engrossed to leave my desk.

Thank you to my fantastic ARC Team (advance reader copy); bloggers, bookstagrammers and everyone in my Facebook Reader Group (Roxanne's Rocks). You guys are all truly amazing and make all of this worthwhile.

To Zsuzsanna at Midnight Readers PR, for everything you do everyday and for organizing the hell out of this release and making this launch such an exciting time for me.

To Betty: for the killer promo graphics and as always, bringing my visions to life with not just this cover but the entire series. You're amazing!

To Francesca: For her unmatched illustrating talent with the background for these covers.

To Emma: My friend and proofreader. I am beyond grateful for your incredible eye and for working with my nutty schedule.

To my Alpha and Beta readers, Kerri, Liz, Stephanie, and Brittni, for all your helpful feedback and for loving this story even when it was a mess.

To my readers, new and loyal. Thank you for taking a chance on my books. Thank you for reading this far, for sticking around for more and mostly, for helping me grow.

Made in the USA
Columbia, SC
01 May 2025